WHITE EMPIRE

SHARON WOODS

For anyone fighting for themselves, dream big and don't stop until you're happy...

CHAPTER 1

ABIGAIL

I RUN IN HEELS, pushing past people, trying to get to my gate on time. I clutch my bag tighter and pick up the pace, but when I get closer to the gate, I take in the lack of people in the lounge, so I slow my run to a walk. Approaching the desk, I stand back to read the board behind the check-in attendant and run my hand through my hair and read the word *Delayed*.

Dammit!

I close my eyes and wrap my arms around my middle, trying to catch my breath. Now with two hours to kill and a dry throat, I stretch my arms out and glance around for a place to call home before finding a drink.

I step over to the side and reach inside my bag to fish around for my phone. Because my bag is overstuffed, I squat down and drop it on the ground and open it up, trying to find my phone. After a few minutes of digging around, my fingers wrap around the cold metal rectangle.

Gotcha.

I stand back up, reposition the bag on my shoulder, and make a mental note to clear out the bag back at home.

I take a breath and check around to make sure no one will be able to hear my conversation. But I sigh with relief to see just the usual hurried passengers getting to their gates. Ever since arriving in the city from my small town Riddells Creek this morning, the number of people bustling around has me taken aback, and it all started from the moment I stepped off the plane and into the airport.

Happy I'm out of the way to be on the phone, I scroll through to find my mom's number and take a moment to give myself a pep talk.

Don't let her ruin your excitement.

I hit the call button and barely hear it ring before she answers, "Abigail, I have been waiting for your call. I am worried sick about you. Surely you could have called earlier?"

My stomach twists and I swallow the lump that's formed in my throat. She's right. I could have called her in the Uber, but I was too overwhelmed with the city buildings and landscapes that calling home slipped my mind. I can't exactly tell her a lie because I'm not good at lying, so I go with the truth.

I look down at my shoes and whisper, "Sorry, Mom. You're right; I should have."

The noise from her throat is of approval before she says, "See, being surrounded by those city people is affecting you. Forgetting about us already. This is a bad idea. I'm sure you didn't get the job anyway. They would have given it to someone with experience."

I wince at her harsh words. It's like a stab to my heart, her words cutting deep. And she doesn't care. She just wants to keep me in Riddell's Creek, to keep *her* dreams and desires at the forefront of my mind.

I cannot move my mouth to respond, so she continues.

"You know we need the money, and you leaving hurts us. Staying and working with the family real estate business is the best future for you."

I watch the people pass me, wondering what their lives look like and where they are going. I bet it's a lot happier and brighter than mine. The back of my eyes burn with threatened tears, so I rapidly blink to prevent any falling.

No, she won't ruin my day. Even though she has a way of hurting me with words, I never talk back to her. She taught me to respect my elders and I take pride because I do. Deciding to appease her, I say. "I will send you money whenever you need it, but the city people are so kind."

I sigh, remembering Eleanor, the lady who inter-
viewed me. She was warm and friendly, easing my
nerves within a few minutes. They aren't the devil like
my mom believes. All my life, she has spoken negatively
about city people, but being here for the first time, I
immediately know she has it all wrong and I'm glad I
applied for the real estate training program because it's
exactly what I need.

"Yeah, well, if you go, we won't have time to replace
you. Being a small town, less work is getting done and
less money is coming in."

It's like a slap to the face, but nothing I haven't heard
before. My mom won't ever hide her truth, even if I think
it's wrong. I won't fight back, though. I just hope I get
the once-in-a-lifetime opportunity to get out and put
distance between us. I'm so sick of being trapped in a
life I'm desperate to leave.

Despite this conversation dragging me down, I have a
good feeling about the interview. I need to wrap it up
and enjoy the last few hours of peace.

"Okay, well, Mom, I was calling to let you know my
flight has been delayed by two hours."

I scratch my head and wait to hear the *tsk* leave her
mouth. I shake my head, knowing she is going to act like
that.

"Let's hope you won't be later than that. You know I go to bed early."

I squeeze my eyes shut, trying to calm the noise that argues against her. I wouldn't dare confront her, but I love to dream. A wicked smile splits my face at a vision of me standing up to her.

I open my eyes and hurry to end the conversation. "I won't, but I need to get going so I can go to the bathroom and grab a drink. I'll see you soon," I say in a fake cheerful voice when, really, I don't want to go back. There isn't anything wrong with Riddell's Creek; it's just not for me. There is more out there for me. I know it.

She sighs. "Okay. Keep me updated and send a text when you're boarding."

I perk up a little, knowing I'm getting off the phone with her. "I will. See you soon. Love you."

I wait to hear the words "I love you too" before hanging up.

I suck in a deep breath and toss my phone in my bag. I move away from the wall and find the sign for the restroom.

Once I've freshened up, I find a large open corner shop with bar seating on the outside and wooden tables and chairs inside. People sit with coffees and either laptops out and are typing away, or phones and books in front of them. I grin widely as I soak up the strong coffee smell and the feeling of being with the "city people."

I walk farther inside and read the menu on the back wall behind the counter. I touch my lips with my fingertips and scan, trying to find something. Deciding to skip the coffee for bubbles and order a glass of Champagne and take it over to a seat at a large table. I select a spot on the end and take a large sip, the sweet, refreshing bubbles hitting my mouth. "Ahh."

I grab my bag and rummage through to pull out my book.

I'm lost in the book and sipping my drink when I hear, "I guess it's five o'clock somewhere, right?" A deep, sexy voice is speaking from behind me. I tense, gripping the book and glass a little tighter and turning my body. My elbow hits a man's groin. "Oh my God, I'm so sorry."

"It's okay, it's not your fault. I shouldn't have been standing so close."

I swallow and crane my neck to find the face to the voice. A flush runs up my neck and onto my cheeks when I see how handsome he is. I take him in, starting with his brown hair finger-swept to perfection, olive skin, and those glossy black eyes that have my pulse skipping beats. He looks to be in his thirties and I'm sure he is just being nice, like everyone in the city has been so far, because I bet I stand out in the crowd. My mouth is hanging open and words cannot form inside my brain. I know he asked a question before the awkward bump, but I'm taken aback by him.

Seeing my reaction, he cheekily winks before a pinched expression hits his face and his black eyes flicker between the glass and me. His large frame moves past me, a coffee cup in one hand and a briefcase in the other.

I shake my head, trying to snap out of the daze. A small smile forms as I answer, "It sure is." I raise my glass to cheer with him.

He offers a nod before he steps around and sits down in front of me. I pretend to be reading, but I'm watching him over my book. He opens his briefcase and pulls out a laptop with confidence. He doesn't look my way, just settles into the chair, dismissing me. I shrug and return to my book and my bubbles.

I'm lost in reading when I giggle loudly at a line in the book, and it turns to a snort. I slap a hand over my mouth and take a quick look around with wide eyes. His gaze, etched with a perplexed expression and accompanied by a tilted head, lands on mine and I wince, embarrassed at being caught, and slowly drop my hand away from my mouth and gaze at him.

He notices me staring and bites his lips, "It must be a good book." He raises an eyebrow in question.

I nod. "It really is. So funny." I have threatened tears from the funny one-liners.

"What's it about?" he asks.

I peer over the top of my book as he leans back and sips his coffee. He's staring at me with intense scrutiny, and I swallow hard as I watch his Adam's apple bob up and down.

That simple movement makes me heat again.

But him asking me about the book has me freezing in the chair. I don't want to tell him what the book is about, instead, I try to hide behind the book. I clamp my lips shut, keeping my reading choices to myself.

But I'm sure he can read the title and Google it, and that would embarrass me further. It's better I just say it and pretend I don't care, I'll never see him again so what's the harm in elaborating.

Own my love of books.

"Ah, well, it's a romance novel. Called *The Takeover*. A single mom who finds love with a guy trying to take over her late husband's business. The children's pranks on the new guy are hilarious. I mean you laugh so hard you can't breathe, kind of funny."

The heat from my cheeks now spreads to my ears, and I'm wishing he hadn't asked.

"Never heard of it, but I can't say I read romance." He smirks and his gaze is so intense, I wiggle in my chair uncomfortably and take him in.

He is wearing a white shirt, which is open a little to his chest, and it's tucked into his black slacks. His cuff links are shining in the shop lights. Normally an over-the-top expensive look wouldn't do anything for me, but his tanned, muscled chest is visible, and I have never met someone who oozes confidence and sex.

After I finish my inspection, my mouth suddenly dries, so I swipe my tongue to wet my lips and ask him, "What do you read, then?"

I expect him to say the newspaper or the stock market.

He leans forward, his hands clasped under his chin. His eyes roam the shop to check that no one is looking at us before he pulls out a book from his briefcase. It's written by J. D. Robb.

I blink rapidly before returning my gaze to his, confessing in a stutter, "I didn't expect that."

His lips open and reveal his dazzling white teeth, and I can't help but smile back.

He is a surprise.

"Most people wouldn't, but I don't mind sharing my secrets with a beautiful stranger I won't see again."

I feel my heart thump harder at the words *beautiful stranger*. It's a compliment coming from him.

He puts the book away in his briefcase before twisting to refocus on me.

"Where are you going today?" I ask, wanting to know more about him.

An incredulous look appears on his face, and he answers, "I'm off on a business trip."

"Fancy."

Of course, you idiot. I want to kick myself for saying something so stupid.

But he doesn't seem bothered. Instead, a smirk appears on his lips, but the aura he gives off intimidates me.

His eyes narrow and he asks, "Do you have a boyfriend?"

I feel a lightness wash over me. Knowing I won't see him again makes me flirty. And I rarely flirt. I blame the glass of Champagne I'm sipping.

"Wouldn't you like to know?" I say and drain my glass.

I glance at my watch, knowing I have time for tea before I need to go back to the gate.

I close my book and stand. His gaze flicks up from his laptop and his firm, intense stare roams over me and I feel naked. I look down to make sure nothing is hanging out and I run my hands over the smooth black fabric of my black skirt, white top, and blazer. Happy I'm not flashing him, I clear my throat and speak. "I'm grabbing a drink. Would you like another coffee?" I offer politely.

"Are you having another Champagne?" His voice rises in disdain.

What?

I pull back and frown. "No. If you must know, I'm ordering a chamomile tea, but you are making me want to change my mind." I glare back at his surprised face.

He shakes his head, answering, "No thanks."

With that, I scoop my wallet up and wander over to order tea, not bothering to tell him to watch my bag. He isn't going anywhere right now; he only just opened the laptop to work.

I stand in line, and I try to recover from the whiplash he gives me. One minute I'm heating up over his words and looks, the next he splashes me with a bucket of ice-cold water. Luckily, I won't need to worry about seeing him after today. Maybe the men in the city are just as controlling as my parents, and that's what I am trying to escape.

I can feel his gaze on my exposed legs. I'm short compared to him, but my black heels give my five-foot frame a little height. I move up and order a tea and a bag of peanut butter M&M's and then return to my seat. As I'm walking back, I notice that his phone is held to his ear, so I sit back down quietly and return to reading my book.

"No, that's not good enough. I'll talk to you when I get back," he firmly snaps into the phone.

I watch him from the corner of my eye, eating my M&M's and watching as he tilts his chin into the air, his other arm squeezing the back of his neck. His shirt is tight over his arm, showing off his toned physique. My number is called, and it breaks me from my wandering eyes. I pick up my tea and return to my seat, taking a sip to wet my parched throat.

I push my fascination with him aside and return to my book, but I look up when I hear him hang up and toss the phone on the table before he madly types away on his laptop.

I'm lost in my book when I hear the announcement for my flight come through the speakers. I drink the last of the tea and put my book back in my bag and rise.

His gaze falls to mine, and he asks, "Are you leaving?"

I tilt my head to answer him. "Um, yeah, my flight was just called. I don't want to miss it and be stuck in the city."

"Shame. I would love to be stuck inside of you," he mumbles under his breath, but I catch it. I freeze mid-movement. My mouth hangs open and I stare back into his eyes in disbelief. I shake my head to push the exchange aside. I thought he was different and genuinely interested in me.

Obviously not.

I decide to not waste any more time, so I step back and say, "Bye," waving before I turn around and put some much-needed distance between us.

Leaving the shop I don't turn around and make my way back to the gate. As I'm walking, I hear my phone chime from inside my bag; I stop and pull it out, staring down at the screen and frowning, not recognizing the number. I take a deep breath and decide to answer.

"Hello?"

"Hi, Miss Crawford. This is Eleanor from White Estate. Is this a good time to talk?"

I raise my brows and peer around, not wanting to tell her it's not. I want to know the reason for her call, so I slow my walk and answer, "Oh, hi, Eleanor. Yes, now is good."

"Okay, great. Well, I'd like to offer you the position in the training program. We believe you would be a great fit for the position, and we would love to have you on our team."

"Oh, wow. Thank you so much. That's wonderful news. I look forward to working with the company."

"No problem. It's our pleasure to have you on board. I'll send you all the information at the email address you provided. If you need anything prior to your start date, give this number a call. Otherwise, have a safe trip, and I'll see you soon."

"Yes. Thanks, Eleanor. I'll see you soon."

I hang up and stare at the phone with complete shock. I put my phone away and continue walking to the gate to board my plane. I know this won't be the last time I see the inside of this airport. The swarm of butterflies in my stomach tells me I have a new adventure on the horizon.

CHAPTER 2

ABIGAIL

A MONTH LATER

I'm standing at the airport with my family. I'm bouncing on my heels with giddiness, still unable to believe my dreams are finally coming true. Of course, it's been a hell of a month, trying to hurry and get my parents' business on top of its workload so they will accept the move. Reluctantly, they agreed, and I promised to help them out with money.

I yawn and rub my heavy lids with my hands. The last month is catching up with me now that I'm standing here waiting for the boarding to begin. I have been dreaming of the new apartment bed that I have so I can catch up on some much-needed sleep.

I organized the apartment from here with the help of Eleanor, so hopefully it's nice when I arrive. It's a fully furnished apartment, so I don't need to worry about finding furniture. I just needed to bring my clothes and myself.

I check the time and smile.

It's almost time.

My mom must sense it and asks, "Are you sure you want to leave?" She gazes down at me with red-rimmed eyes. Her lashes have unshed tears sitting on them.

I look around the small airport, wanting to distract myself from her pain and calm my now knotted stomach. I see only one small plane sitting on the tarmac, a small shop, and a check-in counter. I clutch my hand into a fist and bring it to my chest, knowing there isn't much more for me in Riddell's Creek. I turn to face her and give her a small smile. I nod and say, "Sorry, Mom, but this is a great opportunity I can't pass on. I can bring back some new ideas to turn the business around."

I bite my lip as I watch her for a response.

She clutches her elbows and her face drops. "You promise to come back as soon as the program is over? Please."

She mutters *please* under her breath repeatedly.

But months ago, when I scoured for job vacancies online and this one in the city popped up, I knew this was my ticket out of here.

The announcement to board the plane comes through, and Mom's voice cracks. I step closer and hug her, rubbing my hands up and down her back before pulling out of her hug and straight into my dad's waiting arms.

"I really don't know why you couldn't stay working with us. You're a good agent," he says into my hair.

I sigh before lifting my head off his chest and explain to him, "Dad, this is a big deal. I'll learn so much, and the money is worth it."

"Money isn't everything."

I drop my gaze to peer at the ground, shrinking before I force myself to lift my chin and maintain his eye contact. "I know, Dad, but we need it."

I step back from the embrace and look over at my brother Rhys. His face is stony and unchanged. His arms are crossed over his chest, which is covered by his navy police uniform.

I reach out and rough his hair and say with a tease, "Cheer up, Rhys. I won't be gone forever."

"Promise you will keep me updated," he grunts, swatting my hand out of his hair.

I roll my eyes. "Yes, I will message you as soon as I get into my apartment."

I reach out and grab him and he opens his arms, hugging me back firmly. "Do you have your pepper spray?"

I laugh loudly and pull out of the embrace. I reach into my bag to grab it and wave it in the air between us. "Happy?"

I toss it back into the bag that I never got around to sorting out.

He offers a firm nod and goes back to standing like a stone with his arms crossed and face firm, no expression on it.

I peer over to the line and when only a few people are left, I say, "I better go. I don't want to miss my flight. I will message you all when I arrive."

I keep my excitement at a minimum, but inside, I'm dancing.

I don't promise to call because I will have to hear more sadness in their voices and when I get to the city, I want to soak up all the happy goodness. I want to leave the small town behind for the big city lights and chase my own dreams.

CHAPTER 3

ABIGAIL

I SIT IN THE back of the cab and stare out the window, absorbing the buildings and people walking around the city. I smile and take out my phone, snapping pictures through the window. The taxi comes to a halt outside a tall glass building.

"This is the address," the driver says.

I shuffle in my seat to collect my suitcase. The driver hasn't spoken more than a few words, which is something I'm not used to; Riddell's Creek is filled with chatterboxes.

"Thanks," I say as I pay and then open the door.

I drag the only piece of luggage I brought with me. It's heavy and filled with everything I could squeeze in it. There is still half my wardrobe back home, which Mom, of course, is happy about, because she thinks it means I will come back soon.

I close the door behind me and stand on the sidewalk. I lean back to take in the enormous, modern building.

It is bigger and nicer in person than the pictures I saw online. I'm in awe already.

Making my way to the tower's door to pick up the keys to the apartment, smoothing my blue jeans and white T-shirt down with sweaty palms. I flick my hair over my shoulder and push open the door. Walking with the case behind me and almost skip to the security desk where the doorman is. As I approach, his lips part and a genuine smile erupts. I try to keep my lips together to prevent myself from beaming the whole time. He explains the facilities, then offers a tour, which I decline, wanting to explore on my own later. He hands me the keys and I thank him and move toward the elevators.

Inside the elevators, I whistle the tune I heard in the taxi on the way in, I arrive on the fourteenth floor and read the keys. I step to door number two and open the door and enter. I peer around at the size and beauty of the apartment. I move forward and the door clicks shut behind me, causing me to jump. I pass the small kitchen and dining area and dump the keys and bag on the table, and leave the case next to the chair and walk around, taking everything in.

The apartment is white with brown wood accents, simple and modern, and the view from the living area is spectacular. Floor to ceiling windows allow light and views I have only dreamed about. The little balcony is perfect to sit out on a pleasant night and enjoy my dinner or read one of my books. I walk to the bedroom, and I smile at the large white bed. I step toward it and fall backward, sinking into it.

"Ahh." I close my eyes and absorb the feelings swirling inside me.

After a few minutes, I push myself up and then drag my case into the bedroom and begin unpacking. I'm still trying to believe this is happening to me.

After I empty everything out of the case and settle it all in its new spots, I decide to venture out and explore the neighborhood. I stroll the streets and take in all the hustle and bustle around me. The noise and smell are so different from the quiet, clean air of the small town I grew up in. I can't believe how different the people are. Their clothes, their hair, the number of piercings and tattoos that they have. But as I walk the streets, and grab a coffee from a local shop, I can't help but smile and sip. All these shops are something our small town doesn't offer. I keep sipping the drink and wander around, taking in all the streets and memorizing the layout.

When I finish the coffee, I feel my legs tire from the long day of traveling, so I find a store to pick up some food for tonight. I will do a bigger food shop tomorrow.

I am standing at my apartment door, ready to put the key in the lock, when I hear the door beside me click open and a brunette woman around my age comes walking out. Her hazel eyes hit mine and she offers a warm smile and I immediately smile back.

"Hi, I'm Gracie. Did you just move in?" she asks, tilting her head toward my door.

I drop my hand away from my door as she comes to stand next to me to talk.

"Yeah, today. From a small town called Riddell's Creek. I'm Abigail, but you can call me Abby."

I bite my lips closed to prevent any more word vomit from leaving my mouth. I'm sure she doesn't want to hear about this right now.

Her eyes shine with humor, but she doesn't seem bothered.

"Nice to meet you, Abby. I haven't been here long either, but it's a really nice apartment complex. Sorry, I really must get to work, but we totally need to catch up. I can show you the good places to eat and hang out."

I take in her work uniform and frown. Her hourglass frame is dressed in a tight white crop top, her full cleavage on show, and she wears a tight jean skirt with sneakers. I hope she doesn't have to move much. Otherwise, people might get an eyeful, but where would she work dressed like that at this hour?

I keep my thoughts to myself. Instead, I nod and say, "That would be great. Thank you."

"Okay. I gotta run, but I will speak to you soon."

She dips her chin and steps into the elevator. I stand watching her for a moment before moving back to my door.

Entering my apartment with the biggest smile. I've met a friendly neighbor who has already offered to hang out. I set my bags down on the kitchen floor and take my phone out. I head to the balcony and snap a picture of me with the view in the background.

Sending it to my family with the text.

> *Abigail: I'm here, safe and sound. Settled and already loving it. Love you all, x.*

On Monday, I walk from my apartment to work. I follow Google maps' instructions on my phone and arrive at the address from the email. Standing on the sidewalk, I crane my neck to look up at the tallest tower in the city. It's all mirrored and intimidating as hell. I close my mouth and take two steps back to soak it in.

Every time I think I have seen the biggest building, there is another one I find that's even bigger.

There are many men and women coming in and out of the building through the glass doors. I draw back and shake my head, getting myself to refocus and take one step at a time. Sucking in a breath, I roll my shoulders back, and walk in.

You can do this.

Eleanor is someone I have met before, so it shouldn't be scary, but the nerves are kicking in, causing flutters in my chest. I don't want to let anyone down; I want to prove I can be just as good as anyone else. I'm still grateful I was chosen, considering Mom's constant words of *they will take someone with experience over you* and *you have little to offer.*

Snapping myself out of the negative thoughts, I spot the desk with a receptionist seated behind it. I approach it and she hands me a temporary nametag and calls up to Eleanor to see if I can head straight up to her. I know I'm a little early, but I didn't want to be late on my first day.

I'm smiling back at the receptionist as I watch her talk. She hangs up and tells me to go upstairs because Eleanor is ready.

I walk around the desk and head to the elevators and ride one up to level two. The doors open and I step out onto the polished floors.

The same gray concrete and greenery as downstairs is up here too. It's warm and inviting. I bite the corner of my lip and glance around.

"Hello? Eleanor—are you here?" I call out, taking another step forward.

She must have stood up because her head suddenly appears over the divider of a cubicle. I jump at her sudden appearance and grab my chest. My heart is pounding under my fist.

"Hi, Abigail," she says.

I nod, unable to speak. I'm still trying to recover.

She beams at me, standing tall, and says, "I'd like to officially welcome you to White Estates. Are you excited?"

She rubs her hands together and the light bounces off her nude nail polish. I curl my fingers in a tight fist, cursing because I forgot to do mine. I worked so much prior to coming here for my parents' business that preparing myself slipped completely from my mind.

I hope she doesn't notice them.

Eleanor is a very well-presented woman in her early fifties, dressed in a vibrant yellow modest dress. She re-adjusts her glasses on her nose and I can't help but shuffle on the spot.

Am I supposed to look like her?

Even though she is beautiful, her presence has my shoulders relaxing and the tension melting away.

I smile at her kind word. "Hi, Eleanor. Yes, I'm very excited. Once again, thank you for choosing me."

She curls her dainty fingers, waving me closer as she says, "You deserve the opportunity, and you will fit in here. Now come closer."

I walk closer to her and look down to see she has papers spread out over the table. She looks down as she moves papers into piles. "I have a few housekeeping papers we need to get through, so let's tackle the boring things first, and then I can take you on a tour."

I meet her gaze with a small smile. "Sure."

But thirty seconds later, I'm still standing with my hands balled into fists. She notices I haven't moved and says with a chuckle, "Come. Sit down here and grab a pen. I need you to fill in all this."

She gestures to one of the office chairs, so I don't hesitate. I step over and take a seat. Once I'm comfortable, I pick up the papers and fill them in. Eleanor sorts through her own papers.

When I finish them all, I stack them into a neat pile and hold them out for her to take and say, "All done."

Her gaze lifts, and she reaches over to take the papers. She reads them briefly before lowering them to the desk in front of her. "Okay, great. Let's get upstairs where

I'll show you to your desk, break room, bathroom, and introduce you to Kara, who is head of contracts, and where you will begin the training. And lastly, you will meet the CEO, Mr. White."

My heart jolts with adrenaline. I'm already meeting the CEO and it's day one. I haven't even dressed or polished myself properly. Gosh, this is a terrible idea. My outfit isn't bad, but it definitely doesn't throw the same elegance as Eleanor's.

But there isn't anything I can do right now, so I must fake confidence and put on a smile that doesn't waver. I follow her out of the room; she carries the papers in her hand.

I'm lost in my thoughts when she asks me, "Have you always wanted to work in real estate?"

We ride the elevator up, the conversation breaking the silence.

"My parents own a small residential real estate business, which you know. And I love it, but—" I hesitate, looking for the right words. I'm still unable to gather my thoughts into actual words, so I answer with a simple, "I need more."

I'm grateful when she nods with approval.

"That's great. I started in residential, too. Commercial properties are unique, but I love it and wouldn't want to do residential now. But at least you will know some terms and policies. That's always a bonus. And how are you liking the apartment?"

My smile grows at the memory of me last night, sitting out on the balcony and reading a book. The warm night with views of the lights and traffic noise below was strangely comforting.

"It's better than I could have imagined. Thanks for allowing me to rent from one of the White buildings."

"Of course. He wouldn't want his employees staying anywhere else."

There has been a question on my mind about what happens next. After the year of my contract, what do I do for work? I feel comfortable with Eleanor, so I clear my throat and decide to ask. "I'm excited to grow and expand my knowledge. What are the opportunities after the traineeship?"

Eleanor's face lights up. "You are in the right place. Mr. White encourages growth and development. If you prove yourself, he will offer you a permanent job after the twelve-month contract. But, ah, I will warn you." She pauses a beat and my skin prickles with anticipation.

"He doesn't tolerate mistakes or grant second chances. He expects professionalism and care."

My breath catches and I rub my hands along the front of my red coat. Looking at the building earlier, I expected nothing less, but hearing the words from Eleanor's mouth has my throat constricting.

No mistakes or second chances.

I won't lie. It scares me. If I'm not careful, he could send me straight back to Riddell's Creek, and that thought causes my temple to throb. I say nothing, just nod with understanding.

"Let's go upstairs to your floor and grab your ID swipe card," she says, as if she didn't just drop a bomb.

I walk out with her, looking around at the desks. I'm introduced to Kara and her team before walking farther down to the few desks at the back of the office.

Eleanor pauses at one. "Here is your desk." There is a large white desk with the latest Mac sitting on top. It's simple and modern, and I secretly wonder how long it will take me until the desk is in disarray.

"I have assigned you to George, the other trainee in the program. He started before you. He will help you this week with questions you have. Don't be afraid to ask; he is very approachable."

I don't know who George is, as there is no one at the desk behind her, but a voice says loudly behind me, "Well, thank you, Eleanor."

I turn around and see a blond male walking toward us, a sparkle in his eye and a bounce in his step. He pauses next to Eleanor and smiles at her.

Eleanor smiles back.

George focuses on me. "And you must be the new trainee, Abigail."

"Yes, but call me Abby, please."

He nods. "George. I'm so excited to have you join us. Where did you come from?"

"A small town called Riddell's Creek," I answer shyly.

"Riddell who?" He shakes his head and continues through a chuckle. "I meant, where did you work prior to starting here?"

Okay, the ground can swallow me up now.

I shake my head. "Ohhh, I'm sorry. Well, my parents own a residential office where I grew up, so I was a real estate agent for them."

Eleanor excuses herself to get back to work, leaving me alone with George.

"Come, let's grab a coffee and get to know more about each other."

"Sure," I say back, following him to the break room.

I make some tea and turn around, clutching the warm cup. Sipping I glance over my cup at him as he makes a coffee for himself.

I turn to take tea upstairs and I ask him, "How long have you been here?"

He sips his coffee before he answers, "Only a couple of weeks."

"Really?"

He nods.

"It's a great company. Seriously, and I shouldn't ask this so soon after we met, but if you have a partner, was he or she able to find a job in town too?"

I sip at that exact moment. The liquid goes down the wrong way and I have a coughing fit. When I recover, I say, "No, I'm single."

But I hope he isn't hitting on me. There are no butterflies in my stomach or a heavy desire in my sex like I have read about in books. Which means I have zero desire to go on a date with him.

I look down, squirming and hiding my flushed face with my hair. We step into the elevator.

"Are you single?" I ask.

A heavy sigh leaves his mouth, and he says, "Yeah, unfortunately. I love being wrapped up in the love bubble, but I'm trying to figure myself out. Working on loving myself for a bit."

I smile to myself, admiring the honesty. "I think that's important and great that you can recognize that."

I don't confess that I don't believe I have ever been in love. So, I wouldn't know about this love bubble he talks of. But I have made myself embarrassed enough for one day not to add another one.

He helps set me up at my station, but when his desk phone rings, he rushes to pick it up in a huff. "White Estate. George speaking... Mm-hmm... Okay, see you soon." He hangs up the phone and looks up at me and says, "Eleanor said Mr. White had to run to an emergency meeting, so she will take you to meet him when he gets back. She said to go have some lunch."

"I might go outside for my break. I will see you soon."

"Sounds good. I'll see you when you get back."

He turns back to his computer to work, and I grab my bag and wait for the elevator. When the doors open and I step inside, my mouth drops open and I suck in a sharp breath.

Surely not...

But there is no mistaking the dark eyes, finger-swept hair, and briefcase.

The man from the airport.

The elevator suddenly feels small with him in it. I move to stand beside him and focus on the doors. Luckily, he's on his phone, so we don't have to talk.

"Yeah, I read that, but it still doesn't make any sense."

I'm eavesdropping, but what else am I supposed to be doing in this confined space?

I wonder who he was visiting here?

What does he do for a living?

"Mm-hmm."

I feel my tension release the second the doors open. I exit the elevator in front of him. He's still on his phone, talking.

"I won't be long."

I exit the building and welcome the fresh breeze. The flush from seeing him again is too overwhelming.

There is a nearby park that I stumble upon. Finding an empty park bench, I sit and call Charlotte, my friend from Riddell's Creek.

I pull the lapels of my coat closed as it rings.

"Abby. Hey. I've been waiting for your call. How is everything?"

Mind blowing. Exciting. Overwhelming.

Instead, I simply say, "Incredible. I love it here."

She moans in my ear. "Don't say that. You won't come back if you love it."

"I would say sorry, but I'd be lying." I giggle.

"No. Be happy, Abby. You deserve it. Now tell me, what's the city like?"

I gaze around at the multiple skyscraper buildings, trees, people, cars, and I say, "It's wonderful. There are so many people and so much to do. I don't even know where I want to start exploring this weekend."

"Compared to here, I'm sure you'll find something easily."

"Exactly. Well, I wish I could chat longer, but I need to eat lunch and get back to work. I just wanted to say a quick hi."

"Thanks for calling. Don't be a stranger. I miss you."

I stand and say, "I miss you too."

She is one of the few things I miss about Riddell's Creek.

Because the weather has turned, I decided to eat my lunch in the break room. I pull out my book and read a chapter, and then return to my office and wait for Eleanor.

"Abigail. Are you ready?" she says as she saunters into the room to pick me up.

I run my fingers through my hair, knowing I'm about to meet the CEO and that I need to look like the professional person Eleanor warned me to be.

I follow Eleanor out to the elevator. Inside, I watch the floors highlight and the higher we get, the quicker my breaths climb.

The elevator doors open and I follow Eleanor out. I walk carefully in my low, chunky heels.

Eleanor approaches a desk where a young brunette woman is sitting. As Eleanor says hello, the young woman's smile reveals the cutest gap in her two front teeth.

"Sophie, this is Abigail. The new trainee," Eleanor says.

"Hi, Sophie. Please call me Abby." I say smiling.

Sophie offers me a warm smile in return. "Hi, Abby. Lovely to meet you."

"Is he ready?" Eleanor asks.

"Yes, he is waiting for you both," Sophie answers.

At her words, I run a nervous hand through my hair, fidgeting to calm the flutters in my stomach. I don't have long to prepare because as Eleanor pushes the door open, I hear *him*.

"I have a meeting to get to. I'll call you back," he says.

Oh God. No way.

That deep tone sends a familiar shock wave through me. It isn't until Eleanor moves out of my way that I have a clear vision of the back of him.

"Mr. White, meet your newest trainee, Miss Abigail Crawford," Eleanor says.

He spins and his black gaze locks onto mine. I gasp, my fingers touching my parted lips.

You're kidding.

CHAPTER 4

ABIGAIL

I'M BLINKING, TRYING TO clear my vision. Surely, I'm hallucinating—my eyes are betraying me.

But it doesn't matter how many times I blink; he is still there. The tall frame is folded in a chair, staring at me with an unreadable expression.

I trace my lips with my fingertips in a back-and-forth motion. His intense gaze follows the movement and his hand on his desk clenches briefly, then releases.

"Abigail," he repeats as if testing the name on his tongue.

I can't tear my gaze away from the firm eye contact we share, forgetting all about Eleanor until she speaks.

Eleanor cuts in, but I don't move my gaze away from him. "I've got a call to make. I'll catch up with you later, Abigail."

I part my lips wider and I want to say okay, but the words don't leave my throat.

When the door shuts behind Eleanor, my heart rate increases at the enormous grin that appears on his face.

"My little airport friend."

Of all the people I had to meet, why did it have to be him?

"Be careful. I know what you read, remember?" I say lightly.

A deep, sexy chuckle leaves his chest, and he leans back in his chair, and I take my time letting my gaze roam over him. His gray suit is perfectly fitting, and his white shirt and gray tie show off his chiseled face, and those damn hypnotizing black eyes make me drag my teeth across my bottom lip as I stand there, tingling all over.

"You do, but you're not here to discuss that. I want to talk about your role and my expectations of you working here at White as a trainee." Rising, he walks around so he can lean against the front of his desk. His arms cross over his chest, his gaze firmly fixed on me.

I knew he was a serious businessman from the airport, so the way he is right now doesn't surprise me. I wouldn't say I'm totally relaxed but I'm not intimidated. I nod, waiting for him to speak.

"So, Abigail, let's—"

"Abby. Please call me Abby." I wince at the tone. It comes out breathier than I want it to.

"Abby, please take a seat."

I blink rapidly before I step forward and take a seat, following his order. His lips lift as if he is happy. I didn't argue, but I do want to keep my job and I'm here to learn. If this weren't a business situation, it would be a different story.

"This is a fantastic opportunity. You must have impressed Eleanor."

I clutch my hands together in my lap and say, "I'm very pleased to be here, and also extremely grateful Eleanor chose me."

He nods. "You will rotate into each department every couple of months, learning all the different aspects of the jobs we have here at White. I will call you and George if there are any opportunities that would benefit you both. The team I surrounded you with will be a great help in completing them. I hire the best, so I expect the best."

"Yes, sir."

"Do you have any questions?"

"What departments will I be rotated to first?" I ask.

"You're starting in contracts. Then I will move you two into projection management, land acquisition, and lastly, surveys. How does that sound?"

His question is surprising, and it takes me a second to answer.

"Great. I'm excited for this opportunity. I can't thank you enough."

A small smile forms on his lips before he nods and says, "I hope you learn a lot while you're here. It might seem like a lot at first but asking questions and having George starting with you should help with feeling less overwhelmed. I will check in with you and George for lunches, to see what you're learning and to make sure you're both settling in. Otherwise, you report to Kara while you're in contracts."

I don't have much to say. I'm still a little stunned that I'm working as a trainee in his company. He's still stern, but he seems kind, and I can deal with that. I just want to get to work and see how vastly different it is. I'm keen to learn all new contracts: there were none on this scale in Riddell's Creek. My reason to come to the city was to find myself, so working for a large company and living on my own is a step in the right direction.

He clears his throat, and it reminds me where I am and I say, "Okay."

He walks to his desk, his strong musky scent wafting past me as he moves, causing the hairs on my arms to rise. He takes his seat again and is immediately absorbed in his computer. I hear a noise to the side and realize he is printing something.

His office is impeccably clean, the desk only holding his monitor, keyboard, and mouse. Not a thing out of place, the complete opposite of me.

I sit staring, not moving, not understanding what I should be doing. I'm waiting patiently, but I tear my gaze down to my lap because looking at him causes me to feel lightheaded.

Movement in my peripheral vision makes me sit up straight and watch him. I straighten in the chair, but he walks over to his printer to collect some papers and hands them to me. Taking them, I scan them. A frown forms, trying to understand the contents.

"This is a new contract of mine. Have a read and get familiar with them, discuss it with George, and I'll check in with you to see if you have any questions."

I glance down quickly and say, "Thanks."

"I must get to a meeting now, but if you don't have any other questions, it was nice to meet you, Abby."

"No questions. Thank you, Mr. White."

He dips his chin and walks to his desk and picks up his desk phone and hits a button. "Hi, Eleanor. Thanks; we are done."

I open my mouth. Why did he call her? I could have caught the elevator on my own and gone back down to my floor. I don't need help.

I sit staring, squinting at him, and run my hand through my hair as I wait.

Thankfully, Eleanor arrives and I dive out of the chair like it is on fire and spin, stopping her from entering any farther into the room.

"Thanks, Mr. White," I say as I clutch the papers tightly and hold them against me. I don't turn around for one last look, not trusting myself.

"You ready?" she asks.

I nod.

As I rush out of the office ahead of Eleanor, he says, "Bye, Abby."

And my god. It's the sexiest sound. Damn him and his voice. A man's voice has never been attractive to me, but his voice sends thrills through me, from my head to my toes.

"How did you do?" Eleanor asks as we enter the elevator.

How do I answer that? He was short and demanding, but still totally stealing my breath away.

Unable to say that, I answer the part I can. "Good. He gave me and George a contract to study."

She smiles. "That's good. You can work on it with George, and then Kara will come and read through it with you and have a discussion about it."

I smile, feeling stupidly giddy at getting work to get started on. I reach my floor and Eleanor tells me she will come check on me soon.

I walk over to my desk. George is at his desk, typing away, but as soon as he hears footsteps, he spins in his chair, a knowing expression on his face.

He lifts a brow, and a cheeky grin appears on his lips. "How did you go with Mr. White?"

"Ah, I don't know. Good, I think?" I hold out the papers and say, "He gave us a contract to read. Eleanor said we are to work on it, and then Kara will come and run us through it."

"Yeah, that's cool. Take a seat and let's get started."

I lower the papers to my desk, but something is on my mind. Running my hand through my hair, fumbling, I say, "Is Mr. White always that serious?"

"He is a professional, running a successful business, so yeah—I guess he is. Does it bother you?"

I shake my head. "No. I guess I'm not used to a boss so... stiff? Back in my hometown, my parents were my boss, so I think it's just different."

"That makes sense. The city is intimidating, but I promise Mr. White, Kara, and Eleanor are great. They are such great leaders. You will settle here in no time."

I have no doubt I will and if George says they're great, then I can relax a little and focus on learning.

"Let's get started. Contracts are wordy and require precision."

I nod and take a seat, ready to begin.

CHAPTER 5

JAMES

I'M SORTING OUT NEW client properties into neat piles on my desk when I pause to look at the seat where Miss Crawford sat. Her seductive, light summer perfume still lingers in the air. And the memory of her calling me *sir* has me feeling weak at the knees. I have met plenty of attractive women—hell, I sleep with plenty—but no one causes a flutter in me or has me thinking about them when they leave. I barely think about them at all. But there is something about *her.*

Shaking my head, I try to rid her of my thoughts; I don't have time to think about her. I need to concentrate on reaching the sky with my business. I have goals. White Estate needs to be the most powerful and number one in property development. So, I really can't afford the distraction.

And she is a fucking distraction.

I need to rectify this situation before it's too late. Stop the temptation threatening me like it's choking me of my own breath.

I stand and rub my hand down my face and leave my office.

Hitting the elevator button with force, I march down to Eleanor's office. I need to talk to her.

The elevator feels like it's taking forever and I wish it would hurry. I'm not a patient man.

Eleanor looks at me with wide eyes and asks, "Mr. White. How can I help you?"

I can see her trying to work out why I'm here.

"Can I see Abigail and George's contracts?"

A puzzled expression pinches her face, but she hasn't moved.

I clench my jaw to hold back a bark.

She snaps out of her daze to say, "Sure, but how come? I know you weren't keen on the idea of a training program, but is there a problem?"

She hesitates and I clench tighter and look down my nose at her as if to say *Don't ask, just do*. She nods and goes to her filing cabinet and flicks through until she pulls out a file.

I hold my hand out and take it saying, "No. There's no problem. I'm still not keen on investing our time in young talent for them to up and leave for other companies."

"You can do it your way, as we discussed, so you can make sure White is getting the best value out of the program and I'm—"

I look up from the contract and raise my brow. "And what?"

"I know this is hard after B—"

I clench my jaw, knowing who she is talking about, and I say, "Don't say his name."

"Okay, but since him, you have been set in your ways and haven't mentored as much. Don't you miss it?"

Do I miss it?

Fuck yeah, I do, but I also got burnt by a sneaky prick, who I spent mentoring to be my number two, who then went to work for my direct competition. It's only natural that I'm bitter and set on not doing these programs anymore. It took a lot of convincing, but I can't lie. Even handing over the contract to Abigail, I wanted to sit with her and George and run through it with them. I haven't been hands-on mentoring in my own company because of that asshole. But I told Eleanor I'd try. Now that they are here, I need to double-check the contracts to make sure there is no way they could leave me for the competition. I'm not interested in repeating that mistake.

"Their contracts are for twelve months, correct?"

A deep frown forms in her brows as she says, "Yes. Unless either of them breaks it, like not turning up or breaching confidential information, then they are here for the full twelve months. Is there an issue?"

I rub my brow and then down along my jaw as I think. "No, it's fine. I'm just checking."

Eleanor is looking at me as if I have grown two heads.

"I'll bring these back soon," I mumble, not wanting her to poke and ask me any more questions.

I turn to walk back upstairs, not saying anything else. A few minutes later, I arrive back in my office and lay out all the paperwork and begin reading.

I start with George, who has a fantastic resume with good previous experience, so I move to Abigail's. She has nothing in her closet; her resume is clean too. The contracts are watertight. I assumed this, but I wanted to double-check. I rub my chin as I stare at her papers, trying to think. The sound of my phone ringing inside my pocket makes me flinch. I pull it out and see Joshua's name on the screen.

"Josh," I say.

"What's crawled up your ass?" he jokes.

I have adrenaline pumping through my veins from the mention of the guy who screwed me, and my stomach flips this weird way when I see her, and let's not talk about my cock situation. That's another reason I'm wound up so tight. As soon as we locked eyes, my cock came alive and he can't seem to calm down. It's like I have taken a bottle of Viagra.

I lean forward and put a fist to the side of my head and look down over the file. Damn her and her perfect forms and perfect heart shaped face.

I have rules about not touching my staff, but she is going to be the first one to test that rule.

I blow out a breath and say, "Nothing. Sorry, just reading over the new trainee's file."

"Oh, is she hot?" he asks.

Is she hot?

Yes.

Can I tell Joshua?

Absolutely not.

I'm a private man, so I don't share.

But of course, he reads into that, saying, "She is! Ah, I love how I'm not the only idiot."

He laughs out loud to himself, but I don't find it funny. I grind my molars, tempted to hang up, but I answer, "Excuse me; I have not fallen for anyone. I don't fall in love. I don't have time. No one can ever keep me coming back for more, and definitely not with Little Miss Perfect."

I'm hoping the bit of information will appease him and get him off my case. I don't want him sniffing around in my business.

He snorts. "This is true. You are the filthiest man I know."

I tip my chin up and chuckle, the earlier tension dissipating.

"Anyway, I'm calling to see if you want to grab a coffee?"

I glance down at the files and then wake up my computer to check my calendar. Happy Sophie didn't book any more meetings for me this morning, I answer, "Yeah, I'll be there in ten." I hang up, not waiting for an answer, and pack the file up, then lift the desk phone.

"Sophie, can you come here and take these files to Eleanor?"

"Sure. I'll come in and grab them now."

"Thanks."

I close the files and hand them over, and then tidy my office before meeting Joshua across the road.

On the way down, I'm on the phone to a project manager from one of the jobs when Abigail gets in the elevator. I watch her eyes widen when she spots me. I nod a hello and she smiles back and her nose flushes pink. She dips her head and spins around, her back now to me. Her long blonde hair is tied in a ponytail, and it gives me the opportunity to see over her shoulder, and I notice she has a book in her hand.

She must be having a break and planning to read, and it makes me smirk. I love how she reads in her spare time. I haven't met a woman in the city who reads as much as me. And I can't help but try to steal a look at the name. For some reason, I'm curious what she is reading now, but it's clutched to her chest so I can't read it. I edge closer trying to get a peek, but as I do, I accidentally brush up against her, causing a warm feeling to flood my body. She stiffens but remains silent. And I'm about to say something when the elevator door opens, and she walks out turning in the direction of the park. Shaking off the exchange I go across the road to the shop.

I enter the café, and Joshua is sitting at our usual table. I order a coffee and take a seat, exchanging hellos.

"Did you want to come to Thomas' to watch the game tonight?" Joshua asks.

"I've got a gala tonight. I really hate going to these fancy events, but I have to."

Joshua frowns and asks, "Why? Skip it."

I cross my ankles. "No chance. It's a bad look for me if I cancel at the last minute."

"Fair enough. You don't seem to go to many anymore."

I would rather be working or home reading, watching television, anything else than being out at social events.

My coffee arrives and I take a sip and say, "Nah, I cut back now. I just go to the important business ones and miss the social ones."

I send Sophie a quick text, to get her to make sure my suit is picked up from the dry cleaners today. I will be leaving from the office to go directly there.

"How's Ward tracking?" I ask and drink more coffee.

Joshua has a huge shit-eating grin. "Awesome. Business is booming and thanks for always sending more work my way."

"Always. I would rather give my friends work."

"You don't owe us."

I swallow the lump that's formed at the mention of my past. I clear my throat. "I know."

I'm running the streets at five a.m. with Benjamin. He usually joins me so he doesn't have to do it alone. He is different from me like that because I like to run on my own. It's my only quiet time before my day at the office or trips away. The peace at this hour is something I cherish; there are only a handful of people you'll pass but the rest of the five-mile run is pure silence. The only sound is made from me.

"Are you ready for the game on Sunday?"

"Yeah, I have been training hard. I'm looking forward to some time off."

"Well, we are old men now."

Ben snorts. "Talk about yourself. I'm still young. I don't know what you're talking about."

"Just because your body is fit doesn't change your age, you idiot."

"Obviously."

"I have rented a suite for the new trainees this week."

"How is that all going?" He asks.

"Yeah, they both seem to be enjoying it."

"And you?"

"I'm still a little reserved, but I must admit that after helping Joshua with Ward, I need to mentor again—I've missed it."

A lot.

"Totally. It's you, man. You're so good at it. But it made sense why you couldn't do it for a couple of years."

I want to change the subject, so I turn the conversation back to him. "What's this week's pregame plan?"

"Coach wants us staying together in a hotel. We have some team bonding activities planned."

"I'm sure that's all," I tease.

"Yeah, well, some players need to be kept close. Their extra-curricular activities need to keep us out of the news."

I laugh. "That bad?"

"Yeah, you don't wanna know. Trust me."

We pass a couple getting out of a cab, beaming at their surroundings. I can never understand the fascination; it's like everything is amazing when all I see is buildings, parks, trees, transport, restaurants. People have that in every city. What's so special?

"How's the office?" Ben asks.

"Yeah, busy, but good. I have a three-day trip soon, so just getting organized."

"You're always organized."

"Yes, but unfortunately, not everyone else is, so I have to do things myself." I explain.

We run up to the corner where we split and head off in our own directions back to our houses.

"I doubt that. I think you like to do it; you need the control. You need to enjoy life a bit more. You work too much."

"I do enjoy life; I don't know what you're talking about. Anyway, I'll catch you later." I run off, thinking about what he said... I hang out with my friends, read, work out, travel.

What else could I be missing?

CHAPTER 6

ABIGAIL

IT'S LATE AND I have just stepped through the doors of the ground floor of my complex, when I see Gracie waiting for the elevator.

"Hi, Gracie," I call out and quicken my pace to catch up to her.

She spins and turns with a smile, saying, "Hi, Abby. Did you just finish work?"

The elevator door opens just as I arrive next to her, and we step in.

"Yeah, a new job. Today was the first day."

I hit the button for our floor; it lights up and I step back to face her.

"Ah. How was it?" she asks.

I see her carrying a bag of food, so she just arrived back from the store, reminding me I probably need to get some dinner.

I lean on the side of the wall, trying to hold myself up. "It's fantastic. The people are really nice. I'm going to love it."

I'm still shocked at how nice the people here are. Mom wouldn't agree. She would tell me not to be fooled and that they probably have an agenda and not to trust anyone from the city. I wish she wasn't so negative about the move and would let me enjoy it.

Her smile reaches her eyes, and she says, "That's awesome. Do you know anyone here?"

I shake my head. "No. Just you so far."

She beams. "Well, I think we need to hang out."

Her offer warms me and I say happily, "I would love that."

"Would you be free to go out next week, say... Saturday night? I normally work at a bar, but I have been working for two weeks straight and I finally have a night off and don't want to be cooped up inside my apartment."

The doors open and I push off the wall and exit the elevator, trailing her closely.

Jeez, working two weeks straight is a lot. I'm grateful for my job—only five days, with weekends guaranteed off. I think about her offer, and Mom's *don't trust anyone* enters my mind, but I'm new and Gracie seems so nice. I want to see what the city offers, and I would never go alone, so I think this would be a great opportunity to make friends and explore the city. Despite what Mom thinks, I need to trust people.

"You know what? That sounds perfect." I say.

We pause outside our doors, facing each other, and a thought pops to me, something that I noticed with Eleanor, let alone the nightlife here. So I ask, "What should I wear? I'm not a city girl and I'm sure it's a different type of bar than what we have back home."

I laugh, thinking about the locals in the bar back at home—rustic and original, which I can only guess is the opposite of what they are like here.

Gracie giggles. "Yes, you're right. Just a skirt and top, or jeans and a nice top, or even a dress. It's dressy casual. But you know what... just come with what you think, and you can always borrow something of mine if it doesn't work."

I clasp my hands together and say, "Thank you so much. That would be amazing. Well, I'm tired from today and I want to shower before dinner. I will speak to you soon."

I honestly feel like my legs want to buckle from under me and my eyelids have become heavy.

"Sounds good. Remember, if you need anything, I'm right next door."

I dip my chin and turn to open my door. "Thanks."

Once I'm inside, I toss my bag on the table and take a long, hot shower.

After the shower, my stomach growls and I scan for something to cook, but instead, I grab some dips and crackers and my book, but I pause with a groan. I missed a call from Mom. I pick up my phone and rub my nose and then I close my eyes for a moment, listening to the ringing as I wait for Mom to pick up.

"Hello?" she answers out of breath.

I snap my eyes open and say, "Mom."

Knowing her, she probably left the phone in another room while she made dinner, so she had to rush to pick it up.

"Abigail, I have been waiting for you to call. How are you?" Her tone accuses me as if I haven't called at all.

I softly shake my head and push my food to the side while I speak.

"Good; just about to eat. I walked into the apartment straight from work. I have missed you. How are you guys doing?"

I sit down on the couch while I talk to her.

A heavy sigh leaves her lips. "Oh, you know. More work now that you aren't here, but we will figure it out."

I dip my chin to my chest, still holding the phone to my ear. "Mom, I know, but listen, my first day was so good and I'm going to learn so much that will benefit the family business. I started on contracts today, and I already have some ideas."

The line is silent for a moment and then she says, "That will be good. And what are the people you work with like?"

I lift my chin to that and with a smile I say, "Really good. The people are so sweet, and I have a lovely opportunity already. The team is so welcoming. I even met the CEO, Mr. White."

I feel lighter as I talk about my day, but the mention of him causes my pulse to rise. He is so charming and demanding that I'm left dazed at even the mention of his name. I sigh under my breath, knowing I can't tell her about him without hearing a lecture.

"Oh, well, just be careful. You don't know them, so don't trust them, remember?" she warns.

Of course she brings me down, crashing back to reality. I close my eyes, blowing out a breath. I'm so done with this conversation—too tired to continue the phone call.

"Well, I better get going. I'm so tired. I want to have an early night." It's not a complete lie.

"Okay, but before you go, will you be coming home for your birthday? I need to organize a cake."

At the thought of another birthday in Riddell's Creek, my stomach knots. We have a regular dinner as a family. Rhys will come over if he isn't working, and we have a cake and go to bed.

No.

I want to be exploring the city, not going back there.

"I can't afford to, Mom. The flights aren't cheap and until the program is over, I need to be careful with my money."

The *tsk* leaves her and I know I upset her, but I won't apologize. I need to curb my spending and watch every dollar. I want to spend my money on some new work clothes; the ill-fitting old clothes I brought with me from home aren't making me feel confident. I want to look the part of the successful trainee that I feel.

"Right. Okay. I will speak to you soon, then."

She's not in the least bit happy, but at least I have managed to save myself from a boring birthday dinner.

"Yes, Mom. Say hi to Dad and Rhys for me."

I hang up and toss my phone down next to me and put my head into my hands, the heels of my palms pushing into my eyes.

I take some deep breaths, trying to release some of the tension that talking to Mom produces.

I have spent most of the next morning following George, learning the processes of the company. We arrive in the elevator after a quick tea break, and the CEO's musky scent hits me. I take a deeper inhale with closed eyes and my nostrils flare. I can't help but wonder what he is doing right now. I know he's been in here, and the thought has my pulse rising. His aftershave is becoming my favorite smell.

But when we exit onto our floor, I'm reminded I'm working. I can't be fantasizing about my boss otherwise I could lose this job.

"What're your plans this weekend?" George asks me as we walk to our desks.

"I don't have anything set this weekend except grocery shopping, cleaning, and hopefully reading. I'd like to do some sightseeing since I've never been to the city before. What about you?"

There have been some attractions that I had been looking up online that I want to see. Nothing urgent, but they look fun.

George scratches his chin. "I don't—"

"George. Abigail." I turn to the sound of James' voice; he pauses in front of our desks, looking between us. "How are you settling in?" he asks as he slips his hands deep into his black suit pants.

"Good, thanks," George answers before I can.

James nods at George before he looks at me and asks, "And you?"

"Great too."

He nods. "Good to hear. And how did you two manage with the contract?"

I move papers that are on my desk to find the contract.

"This is why having an organized desk is helpful," says James.

I find it and turn to see he is transfixed by my disorganized desk.

"Yeah, I always start off tidy but then this kind of happens," I say.

James' eyes leave the desk to meet mine, and he says, "It's not even halfway through your workday though."

I shrug with a smile and hand over the contract.

He shakes his head and grabs it. I take the second to absorb his freshly shaved jaw and finger-swept hair, and when he looks up and his dark eyes meet mine, I swallow hard, feeling busted. I need to get a handle on my wandering eye, otherwise my dream job will be gone in a flash.

"Did you have any questions or did Kara help?" he asks.

"No questions. We did as much as we could and then Kara helped us with the rest," George says and I nod, agreeing.

He hands me the papers and I take them back and lower them to no particular spot. James' eyes flick to it before he rubs his jaw.

"Well, let's catch up over lunch."

"Now?" I ask.

He smirks. "Yes, if that's okay with you two?"

"Of course."

I stand and grab my bag before we all leave.

We stand at the elevators together and no one speaks. Silence is normally not an issue with me, but right now it feels awkward and I hope the lunch picks up with conversation. Otherwise, it's going to be a long one.

We enter the elevators and all I can hear is my heartbeat in my ears as I stand in front of him. I'm holding my breath, watching the buttons go down.

Arriving on the ground floor never felt so good.

I'm walking ahead so I slow so I can walk beside them. "Where did you have in mind?" I ask.

"Just across the road to the café." James says.

We exit the building and a phone rings. It's his. He pulls it out with a frown. He looks up with an unreadable expression on his face and before I can ask if he is okay, he says, "Could you please grab a table? I have to get this."

"Yes, of course," I say.

George and I continue walking. When James is out of earshot, I ask George, "It feels a bit awkward, right?"

"I guess a little." He shrugs.

Great. So he doesn't feel it. It's all just in my head.

We arrive inside the café and grab a seat. I grab the menu to scan, and we don't have to wait long before James comes inside and joins us. He takes a seat directly across from me, with George sitting beside me.

He's still wearing a frown, but I don't ask. Instead, we order lunch and then he speaks.

"On Sunday, I have a suite for the football game and the employees come. I think it would be good if you two could come," James says.

A game? In a suite?

"Yes, please!" I say with a grin.

He smiles back and waits until George speaks. "Heck yeah. Thanks so much."

"Just remember you represent White, so this is not a time to get drunk. I'd prefer you didn't drink at all during work events, but if you must, please control yourselves," James says.

A suite would be an experience and I'm trying to do as many as I can. I don't plan on drinking; it wouldn't be something I do anyway. But definitely never at a work event.

"Of course. I'm so excited, but can you explain how the game works?" I say.

"You don't know how the game works?" James asks as he eyes me curiously.

I laugh shyly. "Not at all."

James chuckles and all the awkwardness from earlier has gone.

"Well, lucky you have us to explain it to you," George says.

Our lunch arrives, so we begin eating and then James says, "Okay, so the rules are the player has four chances to advance ten yards; every ten-plus-yard advance gives you four more chances to get down the field to score. And if the team fails to make ten yards in four downs, the opposite team gets the ball."

"Okay, and how long does the game go for?"

"It's sixty minutes split into four fifteen-minute quarters," James says.

"Maybe don't give me any more rules right now so I don't forget them." I say and take a sip of water.

He nods. "Fair enough."

"So, the important question... who will you root for?" George asks.

"I don't know," I say with a shrug.

"You will root for Chicago; there really is no other option," James says.

"We will see," I tease and James offers me a crooked smile back. It feels nice to talk in this relaxed setting.

James checks his watch and then glances between George and me. "We better get back to work. I have to go to a job site and you two need to get back to work."

He opens his black suit jacket and grabs tickets from inside his pocket, handing us each a ticket. Our eyes lock before he shakes his head and walks off. I look down with a smile, holding it as if it's a prized possession.

Two hours later, a desk phone rings, scaring the crap out of me, and I realize it's mine.

"Hello, Abigail speaking." I answer.

"Miss Crawford, can you and George come to my office?"

I close my eyes at the sound of his silky voice filling my ear. It's him. A thrill pumps through me, but it quickly diminishes when the hang-up tune plays in my ear. I pull it away and frown at it before lowering it.

"Who was that?" George asks.

I fold my arms as I look at George and say, "Mr. White. But why does he hang up without waiting for a response?"

He shrugs nonchalantly. "He's busy, and he expects people to listen."

Not liking that answer, I say, "But that's just rude." His face is accusing, and I squint, asking, "What?"

"He ruffles your feathers," he teases.

I shake my head vehemently. "Anyway, we have to go upstairs."

He stands and we head upstairs, and I feel my hands start to sweat. I rub them down on my black dress and give myself a pep talk to stop overthinking. It's nothing bad. George excuses himself to use the bathroom quickly, so I go up alone.

As soon as I enter his floor, I pass by Sophie, his assistant. I wave and smile before I pause a second, to take a breath, and knock on his door and push it open at the same time before walking directly in. He's typing on his computer, not hearing me, so I clear my throat and say, "Mr White."

A firm frown hits his face before he twists. He has his phone in the crook of his neck but mimes, "Where is George?" His hands clasp together as he leans over his desk.

I mime back, "Bathroom."

He nods and finishes his phone call. I watch as he does his usual hang up without saying another word, and I ask him, "Why do you do that?"

He runs his hand through his hair, looking around with a frown before asking, "Do what?"

How is a man this hot and intelligent, this clueless?

"Hang up on people before they have a chance to say okay or bye," I say.

He looks perplexed and I want to kick myself for asking.

What am I thinking, questioning him?

I'm really not wanting to lose my job, but I seem to have words flying out of my mouth around him without giving it any thought.

Softly shaking my head, I whisper, "Sorry. That isn't why I'm here."

He lets out a heavy sigh and says, "No, it's not, but... I actually don't know why I do it."

He frowns as if he's trying to work that out himself. His confession causes me to freeze momentarily before I walk in closer to his desk. His gaze follows my every step and I lower into the seat, trying to pretend he doesn't rattle me.

"Sorry. I'm here," George says as he enters the room and clicks the door shut.

James clears his throat and says, "Now, I had a meeting and there was a new purchase agreement contract that I wanted to show you. It's slightly different, so I thought this would be a good one to show you both."

Neither of us move or say anything.

"Are you two going to come over here so I can walk you through the papers?" A hint of annoyance laces his tone.

Right.

I snap out of my daze and rise as if my ass is on fire and hurry to his side of the desk. George follows.

"There is an amendment to the terms and conditions in this one. Can either of you spot it?" he asks, tapping his pen on the paper before saying, "Actually, George, I might let Abigail guess first because you should get it straightaway, as you have been here longer and therefore have seen more contracts."

"Yeah, of course," George says.

I try to look, but to get a better view of the contract, I need to lean in and that would mean get closer to him, and his presence messes with me.

I point to the paper and ask him, "Do you mind if I have a closer look?"

He hands it to me and I say, "Thanks."

I read but I have only looked at a couple since starting, so I'm not seeing anything different.

"I didn't expect you to get it, so don't worry. It's not a test; you're here to learn. Instead of getting George to point it out, I'm going to talk you through it."

I drop the paper and peer up at him with a relieved smile and I say, "Please."

He places it on the desk, twirling his pen around his thumb. I lean in close to him, pushing aside any other thoughts to allow my full concentration and he explains the contract, talking through each section so we can follow along easily.

His care and patience are captivating and completely unexpected.

When he finishes, we move back to the seats in front of him, and he says, "Now, if you wanted, I can bring you both with me to sign the contract. I want to talk about project managing at the same time because that will be your next rotation, so I figure this would be a good opportunity to get a head start."

"Yes, that would be great," I say eagerly, still enthralled by him.

"Do we need to bring anything?" George asks.

"No. But we need to go now," James says.

I look over at George, who raises his brow.

I smile back, excited to see the project management side of the job.

James picks up his phone and says, "John, I'll be down in ten. Can you be ready out front?" He pauses and then says, "Bye."

A small smile breaks out on my face, and then he looks at me

A sense of pride washes through me.

He did it for me?

I pinch my lips together, trying to hold in a wide grin.

"Let's go," he says.

He picks up the papers and I hold out a hand, offering to take them, but he shakes his head, declining.

He tosses his case on the table, putting the papers and his laptop in there. I watch him tidy his office and tuck in his chair. When he is happy with his office, he walks around his desk and to his door. He holds it open for us.

I haven't moved, so I begin walking behind George. As I pass James in the doorway, I feel the buzz between us. I suck in a breath and keep looking down, walking to the elevator.

I hear him say behind me, "Sophie, I will be back. Call me if you need anything."

"Sure, Mr. White. See you when you get back," Sophie answers politely.

We all stand side by side in the elevator together. I hold my breath and watch the levels light up one by one. I can see him on his phone, texting, and when we stop on the next floor and people join us, I feel my shoulders drop away from my ears. I let out a breath with a long, exasperated sigh.

On the ground floor, the whole elevator empties. I follow him out front and see the black car waiting. He opens the door, George gets in first, and then he waits for me to climb in. I sit back, gazing around, feeling like I'm in a movie.

"John, we need to go to the Browns' office."

I can only see the back of the driver's head. His short brown hair matches my thoughts on drivers. His voice doesn't sound old, but I can't see his face.

"Yes, sir."

"Hi, I'm Abby," I say politely, not wanting to be rude and not acknowledge him.

He turns. A flicker of surprise hits his face. He smiles, saying, "Hi, Abby. John, James' driver."

My mouth pops open, surprised by his face. He is handsome too and around the same age as James; I wonder if they are childhood friends.

"And I'm George."

"Hi, George," John says before he turns back.

I settle myself in the car, feeling James beside me and then George on the other side. I buckle myself in and stare out the window, taking in the city as the car pulls away.

After a few minutes, he says, "You seem captivated by the city."

His voice pulls me away from the window. I peek over at him and his gaze locks on me. A deep frown sets itself between his brows.

"I'm from a small town, so to me, the city is a dream, and more beautiful than I imagined."

His deep chuckle flows through the car and I feel it vibrate through the black leather seat.

It's a deep, sexy sound.

"I don't believe I have heard anyone call it beautiful. I guess I have lived here too long to see it."

"I can understand how different it can be. I wasn't from a small town, but I wasn't from the city," George says.

I turn to face George and I ask him, "Where did you live before?"

"About a thirty-minute drive from here. I moved for the traineeship too."

"But isn't it nicer out of the city? Peaceful, quiet... air cleaner?" James asks. He gazes out the window before coming back to focus on me.

I touch my stomach, covering the butterflies that have swarmed inside, and I say, "This might sound silly, but my dreams and happiness are here. I feel it. The small town just isn't enough anymore, I need more from my life. The career opportunities were limited too."

He sucks in a sharp breath and his dark eyes soften with an expression I don't recognize.

Feeling stupid, I close my mouth and ball my hands in my lap and keep my gaze fixed firmly on the buildings we pass until George says, "I think that's kick-ass. The fact you're twenty-four and you know you need to find yourself and a career is wonderful."

I look at George with a smile. A silent thank you.

"I have to agree with George; it's very admirable."

I turn to him, eyes wide, struggling to comprehend.

Me, admirable?

I bite my lip as I feel the heat tickle my cheeks at their words. Words I haven't heard before, but didn't realize I needed.

CHAPTER 7

ABIGAIL

"How do you think today went?" George asks after we watched James sign the contract.

"Fascinating." Is there any other word to describe it? There is too much to digest, and I still don't know what it all means.

"What do you mean?" he asks, folding his arms and waiting for an answer.

I flop down in my chair and say, "I learned so much. Didn't you?"

Suddenly I'm worried I'm being too transparent, and that he will call me out for my awe of James.

But luckily for me, George is blissfully unaware. "James is great. He's got a different style of teaching than Kara, but equally good."

If I had a choice, I'd take James' velvety voice explaining contracts to me every day, but he's not our direct boss. Kara is.

He inclines his head and says, "I do love how he doesn't have to teach because he has the staff who could do it. But he chooses to teach because he actually enjoys doing it. I bet it's him giving back."

"Reminds him where he started," I finish.

George nods. "Exactly."

I pinch my lips together as I think, then I say, "You can really tell he loves his job."

With that thought, it brings the same question: Where did he start from?

The week at work goes by pretty quickly and I haven't seen or heard from James. Eleanor said that he was away on business, which I'm glad about because it lets me concentrate on learning from Kara and not distracting myself with wandering thoughts about where James is. I came to the city for work, not a guy, so I need to avoid the diversion that James causes.

It's now Sunday morning and I'm just finishing getting ready for game day, so I'm guessing I'll be around him. While I wait for George to pick me up, I have an excited-nervous feeling, and it causes my heart to pound harder. I pull on a pair of tight blue jeans and throw on a basic white t-shirt and sneakers.

Checking myself in the mirror, I think I look okay for the game, but I'm sure George will tell me if I'm not.

Well, I at least hope so...

I move to the bathroom, and I'm finishing the look by applying a small amount of mascara and tucking my hair behind my ear when the intercom buzzes, making me jump.

I hurry to it, "George?" After confirming it's him, I press the button to let him in, and I move away to scoop my bag up from the bed and answer the door when George knocks.

"Hello," I say.

He walks past me, then spins around and runs his gaze up and down me, checking out my outfit.

"You look cute."

I drop my head and look down, then run my hands over my jeans and tuck them into my back pockets before looking at him. "Oh, thanks." I take in his outfit and laugh.

"I see we both match." I wave back and forth between us.

"Don't worry; everyone will have jeans on. Are you ready?" he asks and points to the door when I say yes. My first big city football game, and I can't wait!

We walk up to the stadium with the crowd, and the pure size of the people has the biggest grin stretching my face. I bounce on the balls of my feet and grab George's arm and squeal, "I'm so excited."

He tips his head back and rubs the hand that's gripping him. "I can tell."

He's laughing at me, but I don't care. This is going to be a great day.

"We don't have anything like this back at home," I confess, trying to get him to understand my fascination.

He nods but says nothing else as we continue to walk up to the gates.

The noise of the crowd has me yelling out, "Where do we go?"

George holds the tickets to check the gate, saying, "Through this way."

That sounds like he's been before, and it has me asking, "Have you been in a suite before?"

He shakes his head. "No. This is my first time too."

We pass the ticketer, and I peer around at everyone wearing colored jerseys to support their team. Some spectators have handmade signs and their faces painted. I grab onto George's arm and whisper into his ear, "People really get into this." I nudge toward the overly dressed ones.

We make our way around the stadium. I keep my gaze on the field, watching the staff preparations. The grass is so much greener than I thought it could be, and it's guarded by lots of security.

"Mm-hm. Some huge fans," he answers back as we walk. I'm still gazing at the stadium. It's bigger than I could have imagined.

As we walk, George suddenly stops, and I slam straight into his back.

"Oomph." I bounce back, almost falling straight on my ass.

"Sorry, Abby; I was just checking where we have to go."

I peer around and see a sign. "Just up here," I say, pointing.

We take the elevator and pass security and enter the suite full of people. They're all engaged in conversations, either seated or standing in groups. I can't get over the spectacular views of the field through the glass. It's got multiple TVs hanging everywhere and I'm silent as I absorb every corner of the room.

"Did you want to grab a drink?" George asks.

"Yes, but soda. No alcohol for me." I say, knowing it's a work event and I don't want to be caught drinking at work.

"Good idea. Let's hit the bar."

I nod and we walk up to the bar, leaning my arms on the wood. I stand next to George as he orders our drinks.

The hairs on my neck stand up.

"Abigail. George." His sexy, deep voice vibrates through me.

I turn and I look straight into James' wide-set eyes. His handsome face is relaxed.

"Ah, hi," I say.

"James, thanks for inviting us," George says. I'm only half-paying attention, too busy taking in James' jeans and black t-shirt. The t-shirt shows off his toned arms and broad chest, and I imagine them wrapping around me in a warm embrace. I tilt back to return my gaze to his face after I check him out.

"Jeans suit you." The words fly out of my mouth without a thought.

He is staring down at me, not saying a word.

I stand there, not knowing how to act. I shuffle from foot to foot awkwardly.

"Are you two ready to watch the game?" he asks.

"Yeah," George says.

I nod, and then sip my soda, thankful for the cold liquid soothing my aching throat.

"Did either of you want to get some food before we sit down?"

"Yeah, definitely. I need to try some game food." I look between an amused George and a frowning James, who must think I'm nuts, but I don't care. This is all about experiences and going into a suite and eating snacks while watching the game is a big deal.

"I'll come. I need to grab some before the game starts, too," George says.

"I'll be back later," James says.

He takes off in the other direction and I watch his sexy, tight ass move in his jeans. The man can wear a suit, but the jeans are another version of sexy.

A heavy sigh leaves me, but I turn my attention to the food. There are different options, and they all sound like the most perfect stadium food ever. I decide on a hot dog and soda.

We order and I look over my shoulder to see where James went, and I spot him deep in conversation with two guys.

"Excuse me," I hear a voice say behind me.

I turn and because the guy was standing too close, holding a beer in between us, we bump and before I have a chance to think, it tips up and beer pours all down the front of me. Now my nice white shirt is stained, wet—and see-through.

Oh God.

The guy apologizes repeatedly, and I grab napkins from the bar and try to blot the beer up while telling him it's okay.

"I'll go clean up in the bathroom." I say to George.

He nods. "I'll grab our food."

I push off the bar and when I turn, James' hard glare is on me. He doesn't move; he just stands there with those two guys. I look away and see the sign for the restroom and take off in that direction.

I try to wash and dry it in the bathroom as best as I can. I don't want to miss the game, so I pull my hair over my shoulders and drape it strategically over my chest, but it shifts as soon as I move. A deep sigh leaves me and with no other option, I decide to go take my seat and not move for the rest of the game.

I exit the bathroom and as I walk, I feel his presence before I see him. He holds out his hand and I pause, looking straight up into his eyes. He glances around before meeting my gaze.

"Ahh, I brought you something."

I feel my heart hammer inside my chest. He brought me something.

Why?

"Wow, ah, okay. Well, what is it?" I ask.

He holds out a bag in front of him, and I take it. Opening it up, I look inside and gasp. I look up to meet his gaze and mouth, *No way*.

A deep chuckle leaves his mouth and his smile is so wide it makes him squint. Deep lines form around his eyes.

I pull a purple jersey out of the bag and blink through glossy eyes. A stupid, lopsided grin forms. This is officially the best day ever, even if I'm currently smelling of beer. "You brought this for me?" I choke.

I would have loved to buy one, but it's too expensive for me right now. I'd need to wait a few more paychecks and hide some money from my parents.

"Ah. Um. I can't have one of my employees' wearing beer and flashing everyone. It's not a good look for White."

"Oh, definitely not," I say, frowning and wondering why I'd thought wearing white was a good idea. "I'm putting it on right away," I add and rip the price tag off, then pull the jersey over my soaked t-shirt, smoothing it over my body. I'll have to wash it later to get any beer out that might soak into it, but that's okay.

"What do you think?" I ask and strike a pose.

"Perfect."

An ache in the center of my chest begins, and I say in a whisper, "Thank you."

His hard gaze hasn't wavered from me, and he clears his throat. "You're very welcome."

We stand for a moment longer before he swallows. "The game is about to start."

"Right," I say and watch him walk off toward his seat.

"Purple looks good on you," George says when I rejoin him.

"Thanks. Now I have a team to cheer for."

"Good choice. Here is your food."

I take the fries and get ready to cheer along with the crowd.

CHAPTER 8

JAMES

I WAS SUPPOSE TO be buying food and drinks for the guys but ended up buying her a jersey.

Fuck.

Now I'm returning to the bar to order a round of food and drinks. At the same time, I also ask for a bag of gummy bears and peanut M&M's.

I don't regret buying the jersey. I can't have any of my staff walking around representing my company soaked in beer. It's not her fault. I stood with Thomas and Joshua and watched the accident unfold.

I wasn't expecting to see her nipples erect through her top. I had the sudden urge to cover her. I don't want anyone else's eyes on her. She's trying to make a career for herself and I want to protect her from any gossip. When she went to the bathroom, I excused myself from the boys and went to buy her the jersey.

When she opened the bag, her face lit up like it was her birthday. And I knew I did the right thing. I could say I was just doing my job, and that I would have done this for any of my employees, but, I don't have these protective urges for anyone else...

On my walk to my seat, I peer over to see her. She has the sweetest twist on her pink lips, making them look delicious enough to taste, and it causes me to flash back to moments ago when those green eyes widened when she realized it was me.

Her chest moved rapidly with each breath and when she threw the jersey on, I got to see her curves in something tight instead of her baggy work clothes. I'm jealous of the damn jeans that wrap themselves around her because I want her legs wrapped around me. I can't help but fantasize about the image of her naked and writhing underneath me and, for once, I wish she didn't have to work for me.

But she does.

Which means she is absofuckinglutely off-limits.

I don't touch any of my employees as a rule. I put these rules on myself. Which I could easily break if I wanted to.

And right now, I want to...

But just for a fling? Would it be worth it?

Is that all she would be?

A fling?

And I know the answer is no.

If she is already having this effect on me, then I know she wouldn't just be a fling—she is something else.

Something special.

I shake my head, trying to clear it and start thinking straight before I go back to my friends. I walk up to George and Abigail, who haven't noticed me approach.

"Abigail," I say.

She turns and smiles and I hand her the bag of M&M's and she takes them, looking between me and the bag with a sparkle in her eyes. I don't want to be yelled at for standing in the way during the game, so I hand George the gummies, to which he says thanks, and I take off back to my seat.

Once I'm back, I hand Thomas and Joshua theirs and then take my seat and pull out my phone to check my emails. I see a new one about a new building I want. I send out a quick reply and slip my phone back into my pocket and focus on the field.

"Are we betting on the score results?" Thomas asks.

"Of course—I'm saying we beat them by ten. Usual price?" I ask.

"Oh. I think the game will be closer than that. I say three and yes, a hundred," Thomas retorts.

"Shit! That was my guess, Tom," Joshua says.

Thomas shrugs in a *Your loss* way.

"Okay, I say four points," Joshua says.

We sit as the cheerleaders come on and do their dance.

"Who was that earlier?" Joshua asks, nodding behind me.

I clench my teeth, knowing exactly who he means. God, I wish he couldn't see her now. I'll have to tell him about her and in his little head, he will think she is the one. Since he and Ava are in a fucking love bubble, he keeps trying to tell me to settle down.

But I just don't know...

I need to focus on my goal of becoming the number one real estate developer.

Women are too complicated, and I'm not interested in getting my heart broken.

No, I can't. Even women with mesmerizing green eyes I could get lost in. Ones that keep messing with my brain—definitely not her. She is way too sweet and innocent while me, I'm the older, bossy, and dirty-as-fuck guy. I would scare her, and not only that, she is my damn employee.

With the reminder, I say through clenched teeth, "Just an employee."

His brow raises as if not believing me and he says, "Sure. You seemed to dive to the damsel in distress pretty quick."

I grind down on my molars but say nothing else. Listening to him and Thomas chuckle annoys me. I don't need the questions right now. I'm here for the game.

Thankfully, at that moment, I notice our friend Benjamin.

I point, saying, "There's our Benny boy." I'm trying to distract him, which totally works. He whips around to the field so quickly, I feel my shoulders relax.

For the rest of the game, I keep my gaze firmly fixed on the field, watching my friend play and win. Thomas wins the bet and afterward, as the crowd leaves the stadium, I scan it, looking for her silky blonde hair and the purple jersey, but come up empty. With the amount of people who are here, I don't see her again. A heavy sigh slips out and we leave. I know it's for the best.

It's been a week and today, I'm restless. I pause at the window to look outside at the building below. The view from here is spectacular and a reminder to focus. It's time to get back to work, and I force myself to do so.

A knock on my door has me turning from my computer.

Sophie walks in and says, "Here is your coffee. I noticed you missed it today." She lowers it down on my desk.

I smile. "Thanks."

Glancing at my watch, I see she is right; it's close to midday. I don't drink coffee after two. Otherwise, it affects my sleep.

"No problem. Now, Miss Crawford asked if she could see you?"

Every muscle goes rigid. "Is everything okay?" I hold my breath, and sit back, as if it will make it easier to shift my thoughts.

"Yes. She said Kara isn't around and she wants to talk about a contract."

Work. Good. I can breathe again. Nothing is wrong.

The beating of my pulse comes down from its high and I say to Sophie, "Yes. Tell her to come in."

"Okay. Will that be all?"

I nod.

She exits and a few minutes later, a lighter knock hits the door, and I say, "Come in."

Abigail pushes the door open and smiles and fuck, her smile hits me full force. What is it about her that makes me feel like I could fall on my ass just from a simple smile?

"Hi, James. Sorry to bother you, but Kara isn't around, so I wanted to see if I could show you this contract instead."

I lean on the desk and gesture to the seat in front of me. She sits and I say, "Let me see and talk to me about the client."

"This is a contract for a new developer, and I have filled it out, but I want to make sure the risk analysis section is filled in correctly."

She leans over and hands me the papers. I take them and read, impressed with everything she completed. I pause and look up over the papers at her and ask, "You filled this in alone?"

"Yes. Kara said to."

I nod. "It's very good."

And then I continue reading, knowing the risk section is near the bottom.

I run my finger back and forth over my lip, lost in reading, until I see the risk section, and then sit straight and clutch it with both hands.

"You filled it all out. Which part are you concerned about?" I frown, not understanding.

She stands and comes closer. Her perfume tickles my nose and I hold my breath.

No distractions.

"These two. I want to make sure I correctly estimated." Her finger hits the finance and construction cost risk but I can't pay attention to what I'm supposed to be looking at, because, I have a clear view of her breasts and it's making me hard.

Forcing myself to ignore the ache in my cock, I lift my gaze and she's staring back at me. With her face this close to me, I notice she has specks of honey in her green eyes.

She is way too close to me.

Way too fucking close.

Dangerous territory.

She lowers her eyes, and it snaps my fizzled brain into working. However, the sharp palpitations don't disappear. I push through and focus on answering her question as her *boss*.

"Without knowing all the details of the property, I can't double-check."

"I should have brought the whole file with me."

"Is George downstairs?"

"Yeah." Her brows pinch.

"I'll get him to bring them up and I'll run him through this too."

Her face softens, and she eases back. "Okay. Thanks."

I turn and phone George.

After I hang up, it's silent for a beat before she speaks. "Did you want me to return the jersey or give you money for it?"

Her offer sends a low and pleasant hum through me. *Offering me it back. Offering me money.*

Who is she?

I have never met a female offering me—well—anything.

I raise my brows at her in disbelief. She sits with thin lips, waiting for me.

A flicker of a smile passes my lips and I say, "No. Thanks for the offer, but it's yours."

She smiles from ear to ear. "Thanks."

A knock on the door breaks the chat and I'm grateful for the intrusion, needing to focus on work.

"Hi, James. Here's the file you asked for." George hands over the file.

I take it. "Thanks. Please sit. I'll run through the financial and construction risk cost with you both for this contract."

They both nod so I begin. It only takes a couple of minutes and then they are leaving me to return to their office with the file. Sitting back with a sense of pride. I crack my knuckles and return to work, actually happy they talked me into taking the trainees. I can leave my

ex-friend in the past where he belongs and be grateful
it's lead me to this path I'm on right now.

CHAPTER 9

JAMES

IT'S THURSDAY MORNING AND I'm sipping a coffee, when my phone rings. I take it out of my suit pocket and glance down at the name on the screen.

Fuck off.

I'm not in the mood for this, but I give in. I inhale a deep breath, trying to calm the war that's brewing. Hitting my office door lock button so I can't be interrupted, I answer angrily.

"I need money for food, please," Mom says softly.

It's quiet and I can imagine she is lying on the couch in their house, waking up from the party last night.

I squeeze my eyes shut in frustration. I'm about to lose my shit.

"I give you some every week," I say back.

The son paying an allowance to his parents. What a fucking joke.

"But we need more. Please. I had to pay the gas bill," she says.

I rub the back of my neck, the start of a headache forming. I just wish this wasn't my life. Their fucking reasons are humorous, except I don't laugh. It makes me murderous. Why can't they get their shit together? It's been years of the same fucking cycle.

"How much?" I ask in defeat.

I want to just give them the money to shut them up and get off this phone as quickly as possible.

"A hundred."

I suck in a sharp breath. "It will be in your account soon."

I hang up without waiting, not caring how I seem to them. Just because they are my parents doesn't mean they deserve respect. They lost that when they stopped caring for and protecting me.

I wish I could cut them off, but I can't seem to do it. Only my close friends know I'm still in contact with them and that I still give them money. I do it so I don't live with regrets, even though the constant reminder of pain they bring makes me second-guess it every day.

It's a secret I keep to myself.

Later that night after work, I slip inside the car with John and buckle up. John pulls away from the curb; I see *her* walking on the sidewalk, her blonde hair bouncing in the wind with every step she takes.

I feel my stomach twist at the sight of her.

Why is she walking?

Where is she going?

I don't like that she walks by herself. As I watch her for a moment, I have the urge to protect her and keep her safe.

"John, pull over. Abby is there." I raise my voice.

"Where, sir?" He asks.

Even though I see him as a friend and he is only a year older than me, he knows I'm the boss and to pay respect when he is on duty.

"Abigail. She's right over there. Just stop there," I point and say, aggravated, even though it's not John's fault. I just feel like I want to get to her fast. The pull toward her is so strong.

How doesn't he remember the beauty he drove around?

He pulls over and I dart out of the car in a rush, slamming the door closed after me.

I jog up to her. "Abigail," I say.

She stiffens and turns around slowly, cautiously. When I approach her, a flicker of recognition flashes, and then her face goes slack. "James," she asks curiously. "What are you doing?"

What am I doing?

Why do I have this urge to rescue her and look after her? Pushing my thoughts to the side, I say, "I saw you walking. Do you want a lift home? John is over there."

Her gaze moves to the car. and she squints as if she's thinking about it. I know she is about to decline. So when she says, "Sure," I blink repeatedly, not expecting that to be her answer. We walk over to the car and I open the door for her, she smiles at me for the gesture and it makes my heart pump harder.

She climbs in and I follow.

"Hi, John," she says.

I turn my head and she is smiling at him. Her genuine care of others sends a jolt to my heart, and it beats in a crazy rhythm.

As we sit, her light summer scent fills the car, invading my senses.

She gives John her address and I know I won't have her long. I know that's one of my apartment buildings.

"Why are you walking this late at night?" I ask.

I watch her bite down on her bottom lip, and I curl my hands into fists to prevent myself from grabbing her and kissing the shit out of her.

Why did I offer her a lift? This is pure fucking torture.

My gaze is still on her lips as they move, and I realize she is talking. Catching the tail end of the conversation, I look up at her captivating eyes.

"I was getting a library card."

"You were getting a library card?" I ask.

She giggles, and the sound sends warmth across my chest.

Beauty and brains are a lethal combination. And here she sits, tempting as sin.

"Yes, I just left the library with a card."

"Did you get a book?"

What? Of course she did, dickhead.

She nods. I have to look away to collect my thoughts before looking at her again and I ask, "Romance, right?"

"Yeah."

I smile and I don't bother asking for the book's name, the silence telling me she is embarrassed, so I ask her, "Did you enjoy the game?"

"I did. It was so much fun. I will have to go again."

"I can take you," I say.

What the fuck am I doing?

"And George, of course," I add. I'm so damn loose around her. The words just fell out of me. "I could organize for you two to meet my friend Ben. He plays for the Eels."

She drops her lip from between her teeth. "That would be great."

Uneasiness churns in my stomach at the thought of Benjamin meeting her. She would be better suited to him. He has the easy-going personality that women fall for. Plus, his blond hair and blue eyes that women seem to love. I'm this tall, dark, intimidating person, the opposite of Benjamin.

"Of course," I grind out through my teeth.

She smiles back at me and asks, "Do you watch his games often?"

"Are you asking how soon I can take you?" I squint at her, and I'm trying to tease her even though I'm jealous as fuck that she wants to meet him.

A touch of pink touches her nose and the vision makes my balls tight. Why does every small thing she does excite me?

"No, I'm trying to..."

"Trying to what?" I ask her, desperate to know what she was going to say.

The pink on her nose is turning darker. And she says, "Trying to get to know you."

"Oh." I sit up straighter in my seat and look at the front of the car, surprised. I wasn't expecting that.

Women don't want to get to know me. They want to fuck me.

I don't answer right away because I'm trying to process what the right thing to do is. I decide I can answer a couple of questions.

"I go with my friends to all of his home games, but we watch away games at a bar usually."

"I love that you have such great friends." There is a gentle softness in her voice. But there is a hint of sadness in her expression.

"You don't have friends?" I ask.

Her head drops, and she watches her hands and fingers fiddle.

"One of my friends moved away a year ago and there is one left in town named Charlotte. I worked long hours to help my family out with their business, so I didn't spend a lot of time with them."

I rub my forehead and then I look at one of her hands, thinking about grabbing it and squeezing it. But even though my heart is crushed at the sight of her, wanting to make her happy again, I cannot do that. I have rules.

"I'll be your friend."

Her chin lifts and her gaze captures mine and the sadness is now replaced by surprise.

She smiles up at me and says shyly, "That sounds nice."

The car stops moving. "We're here." John says.

I wish I had more time with her. Talking to her is easy and feels completely natural, not forced in any way.

"Thanks, John," she says and then turns to me. "Thanks for the ride."

I raise my brow at her in a silent question. She smacks my thigh lightly. "Get your mind out of the gutter, Mr. White."

Her hips sway as she exits the car.

And I laugh. God, this woman is a mind reader.

CHAPTER 10

ABIGAIL

I GET INSIDE MY apartment and lean my head back on the door with closed eyes, trying to calm my racing heart with slow, controlled breaths. The feelings he stirs inside me have me feeling breathless. The more I'm around him, the more I respond to him.

This city offers more than I could have imagined in the way of a handsome man sweeping me unexpectedly and unknowingly off my feet.

I push off the door and walk to the bathroom to have a shower before I eat and climb into bed and read.

I wake on Saturday to a loud banging on the door. I try to figure out who that would be. Curiosity gets the better of me and I climb out of bed. I stumble to the door and check the peephole and see Gracie. I pull the door open and rub my eyes.

"Gracie?"

She casts her eyes over my pajamas. Not sexy, but the fabric is so comfortable.

"Sorry I woke you. I didn't think you would still be asleep at lunchtime."

I shake my head. "No, is it really that late?"

She giggles and says, "Yeah. But now you are awake. I wanted to tell you my friend Ava is coming over to do my makeup for our night out. She offered to do yours if you want?"

I smile. "That sounds wonderful. I'm not great at makeup."

I only have worn makeup for this job, knowing I needed to level up to work in the corporate world.

"Ava is amazing. Get ready and come over around four so we can eat, drink, and get ready together."

"Okay, thanks."

"See you in a couple of hours."

She waves and I close the door as she walks off.

I decide to find something to wear, which means I pull everything I have out and throw it straight onto the bed. I find a few options and try them all on. I'm not stressed, knowing she will help me if I don't look right.

Finding a nice outfit was easier than I thought, but the shoes just don't work.

I glance at the time and realize I can run to the store and grab a new pair of heels. I have seen the women in the city, and they don't wear thick, low heels like I do, so I get dressed in sweats and rush out to the shops.

After picking up the shoes, using some of the money I had set aside for my parents, I decide to buy some wine to take to Gracie's later.

I shower and put on a knee-length black skirt and a cream turtleneck top that I strategically tuck in at the front. I put on my new sexy black stilettos and walk to the mirror in the bathroom and brush my hair, but hope the girls can help me with that too. I don't know what to do with it.

I exit the apartment with a small black handbag and the bottle of wine and trek next door. I knock loudly and Gracie opens the door. Her face lights up when she sees me.

She whistles. "Wow, Abby, your outfit is hot."

I look down sheepishly and glance back up, saying, "Thanks," and I step inside. The apartment looks the same as mine.

She closes the door after me and I hold out the wine, saying, "Here. This is for tonight."

She takes it from me. "Thanks. I have one opened, but we will have it after that one."

A girl my age, with red hair and bleached front pieces and a nose ring that catches under the light, smiles and introduces herself when I approach.

I get a closer look at her makeup, noticing she has flawless cat-eye liner showing off her eyes.

"You're beautiful," I say out loud instead of keeping it to myself.

"Aww, thanks. The power of makeup," she answers with a shrug.

"No way. You're beautiful, Ava. A rare gem," Gracie says.

I nod, not having seen someone with a nose and tongue ring before, and it definitely enhances her beauty.

She waves her hand and looks away, saying, "You two stop, will you?"

I smile, loving being around girls my age. Gracie hands me a full glass of white wine and I take it.

Sipping it slowly because I haven't drunk in a while and know it won't take much for me to be tipsy.

"Who wants to go first?" Ava asks, glancing between Gracie and me.

"Me. You know me, so you can do me with your eyes closed," Gracie says.

Ava laughs. "That's true. Is that okay, Abby?" she asks kindly.

"Of course. I was actually going to ask if you girls have something to style hair?" I run my hands through my limp hair.

Gracie wanders to her bathroom. "Yes, I have a curler and straightener, but I think some waves will look good. Come; I'll set it up."

She shows me how to use the curler and leaves to get her makeup done.

I take my time and put some soft waves in and turn the curler off when I finish. Then I rejoin the girls in the kitchen.

I grab my glass from the counter and have a sip, checking Ava's work on Gracie.

"Woah, Ava. That's beautiful."

Now I'm feeling more excited to see what I will look like when I'm done. I'm already loving the results from the curler. It makes my long hair look a little shorter, too.

I stand watching Ava finish, sipping my drink. When Gracie is done, she heads off to get dressed.

"What did you want me to do with your makeup?" she asks me.

I wouldn't have a clue what I would like. This is the first time I will have a full face of makeup.

"I'll leave it up to you," I say.

"I'll order some food," Gracie calls out.

Sitting with my eyes closed until Ava tells me to open them. I almost fall asleep in the chair before I hear her say, "Have a look."

I can't believe how sexy I look with the new heels, outfit, and my hair and makeup done. I feel different.

Rubbing my hands over my hips.

Someone whistles and I turn to see it's Gracie.

"You look hot," she says.

I giggle, saying shyly, "Thanks." And check out Gracie's choice of jeans and white crop top. Her stilettos match mine.

The food arrives, and it's pizza. I take a piece of the cheesy goodness and chew as Gracie pours us another glass of wine each. The alcohol is taking effect and I feel myself relax and a small buzz runs through me.

"Where are we headed tonight?" I ask.

"Let's start at the bar down the street and see where the night takes us." Gracie says.

"Okay," I breathe. This is so out of my comfort zone. I take a big gulp of wine.

I notice Ava is still in jeans and a top. I frown and ask, "Ava, are you going to get ready?"

Shaking her head, she says, "No, I'm going to go home. My boyfriend is coming over."

"Aww," I coo.

I wonder how it would feel to have a boyfriend. Someone you want to spend all your time with. My thoughts drift to James and I can't help thinking of him, even though that would never happen. He's my *boss* and I'm here to work on myself. Not to find a man—even one who is causing a dizzy current to race through me.

"I wouldn't say we're cute," Ava says, pulling me away from my fantasies.

"But you are," Gracie retorts.

I pinch my lips together to prevent a laugh from coming out. If I hadn't met Gracie, I would have been inside my apartment, watching TV. Instead, I'm exploring the city's nightlife. The swarm of butterflies is still in my stomach, but I also can't wait to see what it's like.

We finish our food and wine and all walk out together, saying goodbye to Ava on the street. I still haven't gotten used to how breathtaking the dark sky is when it's lit up by the city lights.

We walk with our arms linked as our heels click along the concrete.

Music is getting louder the closer we come to a corner bar.

I tug on her arm. "Let's go in there first."

I know we don't have set plans, which excites me because we can do anything our hearts' desire.

A couple stumbles out and Gracie chuckles. "Yeah, looks like a fun place."

We enter the bar, and I'm instantly disappointed. It's small and no one is dancing, even though the music is so loud, it's ringing in my ears.

I pull her down so I can speak in her ear. "One drink and let's go find somewhere to dance."

"Yeah, this place is shit," she yells back.

We hit the bar. Not bothering with the menu, Gracie asks the bartender for two shots of tequila.

I grimace. This can't be good, but having a wine here means we have to stay awhile, and it's not where we want to be.

The bartender sets the tequila down and we cheer before downing the liquid and sucking the lime. The burn along my throat is so bad, I choke uncontrollably.

"Are you okay?"

Tears well and I shake my head, saying, "I have never had tequila before."

And I don't think I want another one. It's vile.

"Well, shit. We'll order a wine at the next bar."

I nod. "Good idea. I want to enjoy the entire night." I scan the empty bar and put my lips to her ear and ask, "Are you ready?"

She nods and we link arms again and walk outside. The crisp air causes me to clutch Gracie tighter, and a full-body shiver ripples through me.

"Hang on; I have a friend who is a bouncer at a bar around here. I'll call him quickly to find out if there's a line to get in and if he can let us in."

She's back in just a minute and shows me her phone as it chimes with a text.

A few minutes later, we arrive at a tall office-looking building. I'm concerned that it doesn't look like a bar. "Where is the bar?" I ask her.

"Top floor."

I lift a brow. No words leave my mouth, but I'm a little concerned this is a bad idea.

We step inside, ride the elevator and arrive upstairs. Gracie moves forward and hugs the bouncer. His gaze shimmers and rakes over Gracie's body, clearly interested, but I can tell she doesn't return the same feelings.

He hands her something and when we step in, my jaw drops at the setting. The glass surrounding us gives a spectacular view of the city. The room is lit in a warm yellow glow, a large bar down the left side. Gracie tugs me to the left, and we make our way to the bar.

We step up to the bar and order our wine, then take it through the crowd to one of the glass panels to look out while we drink. The dance floor has a few people, but I frown when we stop by the glass.

"Where is the dancing? People are just standing around talking," I say, worried it's another place where no one dances.

"He said it cranks up in about an hour."

"Okay." But I'm not convinced. The crowd is full of elegant and smartly dressed women and men. I'm feeling this is a different type of bar than the sort I was thinking we'd end up in tonight.

We drink our wine and the room fills with people. I have a really good buzz in me now.

"Let's have one more drink before we dance," Gracie says.

Thinking we have already had a bit to drink, I say, "Oh, I don't know. I really shouldn't."

She shakes her head. "Come on."

And we head to the bar. I sip the sweet liquid and I know I'll regret it in the morning, so I try to drink it slowly.

The music pumps through the speakers and Gracie turns to me and asks with a raised brow, "You ready?"

I nod back at her. I lower the glass down to the bar, half empty. I'll order a fresh one after I dance.

We push our way to the dance floor, my hips following the music. I move my arms, totally lost in this fun night. I'm tipsy, dancing on top of a building at a fancy bar. I feel all the bodies close around me. But as soon as I open my eyes, I look straight ahead and lock gazes with *him*.

James is standing tall with a few guy friends around a table near the back window. His hands are deep inside his black pant pockets and he's staring at me. I should turn away, but I can't stop staring at those blazing eyes. His lips are in a thin line and his hair looks like he's run his hand through it a million times.

His nearness intensifies my feelings for him. I move to the beat slowly, really trying to dance sexily for him. I lick my lips and I know I'm playing with fire here. It could end up with me being humiliated and coming on to someone who doesn't want me, but I feel it deep down in my soul that we share a deep connection. I want to find out more, and the hums pulsing in my veins are urging me to be lost and lose my inhibitions to what feels right and to not use my brain.

I bite down on my lip and really dance; he doesn't move, but he isn't drinking or paying attention to his friends. His dark gaze is firmly locked on me. I get lost in the moment and feel the song and his gaze on me. Gracie is dancing beside me, my mouth is dry, and the damn wine is at the bar. Maybe I should have finished it.

What happens when I leave the dance floor?

Will he come to me, or does he expect me to go to him?

His attitude has me thinking about the latter, but to test the theory, I tug on Gracie's arm. She stops dancing, miming *what?*

I lean to her ear and say, "I'm going to get a drink. Do you want one?"

"No, thanks. I'm going to stay here. Unless you want me to come?"

"No stay. I'll be quick."

"Okay. But come back when you're finished. I'll be dancing here." She goes back to dancing.

"Okay."

James is still watching me; he hasn't moved. I turn and weave through the dance floor until I am out and close to the bar. He is still in the same position. He hasn't moved like I had hoped. So I will have to go to him. I'll drink some wine and then I'll go talk to him.

I get to the front of the bar and lean over it to order. As I wait for my drink, a familiar intoxicating scent hits me... it's *him*.

CHAPTER 11

JAMES

THE WAY HER HIPS moved to the beat of the music had my cock aching. She is such a fucking tease, and she doesn't realize how sexy she is. When my gaze first caught her, I thought I was hallucinating; she looks different. Her natural beauty is hard for me to concentrate on and now, with clothes that hug her hourglass frame, it's even worse. The best part about her dressed up has to be the heels. They're so fucking hot. I have never seen her wear them in the office. Which is a good thing; I need to stay focused on work and not be distracted by her any more than I already I am. I keep imagining her naked and wearing only them, her legs wrapped around my back or up near my ears while I sink myself deep inside her.

I watch her go to the bar. Some guy is eyeing her, and there is no way I want to sit back and watch that exchange. She is mine. I must stop myself from taking her home by reminding myself I don't have time for a relationship. All my time and energy go into my business. I don't want to commit and not be able to give her and the relationship everything I have. I'm not someone who half asses anything. I give every project and person my undivided attention. I support and love them unconditionally.

"I'll be back," I tell the boys.

I don't wait for them to answer. I just stalk over to the bar, where she is bent over with her ass in the air. The vision has me sucking in a sharp breath. She is seriously trying to kill me tonight. I restrain myself from touching her ass by grabbing her waist and I feel her stiffness under my hands, but after the initial shock, she relaxes.

If I didn't know any better, I would have sworn this is what she wanted.

She straightens and spins, and I hiss. Fuck, her eyes are so fucking green. The makeup makes them pop. She watches as I look her over, and when my gaze lands on her mouth, a cheeky smirk arises on her pretty, glossy lips.

"You look ravishing," I say.

I'm still holding her waist firmly. My other hand runs through her soft, wavy blonde hair and tucks it behind her ear. Her pretty eyelashes flutter at the movement. I move a finger under her chin and lift it to crane her head back to bring her face closer to mine.

"Thank you." She smiles proudly.

My gaze drifts to her parted lips and I can't help it. I openly stare, wanting to taste them. Her chest rises and falls, little pants leaving her mouth. Her lips look so juicy, and I so badly want to lean in and kiss her.

"Your drink," the bartender yells from behind, breaking our moment.

She doesn't hesitate. She spins and gulps her wine.

I narrow my eyes and put a hand up to guide hers down, saying, "Whoa, calm down."

She frowns and briefly turns away from me before holding my gaze and asking, "Why?"

"You will be sick and sorry tomorrow."

"Pfft. I feel fine," she says.

"Don't say I didn't warn you."

"I already have a father," she huffs.

I clench my jaw at her reference and I growl, "I know. Because if you were mine, I'd smack your ass for talking back."

I watch her pretty mouth drop wide open. I don't think she has heard many men be so crass.

Well, honey, I'm way dirtier than that.

Her wide eyes are so pretty, and I just want her looking up at me like that from her knees, but I shouldn't go there. I'm barely holding on to my restraint.

She drinks the remaining wine and puts the empty glass down. I cock my head and then shake it at her rebellious attitude, because I know it's not my place, even though I just want to protect her.

"Come dance with me," she pleads, reaching out to grab my hands and tug me to the dance floor.

I tip my head back, laughing, before I straighten up again and then lean over to whisper in her ear. "Baby, I don't dance. I fuck. That's all I do with these hips."

She swallows hard and says, "Come on." Batting her eyelashes and trying to beg, she is so fucking adorable, but I won't change my mind.

"No."

She stares, and then a little smirk forms. "Fine. I'll dance on you. You stay right there and watch."

I open my mouth to speak, but the words won't come out. They seem stuck in my throat.

Is she fucking with me?

I'm still hard. It hasn't gone down since I locked gazes with her on the dance floor. I'm sure I'll blow my load into my pants if she gets too close.

The alcohol is definitely making her braver, making me question just how innocent she is. Despite her acting bolder, I know she wouldn't be able to handle my dirty past. My usual threesome choices wouldn't be something I would want with her. I don't want to share her... I would want to give her every piece of me.

She grabs my hands in both of hers and moves. Her hips and the way they sway hypnotize me. She is being slow and sexy on purpose.

I groan in pure sexual frustration and drop my forehead to hers. "Are you trying to kill me?" I ask through a heavy breath.

"No. I want you to dance with me," she breathes.

I growl. "I told you I don't dance. I fuck."

"Well, fuck me then."

I pull my forehead off hers, snapping back to reality, and I say, "No. I can't do that."

"Why? Is it just about work or is it because I'm not your type?" Her gaze moves to the floor between us, and she lowers her head.

I touch her jaw and lift her face back up to mine and shake my head. Seeing the pulse in her neck beating wildly, I have to resist licking from her collarbone to her ear, feeling the beats on my tongue.

When her gaze locks onto mine, I tell her honestly, "You're definitely my type. But I'm trying to be good here. Work is important to me," I say in a strained voice, trying to get her to understand my internal battle.

"Work is important to me too. I didn't come to the city with intentions to find anyone, but—" She pauses before she continues, "I don't want to be good anymore. And I don't... be bad. I want bad, James," she says.

Fuck my life. This woman is out to kill me. Saying all these perfect things and begging like a good girl and all I want to do is say yes, but it's not a good idea.

I just stay still, at a loss for words. She spins and backs herself up on me and begins dancing. The stilettos help her with height, but I'm still poking her back and I'm sure she can feel it even though she says nothing. I have to concentrate on breathing in and out through my nose, but if she doesn't stop soon, I'm going to let down the people who run the training program and, hell... let myself down for breaking my own goddamn rules. *I'm fucked.*

I spin her, needing her to stop grinding on me. When she is facing me, her gaze is heavy with desire and I can't help but reach out and glide my thumb over her lips, wanting to know what they feel like. She bites down on my thumb as I run it past again and then takes it in her mouth to suck.

Fucking hell.

I raise my brow in shock and my heart jolts, causing me to snap. I grab her face in my hands, tilting her head back roughly so I can lean down and lick over her open, big, glossy lips.

She tastes of strawberry, and if it isn't the most perfect taste. I stare at her soft, delicate face. Her eyes are closed, and she moans the sexiest sound. I need to taste her properly. I can't help but move my hand and bring the other up, to hold the sides of her neck and tilt her head up. I touch my lips to hers in a caress. The warmth and electrical current between our lips has my heart thumping harder inside my chest.

I push my tongue to her lips and she parts them immediately, allowing me to slide my tongue inside her mouth. I groan at the feeling and taste as our tongues dance together, and she is sweeter than I could have imagined. I pull back a little, trying to catch my breath. But I still hold her flush up against me, not ready to let her go.

"You make me feel dizzy," she says through these cute little pants.

I frown, not liking the sound of that, and worried the alcohol might be catching up with her.

"Do you need some air?" I ask.

She nods. "Please."

I kiss her lips one last time, not nearly having enough of her mouth. Grabbing her hand in mine, I turn, hating the loss of her body, but knowing the need to care for her is more important. We walk away from the bar together, our hands joined, and it feels so natural.

She is awfully quiet, and it makes me worry about how she really feels. I don't need her vomiting in the elevator.

I squeeze her hand; she turns to face me, and I ask, "Are you okay?"

"Yeah, but the air will be nice. I won't lie."

A chuckle leaves me. "Almost there."

We ride the elevator in silence and walk out onto the street.

The wind outside is fresh, and she disconnects our hands to rub her arms.

Not ready to stop touching her and wanting to help warm her, I grab her gently and wrap my arms around her shoulders. I warm her with my body, and she sags into me. Her head rests on my chest and I'm sure she can hear my heart thumping against her ears, but she says nothing. I lay my cheek on the top of her head and cuddle her closer. This feels incredible.

"I can call John to take you home," I say into her hair.

"Gracie is upstairs. I can't leave without her."

She reminds me I have totally forgotten about our friends. I will have to text one of the boys to tell them I bailed and went home.

"We can take her home, too."

She is quiet for a minute, so she must think about my offer before saying anything.

"Thanks. I think that would be best. But ah, I think I'm going to be—" She pushes me away with force and runs to the side of the building.

Adrenaline shooting through me, I take a deep, controlled breath and rush to follow her.

I turn the corner and see her hunched over, vomiting, the sheer smell causing me to keep my own bile from rising. I ball my hands into fists, but hearing her dry retching sets me off, and I can't help but move closer and stroke her back, rubbing it up and down in gentle movements. She dry retches again, pieces of hair hanging in front of her face, so I grab the hair and hold it back until she finishes.

"Are you okay? Any more left, or did you want to message your friend and get home to sleep it off?" I whisper.

She uncurls herself and stands, her hand on the wall for balance.

She nods and finds her phone, so I text John to meet us. And then text Joshua to tell him I'm going and that I'll call him tomorrow.

When she finishes texting her friend, she tucks her phone away.

"Are you going to be alright?" I ask quietly.

"Yeah, I have nothing left to vomit now."

"We should go to the front. John will be there."

Her gaze meets mine and the glassiness in her eyes shows me how drunk she is. She sways and I'm trying to calm the anger that's building. I tense up from what this reminds me of...

My *past*.

Something inside me hardens, but I try to remember she isn't my parents. This isn't a regular pattern or is it?

"Do you drink often?"

She turns to look at me. "No, of course not. I left my country town to move here alone, so when a sweet new friend offered me a night out, I took it. This was not intentional." She says.

Her gaze is filled with hurt, and I swallow past a lump that has formed in my throat. I feel shitty for being rude to her, knowing she doesn't deserve my asshole behavior.

This is why I can't be with someone.

I don't say anything else as we walk to the car, but she lets me hold her arm and guide her. It feels like the magical kiss has been erased and replaced with hurt, and it's all my fault.

We arrive at the car, and I open the door. Her face is close to mine and the mix of her gaze and then the smell of vomit plays push and pull with my emotions. I feel like a jumbled mess, but I can't deny she makes me feel so deeply it hurts to look at her. The green of her eyes sears into my brain. I can see her soul just by looking into them.

A girl comes stumbling out. "Abby?"

"Gracie she's in here," I call out.

She eyes me critically, so I step away from the door, not saying a word, so she can peer in.

"Abby," she says louder as she approaches the car.

"Yeah, I'm in here."

I see her shoulders sag and she offers me a small smile. "Thanks James."

She lowers herself into the car, and I jump in and close the door.

I look at Gracie. "Your address?"

"Next door to Abby."

John nods and drives toward Abigail's. I sit in the car with the two girls in silence. It feels like the longest drive of my life. And with Gracie here, I can't talk to Abigail. When the car stops outside their building, I hop out and hold the door open. From where I stand, I watch Gracie look between me and Abigail and walk off smiling. Abigail trails behind her swaying.

I suck in a frustrated breath, my nostrils flaring, and I call out, "I'll be right back, John."

"Yes, sir."

I close the door and go to Abigail. I pick her up effortlessly, and she nuzzles right into my neck, which startles me. My lips press together, and I concentrate on breathing and not on how perfect she feels in my arms. As I'm carrying her, she passes out, and Gracie is nowhere in sight, so I help her get inside her apartment, where I find her bedroom and lie her gently on her bed. Watching her sleep, I try to figure out what to do next. I should go... but I want her to get a good sleep and those clothes look sexy as fuck but don't look comfortable to sleep in, so I cross to her dresser. I wince at the disarray in her drawers but push that aside and find her pajamas. Moving back to the bed, I begin to undress her. Every stroke and dust of her skin sends the pads of my fingertips sparking with electricity and I have to swallow hard and focus on her. Dressing her in her sleep shorts and tank is hard, and I'm feeling fucked up for thinking this way, but when my eyes drop to the curve of her waist and her luscious hips and plump breasts, I throb with heavy desire. I bring the blankets over her body and she rustles, causing her hair to fall over her delicate face.

My chest warms, and I reach over and tuck a strand of hair behind her ear. Fuck. She looks insanely beautiful right now. I lean down and kiss her cheek. Every minute I spend being in her presence but not able to have her, causes my chest to ache. I really want *her*. But I shake my head and leave with a heavy sigh, knowing I can't stay.

CHAPTER 12

ABIGAIL

I TRY TO SIT up in bed, but the pain in my head screams with protest.

I moan and rub my temples, trying to ease the throbbing. When I open my eyes and go to grab my phone from the bedside table to check the time, I freeze. Two Tylenol and a glass of water sit there with a piece of paper.

I didn't get them or put them there last night. I'm totally confused, so I reach for the paper and read it.

Take the Tylenol, drink the glass of water, and rest.

I turn it over, looking for more, but there isn't anything else. I rub my forehead, trying to recall what happened last night. Bits and pieces flash through my mind, but other than that, I remember little right now.

I put the note down on the table and take the pills with the water. The throbbing in my temples is becoming unbearable, so I lie back down and sleep for another couple of hours.

When I wake again, I must admit I feel a lot better. A slight pain sits in my temples, but I can at least sit up without the room spinning.

I try to swallow, but my throat is dry and scratchy, the taste reminding me I threw up last night.

I look over at the note, reading it again. Noticing the handwriting is familiar; it's James'.

I peer down at my sleepwear and grimace at the realization that he dressed me and put me to bed. I'm mortified that he was here caring for me while I was in an unpleasant state. Last night's clothes are nowhere in sight, I wish I remembered him doing it.

I'm sure that instead of thinking how hot I am, he was angry that he was having to deal with an adult woman who passed out from drinking too much. I close my eyes, wishing I hadn't done that last night and that he wasn't here, because when I see him at work, I'm sure he is going to want to talk about how unprofessional I am, even though I wasn't out for work.

I never see him switch off. He is so controlled all the time. So I'm sure he won't tolerate my childish behavior.

I sigh and take the glass to the kitchen and prepare some food. But when I scan my kitchen, there isn't anything appealing.

Thinking of a better idea, I get dressed and walk to Gracie's. I knock on her door and wait.

She opens the door with a smile. "Abby, how are you feeling?"

"Good, but I need a girly chat about last night over some greasy takeout."

She waves me in, stepping back so I can pass her, saying, "Mm, now you're talking to me."

I step through her apartment. It's tidy, with no mess from last night.

I wince and ask, "Are you hungover too?"

"No, but I can't turn down food when I don't have to cook."

We laugh and sit down on the couch.

I prop my arm up on the couch to lean my head on it. "That I understand, but I woke up with the worst hangover."

Her brows crease. "You look pretty good."

"Yeah, water, rest, and Tylenol seemed to help, but I'm still a tad off, which surprises me because I threw up last night."

Her voice raises as she leans forward, saying, "You what? When?"

"Let me order some food. And then I'll elaborate further."

I know if I don't order soon, I won't and I think eating will stop my stomach churning. Pulling out my phone, I order us food, then, shifting to get comfortable on the couch, I swivel and face her. She's eagerly waiting.

Glancing down, I pretend to pick lint off my pants to prevent looking at her while I start to explain, "I barely drink, as you know, so of course I got tipsy really quick. I noticed my CEO at the bar last night, and we kissed."

She gapes at me and asks, "Wait. What? James is your CEO, and you two kissed?"

I pinch my lips together and glance up into her wide eyes. I nod softly, and say, "I don't know what to do because I'm sure he won't be happy with my behavior last night. And to be honest, neither am I. We shouldn't have kissed; we crossed some serious boundaries."

"You weren't at work. He can suck it."

I laugh at her honesty. But even if we weren't at work, I'm still a little worried about how he will be toward me. I'm really enjoying working at White Estate and I don't want to be fired.

"But I do know James through Ava, and what I will say is that he is firm but kind. He would help anyone when they need it. He always puts others before himself and if he kissed you last night, then—"

"Then what?" I ask.

"Then you're someone special, because he has rules about him not touching his staff," she raises her brows, "and, well, to kiss you, it means you got him to break them. And," she laughs, "he would be so fucking mad at himself."

I fiddle with my hair and look away from her gaze, needing a second to collect myself. That was a lot of information to take in, and I need to focus on it being against workplace rules, not that I may be something more to him.

I look back to her and she stays relaxed waiting for me to speak.

"I agree, but more than that, I don't want him thinking I'm a woman who gets drunk every weekend and wipes herself off. Because it's not me. I like to have fun, but I also want to make something of myself in the city."

A deep frown forms in her brows., "You don't owe him an explanation; you could just say it's not the norm for you. But don't kiss his ass."

"Mm." I'm still not a hundred percent sure what I will say to him.

"Now tell me about how you ended up locking lips with him. That's what I really want to know."

I feel my cheeks burn up and I glance down at my fingers before slowly meeting her gaze. "Well, he was watching me dance and when I moved to the bar, he came up to me. I'm trying to remember all the pieces, but it's taking a while to piece some stuff together. Anyway, he ended up kissing me and I tell you it was—hot." I fan myself and my cheeks turn crimson from the memory.

She wiggles her brows, and there is a sparkle in her eyes. "He is hot and experienced. If he can do this with just a kiss, what would the sex be like?"

Intense. Hot. Addictive.

"Yeah." I nod, saying, "He blows guys my age out of the water. I really didn't expect to meet a guy when I moved. My goal was to get out of my hometown and further my career."

She waves it off, saying, "You can still do that. It's just a kiss. You don't have to want more."

But I know that kiss wasn't nothing. It wasn't anything I have ever felt before. The level of connection we shared was unnerving.

I blow out a breath. "That's the thing. I don't know what I want. I'm so confused. He confuses me."

She laughs. "You so like him."

"I know." I cover my face with my hands, and mumble, "I'm officially screwed."

It's Monday, and I have been on edge pacing the office, taking longer on tasks that I could normally do in my sleep. All because I'm wondering if he will call and ask to talk to me, and then I practice what I will say to him. But so far, it's the afternoon, and I have heard nothing.

I'm looking through my phone on my break when a gossip site I follow online has a picture of him at a corporate event with a stunning brunette. The picture is of him, in a tux and bow tie with a white shirt; he looks delicious with his hair neatly styled and his stony expression set, but under that hard exterior is a kind man. I have seen it when he works with me and George.

Unfortunately, the woman draped over him is hard to miss. Her eyes sparkle up at him, as I'm sure most women do when they look at him. It's hard not to fall for him. She is around his age and dressed up in designer clothes, matching him with sophistication and elegance. They make a powerful couple. It's like a punch to my gut, but I can't help but click on her and scroll through her pictures, and after I finish browsing as many sites as I can find on her, I scroll through all the gossip pages about him. I should've closed the browser, but I couldn't help myself, and now I'm on one article that discusses him leaving a gala with two women on either side of him. I scrunch up my nose and a sinking feeling hits my stomach as I agonize over the words in the article.

I'm utterly confused. Is this who he really is? Or is this the media twisting information? I know who would know the answer to this question—Gracie.

But she's not here, but George might know and he's here, thankfully.

When I get to his desk, I say, "I have a question."

He swings around in his office chair, his eyebrow raised. "Shoot. What is it?"

"Does he date a lot?" I whisper.

I feel my muscles tense, waiting for the answer.

He leans back and looks at me, baffled, asking, "Who is he?"

"James."

"Ahhh," he says as his eyes gleam and a knowing grin appears on his face. "You want to know about his love life?"

I swallow. Maybe I shouldn't have asked. "No, I'm just curious."

"Right..." He's eyeing me suspiciously but continues, "I know he hasn't had a girlfriend for years. Rumors are that his last girlfriend cheated on him."

I stare at him wordlessly.

Surely not.

"Who would cheat on him?" I mutter under my breath.

Why would they cheat on him?

"He caught her sleeping with his business partner and friend."

I gasp and my body stiffens. I'm desperate for more information about his ex, so I ask, "Where? Did he, like, walk in?"

He shrugs, saying, "No idea. That's all the information I have about the ex. Now, when you talk about James and the casual sex, it makes sense. Yes, there are those rumors around, but I can't blame him. He is a busy man, and it wouldn't be easy to trust after being cheated on. And most women would only want to date him for his money."

I put my fingers to my lips and brush my finger along them before I squeeze them between my thumb and forefinger, thinking about this. I would have to agree with George that it all makes sense. But to me, money isn't everything, and it's not my motivator in life. I want to be happy and chase my own dreams. Being here in the city confirms that because I have never been happier.

"It's sad. I don't understand. Money isn't as important as happiness."

His eyes glow and he says, "You're a rare one. Most people love money."

I smile. "Thanks. I better get back to work. It's almost quitting time."

A few hours later, I'm sitting on the couch, watching television before I need to have dinner and get into bed. I feel tired from the adrenaline that pulsed through me today. The anticipation that we would talk tired me out, but I didn't see him today and if I'm honest, I'm now a tad disappointed, wishing he wanted to talk to me, check on me.

My phone rings. I reach for it and see *Mom* flashing across the screen. I squeeze my eyes shut and sit up, answering.

"Hi, Abigail. How are you?"

"I'm good. Just working and exploring the city. You know, all that fun stuff," I say cheerily. I don't tell Mom how I really feel. I never want to give her a hint of worry or doubt, something she can turn against me and tell me I should come home. I haven't been calling daily because I don't want to be listening to their complaints about being overworked, or them asking for money.

"That's good. Wish you were here. We are missing you. Work is a lot right now."

I dip my chin to my chest and scratch the side of my face. I hate hearing the struggle and strain I'm putting on my family. It makes my stomach upset.

"Sorry, Mom," I whisper, not knowing what else to say.

"Would you be able to give us any money to help with some bills?" she asks.

A pressure builds in my chest and I expel an audible breath. "Ah, um. Sure."

"If you could transfer it tonight, that would be great."

"Okay. I will do it as soon as I get off the phone with you, but I can only transfer one hundred. You need to be careful until my year is up in the program, and we can work on turning the business more profitable."

"I was just ringing for that, so I will let you go so I can cook your dad dinner and if you transfer the money, that will help."

I rub my face, disappointed she only wanted to ask about the money. She didn't want to call and see how I am or ask questions about the job.

She hangs up and I drag the phone away from my ear and look at it for answers before transferring the money and having a shower and climbing into bed to read. My earlier appetite has vanished, and I don't feel like dinner anymore.

CHAPTER 13

ABIGAIL

THE NEXT DAY AT work, I'm a walking zombie. I'm still tired and lost from the phone call with my mother. She knows how to make me feel shitty for leaving them to come here.

I'm sitting at my desk, working in silence, waiting for George to turn up.

When my phone rings, I expect it to be George, but the voice booming through the phone turns me upside down. I'm no longer a zombie. I'm on the edge of my seat.

"Miss Crawford, can you and George please come to my office," James says.

"He isn't here right now."

"Well, just yourself."

"Ah, yep, sure. See you soon," I say, a little too high for my liking.

I expect the hang-up tune in my ear, but he says, "Okay."

It's not a thank you, but it's a big deal. He actually listened to me. I feel instantly lighter and savor the feeling as it spreads across my face in a smile. How can he turn my day around with a simple sentence? I'm still a tad queasy about what he will say about the drunken night and our kiss.

I run my hands through my hair and down over my clothes and walk to the elevator. I watch the floors light up, and my breath quickens the closer I get to his floor.

The doors open and I smile at Sophie, who nods for me to go in, and I take a breath and knock. Waiting for him to call out feels like forever, but when he finally does, I open the door. I'm trembling as my gaze catches his. His face is soft, which surprises me; his usual hardness is nowhere in sight. I close the door behind me and move farther into the room. He watches every step I take, but his body doesn't move an inch.

I take a seat in the chair opposite him and clasp my hands tightly together on my lap. "Hi," I squeak.

He offers me a smile and then says, "Hello, Abby. I called you here to talk to you about a contract. Kara isn't in today, so I will give you and George work to do."

I move to clutch the chair's arms and tighten my grip to steady myself, not believing what I'm hearing. He is working with us today.

Surprise is making my stomach do somersaults and I stumble to speak. "Okay. Umm, thanks."

I don't really have many words for him. I'm still scared to mess this job up, but he won't be giving me a project on my own, so I need to calm down. I have to trust him and have confidence in myself.

"I'll grab you the file and you can take it downstairs, and you and George can have a go before I check over it. I'm here if you need any help, but I want you to figure most of it out yourselves. It's the best way to learn."

He stands and I can't help but run my eyes over him. He's in a black tailored suit that fits him perfectly. His brown hair is styled neatly and when he turns and walks over to me with the file, I cast my gaze down to the floor, wanting to hide my blushing face.

When I see his feet in my peripheral vision, I look up, and he has a big smile on his face and he's staring at my parted lips. But he doesn't comment on it. He hands me the file and I take it, dropping my gaze to scan it to avoid turning crimson.

I stand, clutching the file like it's a lifeline to hold me steady, and say, "Well, thank you for the challenge. I will go down and we will get a start on it."

He clears his throat, causing me to pause, and asks, "Also, I called you here to see how you were on Sunday?"

I shudder with humiliation, but also a bit of hope hits me. He wants to know how I was.

"Hungover, but that's what I deserve. But ugh, thanks for the medication, water, and the—clothes." I stumble over the last word.

His eyes widen as if not expecting me to mention that he changed my clothes.

The blood pounds in my temples and I say, "I definitely felt better by the afternoon because of you. And I'm really sorry. I didn't come to the program to get involved with the CEO; I hope you know that."

I want to say more, but I don't want to ramble. I figure with a sorry, he will either accept it or not.

He nods and just stares at me. I feel uncomfortable standing here. I'm walking away when he asks, "Ben has a game this weekend. Would you want to go with me and then meet him after?"

I break into a wide smile as a warmth flows through me, and I say, "Yes. Ah, that would be amazing."

"I'll ask George when you two bring me the contract to look over."

George... right.

Which is the correct decision, but it doesn't mean I don't wish it was just him and me.

"Good idea."

He smiles too, and he dips his head, pulling out his phone. He asks, "Can I have your number to organize a pickup time?" His voice is hesitant, like he's unsure.

I blink at him, startled by his question, then I give him my number and he taps it into his phone.

Standing there, blank and amazed, I ask, "Is there anything else?"

He shakes his head. "No, that's all. I'll see you and George when you have completed the contract."

With nothing left to say right now, I think it's best to leave. I turn and say, "Okay. Bye."

I exit his office, but with a fresh spring in my step. I'm going to another game, and I get to spend more time with James.

———

Two hours later, George and I are riding the elevator to James' office. I hold the file and I'm proud we managed to complete the form together.

Sophie phones James and lets us in. It doesn't matter how many times I see him; the swarm of butterflies hits me full force. I clutch the file harder as he points to the chairs in front of him. His gaze flicks between George and me.

"How did you two do?" he asks.

"Excellent," George answers.

I shift off my seat to hand him the file. He grabs it and offers a thanks. I sit back and watch him flick the pages, reading.

"Mm."

"We weren't confident answering one of the articles and thought we would wait to ask you," I say.

He looks up and smiles before returning to the pages. "Brilliant. This is what I like to see. You two have done an exceptional job." He flicks through the pages until landing on the empty section and then explains it in detail.

I nod in understanding, grateful for his thorough explanation.

When he finishes, he closes the file and says, "Eleanor will watch over you this afternoon and you will have Kara back tomorrow."

We stand and thank him for his time. I wish I were spending more time with James White, the CEO. The way he mentors is like music to my ears. Not only is he kind, commanding, and knowledgeable, but he is hypnotizing in the way the words roll off his tongue. It makes me want to stay and listen to him for hours, but he's excused us, so we need to leave.

George and I turn when he speaks.

"George, did Abigail ask you about Saturday's game?"

George beams and says, "Yes, she did. And I would love to come along."

The rest of the week is a drag—hurry up weekend. Benjamin's game is Saturday night, so I have plenty of time to get ready. I'm still in shock that he asked me and George to come to another game. He isn't the type of CEO I expected and now I have to wonder if he's the exception or the norm—although there has to be a better way to find out than working for someone else. I would be perfectly happy to work for James for my entire career.

Friday after work, I decide to venture to the bookstore. I finished reading a book last night and I need a new one for tonight. Having been to the library, I want to see the nearby city's bookstore. I googled the nearest one and it's not a far walk, so I change from my work clothes into a pair of pants and a top and head out.

Arriving at the brown brick store, I step inside, where I'm hit with the smell of books, and I can't help but break into a big fat grin. This is a bookstore of dreams. We have a convenience store in Riddell's, but nothing like this. This place is huge.

The floor to ceiling bookshelves hold thousands of books. I move slowly, reading all the subheadings. I pass a wooden ladder and I imagine stepping up and grabbing a book off the top.

Imagine working as a librarian in here.

What would I need to do to become one? I don't even know that.

I shake my head.

What a stupid thought.

I'm expected to bring back ideas to turn Mom and Dad's business around. I don't have time to fantasize about another job.

There are tables stacked with books too, so I browse and read different titles. I start with the romance section, picking up a few, but I know I can only spend a little of the money saved for my parents. After reading the synopsis of a couple, I decide on one before walking into the thrillers and then seeing a section for destinations. I see a New York one, so I tuck the romance book under my arm and reach for the New York one and begin to flick, lost in looking at the things to do section. I'm engrossed in the images when I hear his voice say, "Abby."

I startle. The book under my arm drops to the floor with a thud, and I grip the book I'm holding closer to my chest. I feel my heart beating a million miles an hour at the surprise.

James bends down and picks up my book and scans the title. Our gazes lock and my pulse isn't slowing down. "Sorry. I didn't mean to frighten you."

"It's okay. I was miles away." I say.

"To New York?"

I frown.

He points to the book I'm still clutching, and he asks, "Are you looking at going to New York?"

I pull it away and close it, looking at the cover photo. *I wish.*

"No. But I have heard about the city and wanted to see all the attractions you can do there."

"I've been." He says.

"To New York?"

"Mm-hm."

"What was it like?"

He gives a soft shake of the head and a smile. "I have been more than once. It's a city."

I roll my eyes playfully and say, "Trust you to say that. But do you go for work?"

"Yeah, always."

"That's your problem. You need to go and be a tourist."

His face lightens with a flash of amusement. "And what would be the first thing you would do?"

"One thing?" I ask.

He nods.

"I can't choose just one, but I would go to a Broadway show, walk to Central Park, and in here there is a New York city lights and skyline cruise on a yacht that sounds amazing."

He squints at me for a long time, but then he smiles saying, "I must admit, I've never done the cruise, but it does sound intriguing."

I put the book away before holding out my hand.

He frowns.

"My book please." I say.

"Right, sorry. Here."

I reach for it and ask, "What are you looking for?"

"Are you going to help me find a book?"

"I can. Unless—"

"Unless what?" he asks when I don't finish my sentence.

"You would prefer me not to."

He shrugs and says, "You're here. I'm here. On a Friday night. Why not?"

When he puts it like that, it's hard to resist.

"Okay. Well, have you read the latest J.D. Robb? The one you read at the airport wasn't the latest release."

"You remember that?"

I suddenly feel a wash of embarrassment hit me and my cheeks burn. "Ah, yeah."

"I bought the newest book last week and finished it. I need something new for this week."

"You read that much?" I ask.

"Yeah. Why is that so shocking?"

"Most guys I know don't read."

"I'm not most guys."

Oh, I know that.

"I like that you read too," he says, surprising me.

I turn and face him. "Um. Thanks."

I don't want to make any more embarrassing slip-ups with him, so I keep my lips sealed and I focus on the books.

"You prefer crime books?" I ask and begin walking past the rows of subgenres. He follows me closely and when I get to the Crime section, I pause.

"Yeah."

"Why?" I ask.

"Why what?"

"Crime books and not business?"

"I want to be unwinding, not working. But it's the suspense aspects that I enjoy; I'm not a serial killer."

I laugh. "I'm just checking."

He called me Abby, which I really like. But I don't want to indulge in a fantasy, so I focus on the task at hand.

I turn to read the spines until I stop on one and hand it to him.

He reads it. "*Misjudged: A Legal Thriller.*"

"Have you read it before?"

"No."

"Good, because if you like that, he has more."

"You are very good at this."

I smile and say, "Thanks."

"Have you finished shopping?" he asks, peering down at my romance book.

"Yeah. You?"

"Yes. Can I get John to drive you home?"

"I can walk."

"I'd prefer to look after my staff. And we pass your building, so it's not out of the way. But it's your choice."

I smile and say, "Why not? It means I can get home and get into my sweats quicker and get reading this." I wave the book in the air.

He nods and we pay for our books and walk outside to the car.

Sitting inside I struggle with the seatbelt, it won't latch. He leans over and my breath catches at his nearness. He buckles it for me and pauses, his eyes lift to meet mine and he stares with such intensity that, it has my entire body tingling. I press my thighs together trying to ease the ache in my sex. The tension in this car is high, so I need to talk to fill the air. "Do you go to the bookstore every week?"

He turns to face me as he answers. "Not every week. It depends how quickly I get through a book."

"Why not shop online?"

"You ask a lot of questions."

I shrug and say, "Sorry."

I don't think he'll answer because he turns to face the window, so when he speaks, it surprises me. "I like the bookstore. It's filled with like-minded people. It's quiet, and it's a good place to think."

I smile at his answer and peer out my window, totally absorbed in how much he echoes my own thoughts.

We arrive at my building, where he holds open the door and I say goodbye, knowing I'll see him tomorrow for the game. Deep down, I can't wait to speak to him more.

The more I know about him, the more I like.

I fell asleep early last night and woke to a message from James.

> **James:** I will come and pick you up at 5:30 p.m. sharp tomorrow. James.

I smile at his simple message and quickly type out a reply.

> **Abigail:** That sounds good. I'll be ready.
> See you soon. Abby.

I know I won't get a reply, so I go about my day, cleaning my apartment and going out for a walk. Along the way, I stop to grab a coffee at a local coffee shop before making my way back to get ready.

I decide on a pair of dark wash jeans and the jersey he bought me. I'll take a jacket, and I put my hair up in a high ponytail. I'm applying my favorite lip gloss when the door buzzer startles me. I screw the lid on the gloss and let him into the building. When I let him into my apartment a few minutes later, my heart jolts at the sight of him. His gaze travels over my face and slides down slowly and seductively over my body, gently stoking a growing fire through me. I rake my gaze boldly over him, drinking him in. His blue jeans and green shirt complement his dark hair and smooth skin. When I meet his compelling eyes, they rivet me to the spot.

"Abby." A delightful shiver of want runs through me at the way he says my name.

"Hi."

"George had to cancel this morning. Are you still okay to go?"

An easy smile plays at the corners of my mouth and I say, "Yes. I wouldn't want to miss it."

I feel bad for George and I hope everything is okay, but I wouldn't miss another game and more time with James for anything.

"Okay. Are you ready?"

I nod and fix my bag on my shoulder and close the door behind us. "I'm excited about today. Thanks for taking me."

"My pleasure. I love your genuine excitement about the game. Only my friends have this level of love for the football. It's nice to meet a woman who loves it too. But before it starts, I thought we could have an early dinner. I know you are new to the city, and there is a nice restaurant I love that I thought I would take you to."

"Sounds good." I say looking up and flashing a smile of thanks.

He rewarded me with a larger smile of his own as we exit and walk toward the car. I stay quiet after that and when we approach the car, he opens it. I sit and peer out the window. But he bumps me and I look down and then up to his smoldering gaze. It startles me, and then a tingling in the pit of my stomach forms and I have to fight the overwhelming need to be closer to him. I settle back into the car with a feeling that tonight is about to take my breath away.

CHAPTER 14

JAMES

I sit in the car in awe, unable to comprehend that she is real; women like her don't exist. At least, not in my world of corporate events and parties. And I don't go to many events; I keep to myself and stick with my friends or work. Women that I meet see the dollar signs and swanky suits.

No, I want someone like her, who can strip me bare with just her words. Her drive, intelligence, and her love of books are captivating me.

I want to know more about her tonight, and knowing how excited she gets over little things, I figured this place would be perfect.

We get out of the car and I glance at her lit-up face, and it makes me just want to kiss her. But I resist because I can't cross my own rules again, and what would my colleagues think? No, even though I'm developing this ache in my chest for her, I need to fucking resist.

I open the door so she can walk in first. I scan the restaurant through the crowd of people for a place to sit and talk. Nothing is available, but I see two empty stools at the end of the bar. I lean down, inhaling her delicious, sweet scent, and speak into her ear. "Let's go there." I point toward the stools.

"Okay," she calls back.

We squeeze our way around to the seats.

"What do you want to drink?" I ask when we both sit.

She looks around, soaking in the place. When she returns to me, her eyes narrow, and she asks, "Are you having a drink, too?"

"I'll have one."

As soon as the words leave my mouth, her face softens and her posture relaxes. "Okay then. I'll grab a beer."

I glance at her, then at the bar and back at her again. I shake my head in disbelief.

I wave down a bartender and order two beers, then I prop an elbow on the bar and my hand under my chin to give her my undivided attention. "You drink beer?"

"I grew up in a small town." She shrugs and continues. "It's normal to drink beer."

The bartender drops the beers off, and we pick up our drinks. She holds up her glass as a toast. "Thanks for taking me to another game."

Her mouth twists into a sexy grin, and we clink our glasses together and take a sip.

"So how come you don't drink?"

I watch her take a drink of her beer, and then her gaze focuses on me.

"Well, this story will surely bring the excitement down," I say, not wanting to go there right now.

"No, it won't. Please tell me."

She covers one of my hands with hers and gives me a gentle squeeze as if encouraging me to continue. The electric current hits me hard and has me spilling my secrets.

"My parents are addicts."

Her eyes bulge and her hand covers her mouth, but not before I notice it's fallen open. I expected that kind of reaction; it's not something anyone expects me to say.

I feel a little lighter because I'm finally sharing this with someone other than my closest friends. With her, it's different because I know she won't share this infor-mation and that she genuinely wants to know.

"I had to care for myself growing up. I don't have brothers or sisters, but I relied on my friends' parents a lot. The strangers that came to my parents' house... weren't nice. I didn't feel safe, so I stayed at my friends' houses most of the time."

"Did your friends' parents know?"

"Yeah, but they couldn't do anything unless I wanted them to. But I didn't. For some reason, I still carry a shed of hope at thirty-four that they will change." I laugh, but it's a choke, knowing it's ridiculous.

She tilts her head to the side and edges closer, asking, "How did you become so successful?"

I shake my head and offer her a weak smile and say, "I wanted to be better than them. I didn't want to be another statistic of *if your parents are one, so will you*. I studied after school, and all my spare time spent learning real estate or reading books or upskilling by reading online articles. Then, after school, I started in real estate and worked my way up with the help of some extraordinary bosses. They gave me many opportunities, and I pushed myself to work lots of hours and go through college."

She sits staring at me before saying, "You're already better than them. You acknowledged their wrong and chose a better life for yourself. Your commitment to work hard is something I admire."

Her sweet words make my gaze drop to her soft, pouty lips and I swallow thickly. I want to break my rule and kiss her until she forgets she's ever been kissed by anyone other than me, but I don't. I hold on to the deepening desire I'm developing for her and instead, I pick up my drink and wash down the inferno that's brewing with some ice-cold beer. It doesn't help, but at least it's refreshing.

"Do you have any siblings?" I ask her.

I would have loved one growing up, but on the other hand, it wouldn't have been fair for another person to have lived through what I did. But my friends are like brothers I never had. They might not be blood related, but they might as well be.

Her smile is wide, and she dips her chin and says, "Yes, I have an older brother. He is a police officer back in our hometown. I actually haven't spoken to him since I moved here." Her voice trails off and her color pales.

The look on her face makes my stomach harden and I reach out and use a finger to raise her chin so I can gaze deeply into her green, glossed-over eyes.

"He will understand you are super busy settling into a new job and place. You can call him tomorrow."

She smiles at that, and I move my hand to cup her face. She leans into my hand, and I softly caress her cheek with my thumb in soft small strokes as she gazes back at me. I retract my hand, and a shiver runs through her body.

After our beer and dinner, we walk into the stadium toward the VIP section, but I point to the food vendors. "Let's grab some snacks to take to our seats."

I know her love of peanut M&M's.

"Good idea."

During the game, I keep taking glances over and watch her face light up. When the game ends, I lean over to ask, "Are you ready to meet Ben?"

She nods vehemently and we rise. I lead the way to the players' locker room. Benjamin already knows we will be coming; I spoke to him yesterday.

We get past security and into the locker room. Half-dressed players wander around with only small towels covering them.

I purse my lips and my breath becomes coarser and faster as all the players eye Abigail. I'm turning into a green-eyed monster and feeling very protective.

She's mine.

Seeing Benjamin makes me walk faster. He hasn't noticed me. He is too busy rubbing his knee as we approach; he drops his hand and smiles.

I give him a man hug and slap him on the back. "Congratulations on the win. An awesome game, as always. Proud of you."

"Thanks, man. It was a good game. This must be Abigail." His gaze moves to her, and he holds out his hand and says, "Ben. Nice to meet you."

They shake.

"Please call me Abby. Nice to meet you too, and thanks for allowing me to come to meet you. I'm sure you must be tired after the game, so I appreciate it."

His eyes grow wide, and I know what he is thinking. It's what I keep thinking: How is a woman this hot so kind? Don't worry, Benny boy. I keep asking the same thing.

"Have you always wanted to be a football player?" she asks.

His eyes gleam as she waits for his answer. "Yeah, I did. I love it. My dad was a player when he was younger, too. And I remember from a very young age, I always had a ball in my hand, playing with him any chance I could get."

A woman approaches us and Benjamin stiffens as she asks, "Are you ready for me?"

I flick my gaze between the two and say, "Yes, we must go anyway. I will speak to you soon. Great game." I raise my chin and shake his hand.

Abigail waves. "Nice to meet you."

We walk through the locker room as fast as possible. When we get back to the car, I pause before opening the door. I turn her around to face me. She looks more delicate and unreal in the dim light of the night.

I step close to her and feel my blood coursing through my veins like an awakened river, sweeping her weight-lessly in my arms. I want to claim her lips and crush her body to mine.

My reason for not pursuing her vanishes with every second I stand here with her. Fuck my stupid rules; this wholesome, beautiful woman has only shown me how different she is from the usual women I meet. I could fucking make time for her, I could give her commitment, all of me, including love and support—if I want to.

And fuck, I want to.

I want her.

Right now.

"Can I kiss you?" I ask as I run my hands along her jaw to cup her neck, waiting for her answer.

She breathes, "Yes, please." And she flutters her eyes closed and leans in and I take the opportunity to meet her lips in a mind-blowing kiss.

Our first kiss was unbelievable, but this right here is heart-stopping. She opens her lips, and I thrust my tongue and explore her mouth, tasting and licking every inch of her. I feel my cock swell and a need tingles up my spine. I pull back an inch with closed eyes and I hear our quick breaths fill the night air.

I skim her lips with my tongue and ask her, "Will you come back to my place? I haven't had enough of your sweetness yet." I open my eyes to read her reaction.

She bites her lips and huskily answers, "Yes, I would love to."

And that's all I need to kiss her with a savage intensity.

The pain in my cock and the heaviness in my balls have me tearing my lips from her. I peer at her swollen lips, and I dust my thumb over her bottom one, mesmerized by how I did that. I drop my hand to the door and open it for her.

Her chest rises and falls before she turns and gets in, and I hop in and take us to my house. I'm trying to recover from the onslaught of passion and just take her hand in mine and run my thumb over the back of her hand in a soft caress.

When we step into my condo, I feel my heart thundering inside my chest. I'm trying not to pounce too quickly on her and give her time to make the decision she is comfortable with. She steps in, her eyes gazing around and her mouth wide open.

I step farther in, and she follows and walks straight to the glass, looking at the city view and lights, saying, "Holy shit. This is your place?"

I come up behind her and wrap my arms around her waist, pulling her close to me. I rest my head on top of hers and I stare out at the night sky. I have never enjoyed my house until right now. This view is even more spectacular now that I can share it with someone who truly enjoys it. Her vibrancy and excitement are rubbing off on me.

I lower to smell her, soaking in her perfume. We stay like this for a while until she twists and then I untangle myself.

"Do you want to see the rest of the house?"

She nods. "Please."

I take her around the house, showing her each room, and when she sees my library and office, I swear it is like she walked into her own surprise party and can't wait to say hello to everyone. She can't enter the room fast enough, scanning along the spines of the books, running her index finger over them.

I know her love of reading, but I don't read romance. My shelves are filled with non-fiction and thrillers.

"This room is a dream."

To me, it's a room with books, but I try to look at it through her eyes and I can't help but smile. All these materialistic items are inconceivable to her, rather than expected.

"I guess it's pretty cool."

I watch her move around until she has had her fill. And when we finally leave that room, I walk her into the last one—my bedroom. Because the night sky lights up the room, I always leave the drapes open to enjoy the view. She steps in farther and enters slowly. I follow her like the dog that I am.

She pauses at the end of my bed, her tempting mouth curved with a sudden boldness. She glances between me and the bed, biting down on her lip.

"Do you want me?"

She nods confidently. Her gaze never moves from mine. We are toe to toe and her chest rises and falls in anticipation. She wants this as much as much as I do. I grab her ponytail and yank it down, tilting her face up to me.

"Oh" slips out of her delicate mouth.

I lick from the base of her neck all the way up to her ear before nipping just under her ear. Breathing into her skin. "Is that a yes? I can't hear you, baby."

"Yes, yes. Please, yes," she moans.

I grin, loving how she's already affected by me and a simple touch. I want more. I need her to beg me for release.

I trail kisses back down her neck and across her skin as I ask, "Are you soaked and ready for me?"

When I finish with a kiss on her shoulder, I stand and enjoy the way her lips are swollen and parted, her eyes are hooded before she closes them.

"Oh God." She says through pants.

I lean into her ear and whisper, "I bet you're drenched and achy, waiting for my cock, or would you want my fingers?"

Her body shivers at my words and I pull back.

She shakes her head.

I frown and ask, "What do you want?"

"Your mouth on me."

Well, fuck me. She's letting me take charge.

A deep chuckle leaves my chest, loving her honest answer. I kiss the crook of her neck and my mouth waters.

"You got it. I haven't had my dessert yet, and you would be delicious. The smell of you has my mouth watering."

Her sexy groan snaps my restraint and I lift her in my arms and throw her on the bed, getting to work on removing her jeans, tossing them across the room. She's wearing pale pink lacy panties and I swallow. They are so hot on her skin; I run a finger down the edge in a feather-light touch. Her back arches off my bed and she moans.

The sound of her moan is perfect and I make a promise to myself to make her moan more often, just to hear it again.

"I haven't even started yet."

I smile to myself as I grab her panties and pull them off. She closes her legs as if embarrassed.

"Part those pretty thighs and show me your pussy." The desire I feel causes my voice to be a lot deeper than usual.

I help her part them and I close my eyes and suck in a breath. When I open them, I'm greeted by her pretty pink core glistening with desire.

Fucking perfect.

I lower and kiss her inner thigh, making my way up to her center and sweep my tongue along her and say with a growl into her opening, "Drenched for me."

Her back arches again and her legs tremble under my hands. Her scent is so sweet, I feel drugged.

Settling between her thighs, I drag her body to the edge of the bed. I put her legs on either side of my head and rest them on top of each shoulder. My hands skim down her soft, silky thighs and trace my fingers up and down through her soaked sex. I continue the stroking until her moans increase and then I stop at her nub and rub it in hard circles before finding her opening and entering two fingers.

"James," she calls out loudly.

I love the sound of my name when she is needy and achy for me. She is so close to begging, I can almost come. I love pleasuring her and watching her wriggle. This isn't something I have enjoyed before; normally women pleasure me, but I want to please Abby.

I move my fingers in and out slowly, her walls clamping down on them with every stroke.

"Does this feel good?"

"Yes," she pants.

"Good. I can't wait to fuck your tight pussy. But I need you to come on my hands and mouth first. I want to taste your orgasm on my tongue."

She moans and I pump my fingers in and out, hitting her G-spot repeatedly as she shivers, and it causes goosebumps to appear on her skin. I lean down and lick her nub and then use my tongue to rub her clit.

"Please."

"Please what?" I ask.

"Let me come."

I smile. There is the magic word.

"I know, baby. Come now."

She grabs my hair in a tight grip, as if to hold me there, scared I'll stop. But I couldn't stop if I tried. "I'm going to come," she says in a ragged breath.

I pump harder and bite her nub gently. That's all it takes for her to scream my name over and over like a chant and thrash underneath me. I keep pumping my fingers and then when her orgasm finishes and her body stills, I slowly remove my fingers and spread her wide so I can lick up all her juices, starting from her puckered hole to her clit. It's the most perfect taste.

She bucks her hips, but I hold them down and moan loudly, saying between my last licks, "The best damn dessert I have had the pleasure of eating."

Her body shudders involuntarily, but she doesn't say a word. I kiss her sex and inner thighs before crawling over her. When I'm hovering above her, her eyes are closed, but when I lay a kiss on her lips, they open wide, and they are so clear and bright from her orgasm.

I stand up and remove my top and toss it on the floor. Her gaze trails over my chest and down my abs, her pink lips parted, and when I unbuckle my jeans and push them down, I watch her mouth open farther and I ask, "You like what you see, baby?"

Her gaze flies up to mine, and she nods, her mouth closing, and her throat bobbles as she swallows. Seeing that, my cock aches. It's been rock hard since she entered my bedroom, and I can't wait to have her shatter on my cock. I push my briefs down and she sucks in a breath; I stroke my cock a few times, enjoying the heated flare of her gaze. She loves it. I walk to the bedside table to grab a condom.

I tear it open and cover myself and step over to her, asking, "Are you sure?"

"Yes," she hisses, and her eyes sparkle with anticipation.

I know she wants this as much as me, so I lean down and slam my mouth on hers, swallowing her cute little moans and letting her taste herself on my tongue before I pull away. I lean up on one hand and grab the base of my cock with the other and rub my tip along her opening; she groans and wiggles, but I don't make her wait any longer and I thrust inside. She screams my name and I feel like I'm in heaven; her warm, slick pussy is better than anything I could have imagined.

I move, my thrusts getting harder each time, her fingers and nails finding my shoulders and back and begging for more as she claws me, marking me. And fuck do I want to wear her marks loud and proud.

With my heart aching from how spectacular we fit together, I fuck her hard, and she screams, "Harder."

I have to close my eyes and concentrate on slamming into her with every thrust. "Baby, you will get what I give you. I promise I'll take care of you".

Her walls spasm and tighten around me and her toes curl and I know she is close, so I rasp between slams, "Be a good girl and come for me now."

"James," she screams, shattering beneath me.

Her pussy milks me, and I can't hold on any longer. It feels way too good; I moan as my dick pulses, emptying.

When I'm finished, I gaze down at her face. I'm breathing hard, and she smiles. It makes my heart thump.

I kiss her softly and I lie down next to her, pulling her to me, wanting to hold her close while we both come down from that amazing sex.

A layer of perspiration covers our bodies and I push a wet strand of her blonde hair away from her face and ask her, "Are you okay?"

"Yes," she says with a smile. "More than okay."

I smile. "You ready for a shower before bed?"

She nods. "Yes."

And with those words, I scoop her up and carry her to the bathroom to shower.

CHAPTER 15

ABIGAIL

I'M TANGLED AROUND A six-foot-one man whose steady heartbeat pounds underneath my ear. His steady breath tells me he's asleep. I lie there thinking about our awesome date yesterday and then the full night of pleasure. He is by far the best lover I have ever experienced. He worships every inch of a woman's body and the soft kisses afterward show me that tender side he doesn't show the rest of the world.

"Good morning," his raspy voice grumbles under me.

I turn to smile at him, saying, "Hi."

"How are you feeling?"

"Really good."

I move closer to take his lips in a long, sensual kiss. He hums as I drag my teeth over his bottom lip, and then I kiss him again. His lips are so soft, and they feel so good against mine. I could kiss him forever; there is something about kissing him that makes me feel connected. His hand grabs the back of my head to hold me there, and his tongue takes control. A moan leaves the back of my throat in appreciation.

After a minute, I need a breath, so I pull back and he says, "Mm, that's good. Not too sore for another round?"

I giggle. "Oh, no way. I'm spent. My body needs to recover."

His grin is proud. "Well, let's get you some breakfast and showered before we go do something for the day."

I gape and jump up on my knees, staring down at him. "Are you serious?" I ask.

He dips his chin and reaches out and strokes between my breasts toward one nipple, then the other, causing a full-body shiver and my nipples to pebble. "Yes, I'm serious. Let's go eat so we can start exploring."

I don't say anything. I just gaze at him, wondering how he is even real. I shimmy back and get off the bed, about to pick up my clothes, but I pause and ask, "Do you mind if I freshen up first?"

He gets off the bed and comes to stand in front of me, tucking my hair behind my ear, and I look up to face him. He pecks my lips and says, "Not at all. I'll start with breakfast. Come find me when you're done."

He leaves one last soft kiss on my lips and then walks away; I watch his naked ass and muscled back walk out of sight. A small sigh leaves me, and I scoop my clothes off the floor and walk toward his bathroom. After the shower, I walk through his divine house passing the formal lounge that has a gigantic chandelier hanging in the middle of the room, and I smell the sweet food as I enter the kitchen. The all-white kitchen looks brand new. He stands with his naked back to me while cooking.

"Your house is gorgeous. It looks like it belongs in magazines. I have only ever seen houses like these in movies."

He spins to face me. "I'm glad you like it. To be honest, I don't enjoy it as much as I should."

I stand with my hands on the counter. "You work hard. So, what are you cooking? It smells so good. Can I help?"

"No, I'm good. Just sit down and talk to me. I'm almost done with these."

I pull out a chair and sit. "Well, I do have a question I wanted to ask you."

"Yeah, what is it?" he says over his shoulder.

I play with my wet hair, watching him, feeling a tad queasy about asking. "So, I wanted to ask you about your ex."

"Ask away," he says with a nonchalant voice.

"Well, um, I heard she cheated on you."

He freezes for a moment before continuing to flip a pancake. "Who's telling you this?"

I don't want to say George and risk him losing his job.

"It doesn't matter who told me. But if it makes you feel better, I think she's an idiot."

He smiles broadly at that. "What about your ex?" He asks.

"I can tell you I haven't dated much." I laugh. "I have had one serious boyfriend. I was with him for a few years, but he took a job out of town and long distance didn't work."

His gaze turns hard. "So you still would be with him if he walked in tomorrow and asked for you back?"

"No, after we broke up, I realized we weren't meant to be a couple. We are better off apart. I'm the happiest person right now."

"Good because I'm also very happy right now." He says and turns back to the stove and stays silent.

I watch him move about his kitchen with a stupid smile on my face and if I wasn't tired from our romp last night, I'd beg him to eat me for breakfast.

He takes the food to the table and says, "It's ready. Come sit."

I do, and as I take my first bite, he says, "My ex cheated on me with my ex-business partner and so-called friend. I walked in on her having sex with him in the office. She wanted me to propose because we had been together for three years and practically lived together, but I was twenty-eight, and not ready. So, of course, we split, and that's it. I never heard from her again."

I sit still and say nothing, waiting for him to finish eating, but he doesn't, so after a few minutes, I ask, "Have you dated anyone else since then?"

"Not exactly dating. No one has caught my attention to consider more—well, not until you."

"Why? I'm nothing special." I say with a shrug.

He shakes his head. "I disagree. You came to the city to further yourself in your career, leaving your family and friends. You work hard, you're honest, kind, intelligent, and there is this sense of calm I get whenever you're around—it's as if I can be my true self."

I watch him curiously before speaking. "Thank you. They are the nicest words anyone has ever said to me."

"That's a shame. You should be told all the time how special you are."

He smiles at me and my heart swells inside my chest. He's back eating his pancakes. The silence is causing the food to feel caught in my throat. I wash it down with the juice he put down on the table and try to eat a little more. His tender words were not something I expected to hear, but they were a wonderful surprise.

"What did you have in mind today?" I ask, turning the conversation away from his ex and feelings.

"First, I'll take you to get the best coffee and then I thought there is a museum I have always wanted to go to but have never been to, and then have a bit of lunch. What do you think?" He eyes me curiously.

"I like that idea—a lot."

He comes over to me and kisses my forehead and says, "Let's go, then."

After he showers, we walk out of his apartment hand in hand. He explains certain buildings or gives me facts about the city. It's fascinating, and I love how he knows so much about it. We arrive at his coffee shop, but don't stay. We clutch our coffees and sip them while we continue sightseeing.

"The museum is just there." I follow his finger across the road. "But let's finish our coffees in the park first."

We wander into the large park, which is filled with trees and flowers and people jogging past. We find a bench and take a seat, sipping the drinks. It's so peaceful. The smell of grass and open air fills my lungs, having a relaxing effect on me.

"Do you think you will ever return to your hometown?" he asks.

I ponder his question before turning to him, shaking my head. "No, I don't see myself ever returning. I have never felt so free since living here."

"Why didn't you feel like that at home?"

I sigh. "I worked all the time and my parents always dictated what I would do and say. They love me, but they smother me too."

Watching families play ball in the park makes me smile. I don't have fun memories like that.

"Are they like that with your brother?" He asks.

"Well, it's different with him. Mom is always meddling in his life. He hates it." I chuckle, thinking of my family.

I lay my head against his shoulder. His coat is soft against my face and his scent is stronger now that I'm this close. We sit in silence, watching the world go by. The peace I feel inside me is a moment I won't forget. He makes me feel like I have never felt before, a mix of butterflies and ease.

I didn't come to the city to find someone, but it seems the city has other ideas. It brought me to him.

"Are you ready?" His voice vibrates through me.

"Mm-hmm."

I sit back up and drain my cup. We hold hands and throw our cups in the bin and walk silently toward the museum.

A few hours later, we walk out of the museum in awe. I can't believe the history of the city. I have a wide grin on my face.

"You ready for lunch?" he asks.

"Definitely. I'm starving."

He leans down and whispers into my ear, "You know I'm starving too, but the only thing that will satisfy me is your pussy."

A shocked gasp leaves me, and I cover it with my hand before I smack his chest playfully. "James."

"It's true, but since you want food, I have a restaurant in mind. It's not too far away. Are you okay to walk?"

My heart beats harder. I can't get over how thoughtfully he's planned for our day. "Yeah, I'm good."

He nods and when we arrive inside the Italian restaurant, I run my hands down my jersey, feeling stupidly underdressed for a place like this.

"You look cute. Don't stress."

I peek up at him from under my lashes and smile bashfully. He knows what to say at exactly the right time.

We are taken to our seats where I sit, and suddenly I feel hot and my throat constricts so I take the glass of water and drink. He sits there looking like he belongs, even in his casual look. He looks at me with a blazing stare and I know he doesn't mind the jersey.

"Hi, what can I get you two to drink?" a waitress purrs behind me.

I swivel in my chair and smile at the brunette woman who looks to be in her late twenties. She hands us both a menu and I sit quietly reading it, but James interrupts, "What would you like Abby?"

I look up and he nods, encouraging me to order first.

My gaze hits hers, and she pops a brow as if to say, *Are you going to order?*

"Yes, ah, can I get a sparkling water?" I squeak out.

"I'll have the same." James politely replies.

Her face splits into a fake smile and I shrivel into my seat, nibbling on my lip. But her focus is directly at James. His body is tall, powerful, and unmoving. He isn't indulging her. Instead, he keeps his gaze fixed on me.

"I'll be back with your drinks."

His gaze flicks briefly to her before locking with mine. I flush, crimson.

He offers me a crooked smile, and his gaze bores into mine with a hint of something I don't recognize. "Are you jealous, Miss Crawford?"

"No. But it isn't something I'm used to."

I read the online article, and George has told me about his past and I can't help but wonder will he ever be able to settle down with one woman? And would I be enough? But I shake my head, clearing the stupid thoughts that enter my mind. And Gracie confirmed that I'm special. I've got to trust him. He wouldn't be risking our work for a wasted fling; work is important for both of us, which is why we didn't act straight away.

"I have no desire for anyone else. The only woman I am interested in...is you."

He fixes his gaze on me, and I feel my heart beating in my ear. I'm unable to talk, sitting frozen in the spot as a smirk breaks triumphantly on his face.

The words he speaks are bringing me to my knees and patching up my silly heart. *How did I get this man's attention?*

I'm sitting here a world apart from my small town with a handsome man who is telling me he is interested in me. Someone pinch me.

When we get home, we barely make it inside the door. His gaze is roaming up and down my body, and he grabs my hand to bring me toward him.

"Do you know how much I want you?"

I bite my lip and shake my head slowly, peering up at him from under my lashes. His mouth crushes mine in a heated passion. Our tongues are dancing hungrily and I want more. I have a burning sensation in my core that needs him. He's flush up against me, but it still doesn't feel close enough. He kisses and nibbles along my jaw toward my ear, where his teeth graze my lobe and tug it sharply between his teeth, and then he continues the attack on my neck, moving to my collarbone. Running his hands through my hair, tugging my head to the opposite side so he can continue his path of kisses and nips.

His hands run along my back, leaving a trail of goose-bumps where he touches. Grabbing my ass, and squeezing each cheek roughly in his hands, urging me to jump on his hips. He pushes my ass against his hard length and my clit lines up perfectly on him and I grind him through our clothes.

"Oh, James, God," I say.

He growls into my ear, "I love that pretty little mouth, soon I'll be filling it full of my cock."

I shudder at his crass words and his warm breath on me. My arousal peaks and another moan slips out, so I capture his mouth again in a rough kiss.

He is quick to remove my top, pulling it off over my head and dropping it to the floor. I pull back with wide eyes.

He hisses. "No bra, you naughty girl."

I feel my face flush crimson, loving how much I can affect him. Here I was thinking it was just me feeling swept up in attraction.

He takes my breasts in his hands, my nipples pebble into hard buds, and I'm soaked. He squeezes each breast and rubs his thumb across my nipples.

"Ah, shit," I say, and then I slam my lips shut, trying to stop myself from talking. The sensation hitting me straight between the legs makes my body ache painfully.

He continues his assault, rolling each nipple between his forefinger and thumb, and I don't know how much more I can take.

He lowers me to the floor, keeping me close, and begins unbuttoning my jeans. He pushes them over my hips, dropping them to the floor. I step out of them and stand there naked because I didn't have any fresh panties with me.

"No panties either? A very naughty girl."

There is a fire in his eyes and a strain in his voice. That makes me flush from head to toe.

"You want my cock, don't you?" he asks. He skims his fingers over my hips and ass, gently, just a whisper of contact, and I quiver and wish he would move lower, in between my thighs, to take away the ache.

I nod, tugging my bottom lip, unable to say the words. I stare hopelessly into his eyes not caring if I seem desperate because right now, I feel needy for him. Knowing how good he can make me feel, I chase it again.

Standing there completely bare while he is in all his clothes. I reach out and he helps me remove them. When his shirt is off, I skim my hands over his warm, naked chest and down over each ab to his prominent V that shows me the line to his cock.

I grab his jeans roughly and drop to my knees, peeking up at him from under my lashes.

He stares back at me with wonder. "Fuck, Abby." He growls and I smile back with a thrill.

"You're excited, aren't you?" He asks with a devilish grin.

I don't bother answering him with words. Instead, I pull his jeans down over his thighs and down his legs until they pool at his feet.

He kicks them away and I pull his briefs down, releasing his heavy, thick cock from the material. I run my hands over his thighs, feeling his dark hair under my palms, and he tenses when I'm close to his swollen cock. A gruttal *Mm* leaves his mouth. I peer up under my lashes and the view makes a soft sigh escape. He is watching me with an open mouth, his breaths short and sharp, which causes a longing in me.

I grab the base of his shaft and lick along the underside before pulling back and saying, "This cock is as perfect as you." My voice is husky and I know I'm playing with fire, but I want to drive him to the edge like he does me.

A frustrated growl leaves his chest, and he says, "You're trouble, with a capital T. Now show me how perfect it looks as you take me deep into that pretty little mouth of yours."

I swallow hard from his words. They send the blood rushing to my sex and I hide my grin.

With pleasure...

I love the fact I'm in control of him right now. Grabbing him again, I lick his shaft and twirl my tongue around the head. His cock pulses in my mouth and I love that his body is showing me what he likes.

I lick his shaft again and after another twirl, I take him all the way in until I can't take any more and I tug up on the base of his cock. I drag my tongue underneath him all the way out and then, with my hand, I pull him down. The tug-of-war, push and pull, doesn't last long before his hands are in my hair, tightening, and I hear him suck in a sharp breath.

"That's it, like that," he rasps.

I have one hand on his thigh and am squeezing it, but as he grows in my mouth, I feel the taste of his salty pre-cum on my tongue and I moan. The vibration of it causes him to tighten his grip in my hair until he pinches my scalp.

"Fuck, baby. I'm going to come down your throat in a second if you don't stop right now."

The ache between my thighs becomes uncomfortable, so I close them, trying to ease the pain. I know I'm wet and ready for him, but I need him to come first.

I need that power over him. I keep up the same rhythm, ignoring that he is trying to hurry by thrusting into my mouth.

A few minutes later, he grunts at me. "I'm coming." And I take him as much as I can and when his hot orgasm hits my throat, I swallow it all. When he stops, he lets go of the harsh grip on my hair and strokes it down, and I slowly release him.

I sit back on my heels; he gazes down and shakes his head. "You are going to be the death of me. Get on your knees on that bed now."

I twist my lips into a knowing grin and I scramble off the floor, eager for release. I get on the bed and peek over my shoulder, watching him come to stand behind me. His hand reaches out to stroke my clit and I nearly jump off the bed. That's how sensitive I am.

"I love how responsive you are to me," he growls.

He runs two fingers along my clit to my opening and thrusts them in; I let out a feral cry. He moves his fingers in and out, hitting my G-spot with each stroke. I feel like I'm going to combust with desire; the walls tighten up and I'm clenching hard on his hand, but he doesn't stop. He keeps up the pace and moves his thumb to my puckered hole.

At the movement, I hitch a breath.

He stops and moves away, asking, "Are you sure you're okay with this?"

"Yes," I breathe.

"Okay, but don't move."

I nod.

A minute later, he returns to me and I gasp from the cold lube but as if sensing my fear, he whispers, "It's okay. I got you, baby. But do you want to stop? We can do this another time."

"No. I want this, please," I say.

I'm grateful that he cares about me, but I want to try this, and who better than to do it with than someone I like and trust.

"I'll make you feel good. I'll take it slow."

This is a territory no other man has gone before. I have always said no, but with him, I want to try. Everything we have done so far has been incredible. So I don't take long to nod and let out the breath I was holding and say, "Okay."

"Good girl."

He rubs his thumb in lazy circles, and a tingle runs through me. My regular breathing returns and pleasure is ripping through me. Newfound pleasure takes over and I don't think I can hang on much longer.

He slips two fingers inside my pussy as he continues stroking the back entrance with lazy circles. "Does this feel good?" he asks.

"Hm-mm. Yes, so hot."

"Good. I want you to enjoy this."

I moan in response.

His fingers don't stop and I'm so close to orgasm.

"I want you to come all over my hand." He speaks into my neck as he presses his thumb inside me. I feel a slight sting, but it quickly subsides to an intense pleasure.

His words and thumb send me off the ledge and I'm groaning loudly and my release ripples through me. The orgasm hits me harder than I've ever experienced before and when I come down from the peak, I'm breathless and I drop to my forearms and lay my head down, trying to recover.

But he doesn't give me much time. He rolls me over and I gaze at his dark, hooded eyes. He kisses me until my lips feel raw and swollen.

"I can't get enough of you," he smiles, reading the shock on my face.

Well, how can I deprive him of what he wants when my body will love him for it soon?

He grabs a condom and rolls it on before gently sliding into me, inch by inch, and I welcome him with a shudder of pleasure. Once he is flush up against me, all the way in, and I'm adjusted, he pulls out and thrusts in the most perfect rhythm. He becomes harder and faster with each thrust. His grunting and masculine scent fill my nose.

He growls at me. "Come on me, baby. Let me have it."

I'm too breathless to talk, the orgasm building fast. My walls are spasming around him, chasing the release it is desperate for. I'm gripping his shoulders tightly for something to steady me, losing control. I arch my back off the bed and I release a long moan.

"Fuck," he grunts and I feel him pulsate inside and know he is coming too.

When he is empty, he leans forward, kissing me so softly, it causes me to shiver involuntarily. I run my hands down his shoulders and up his muscular arms, enjoying the feel of this man over me, controlling my pleasure. I love it; it's the most intense sexual experience I have ever had. He worships and pleasures me like he was born to do it.

He kisses my forehead and then over each eyelid and then hovers over me, waiting for me to open my eyes. When I flutter them open, he smiles and lays down pulling me with him. He grabs my waist and holds me close, never letting me go.

CHAPTER 16

JAMES

I WALK INTO MY dark office a little earlier than normal because I did not complete the usual extra work I normally do on the weekends. I don't regret it, though. I can't remember the last time I had two days off work and actually enjoyed myself. I never even thought about opening my emails or my laptop. Abigail distracted me in the best way possible.

I smile as I think about her and I shake my head, getting back into work mode, as I have a lot to do this morning. I flick the lights on and sort the paperwork in order.

Once I'm organized, I sit down and begin emailing the to-do list for Sophie before responding to the mountain of emails that I received over the weekend.

I'm deep in a new contract when Sophie enters my office. I'm listening to her explain her weekend antics when my mind travels back to my weekend.

The way Abigail's body responded to my touch, the soft moans and sounds coming from her sweet mouth sends a rush of blood to my cock that's borderline painful. I feel my balls become heavy and achy with needing her again. When will I ever get my fill? This longing for a woman is a new feeling for me.

There is a tightness in my chest as I think about how vulnerable I am with her. How I can tell her things I don't even tell Joshua, Benjamin and Thomas.

I couldn't turn her away even if I wanted to. There is something in her green eyes that has me second-guessing my theories about relationships. She is so different from anything I could have imagined. I wasn't looking for a relationship, or wanting one, but she barreled into my life and forced me to question everything that I want.

I have lost concentration and have no idea what Sophie is talking about. So, I do the only thing I can do. I nod and say, "Mm-hmm," and she continues, not realizing my lack of attention.

When she leaves, I go back to the contract, but my phone rings. It's Joshua.

"I'm going for a coffee across the road. You free?" he asks.

"Yeah, I'll come now. I can fill you in on the little minx working for me. Who was sent to fuck with me."

Joshua lets out a roar of laughter that makes me smile. I know he and the boys will have a field day knowing I'm pussy whipped, just like them.

"As if you can talk. I'll see you soon."

I hang up and grab my jacket, then pack up my desk.

Passing Sophie, who is on the phone, I tell her, "Going for a coffee."

She nods.

Taking the elevator, I stare at her floor number and I can't help but be tempted to push it, shaking my head, I remember my position as her *boss*. I press the ground floor and hold my breath until I pass her floor and the elevator stops and opens at the bottom.

I wait in front of Joshua's building and get absorbed in my phone. His booming voice tells me he's arrived.

"I hope your day is better than mine," he moans.

Well, it hasn't been too bad. The only bad part is having a boner half the day, thinking about *her*, but I keep that to myself.

"I can't complain. I'm sealing contracts, building properties, and making money. Life is good."

More than good, but I bite my tongue.

We walk across the road to our favorite local café and order our coffees, then take our usual table in the far back corner, preferring to discuss business away from others.

I sip my coffee and ask, "What's made your day so shit?"

He lets out a deep sigh. "Just another building delay. It's the third time for this one project. And then they hound my guys when they finally can get in to do the work like they need to work faster."

"The fun of running a business. And how's my favorite vixen?"

I watch his face light up the room. The love glows real. I finally see why Joshua and Thomas wear stupid grins on their faces when they talk about their women.

Ava is perfect for Joshua. She pushes him to be better and argues with him—that is definitely my most favorite part. She has a no-prisoners approach, and she couldn't care less if it's her boyfriend or a complete stranger. He met his match in Ava.

He runs his hand through his hair, saying, "She is good. She is helping me with my dad, trying to find some common ground and have a relationship."

I purse my lips, trying to not say anything on the subject. I don't agree with how his dad treated him, and he has worked hard to get the company to where it is today. But I can't comment about his parents when I still give mine money whenever they ask. They always say the money is for food, but I know it's code for alcohol or drugs.

"She is good for you."

That is all I can say about that subject.

He watches me carefully with a raised brow and asks, "What about you? You mentioned a minx twisting you up. And you talking about a woman like that is—strange. I need to know more."

I sit forward with my elbows on the table and rub my face. "I wish this coffee was a beer right now." I laugh and take a sip.

"Ha, keep dreaming. Tell me."

I look around, making sure no one will be able to hear us, and say, "Well, you know the woman at the football game?"

He claps and punches the air, excitedly saying, "I fucking knew it."

I roll my eyes. "Calm down, dickhead."

He settles back into his seat, eyeing me.

"She's in my new training program. However, we actually met at the airport once months before. And the little conversations we have shared intrigue me. Fuck, she intrigues me. So we went to Ben's game on the weekend and I had the best time. We talked and—" I scrub my hands over my face, trying to find the right words.

"And you, my friend, are fucked." Joshua laughs.

I chuckle. "I guessed I was going to cop it from you boys. Joining your pussy-whipped asses, but I'm still working out what's going on."

"When are you catching up with her again?"

"We haven't set anything up yet, but probably this weekend. I told her that at work, I won't treat her differently. I don't want her singled out for seeing me, and I still expect her to do her job, even if we are together."

"I get the whole she needs to perform at her job, but you're missing out. Sex at work is hot."

I shake my head. "I'll take your word for it. There will be nothing in my office. At home or out is fair game, but work is work," I confirm, as if to remind myself and him.

He shrugs. "Your loss." He returns to his coffee before asking, "Does she know about your parents?"

I sigh, saying, "She knows they are addicts, if that's what you're asking. Wish I didn't have to, but it's not like I can avoid it forever."

He eyes me with pity, knowing how shit they are and there isn't anything anyone can do.

"But at least you're being honest."

CHAPTER 17

ABIGAIL

I WANDER INTO MY office and falter. I'm surprised to see James is waiting near my desk, his back to me. I run my gaze slowly down his black suit, admiring him, but my gaze stops at his taut ass. His hands are buried deep in his pockets, pulling the fabric of his pants firm against his ass. He wears the suit; the suit does not wear him. I can't seem to stop myself from turning up to an uncomfortable heat, remembering his body from a few days ago and how he uses it so well out of work. I wish I were back at his house in a lust bubble and not here perving and secretly worried about the work-mode James. I won't lie; he intimidates me.

I force my feet forward and as I come closer, he spins around. His face is the usual stone, but there is a change in his eyes. A hint of warmth, appreciation, and I feel my heart grow inside my chest. He shares these hidden looks I know no one else gets. There is a sparkle only for me, and it makes me fall harder. I think I might be the one who's all in and if I'm not careful, it will leave me heartbroken. The fact he hasn't had a relationship since his ex-worries me; he may never be able to commit to me.

"Abby."

His deep voice fills the room and I feel it deep in my body, all the way to my toes. I walk closer so I am standing beside him. George is in his seat, watching. I can imagine what he is thinking. I internally roll my eyes and I want to tell him to disappear, but he wouldn't miss this.

"Seems you have..." He trails off and clears his throat and continues speaking. "Passed contracts. Kara said you have exceeded the program and would benefit in being moved to project management early." His face softens and a grin appears on his face.

I beam triumphantly back, knowing I did it. I put that happiness and warm acceptance in his gaze.

"I did?" I ask.

He reaches out to touch my face and my eyes widen. His hand is so close to my face. It's like he suddenly realizes where we are, and that George is watching us. His eyes flash with horror and he instantly drops his hand, curling his fingers into a fist and stuffing it back inside his pocket. His whole body tenses up.

"Ah, well, I'm eager for the second part of the program. I have learned a lot about contracts," I say, hoping to smooth the awkwardness that now fills the room.

He nods, but still continues to stand like a statue. As I wait for him to say or do something, my breathing increases. After a moment, he speaks again. "Well, thanks. You two are exceeding my expectations." He clears his throat. "I need to get back to my office."

"Mm-hmm," I mumble, not knowing what else to say.

He turns and leaves the office, when his phone rings. He pulls it out and answers, "Vixen."

I feel my heart shatter like glass, splintering into a million pieces. I drop my chin and think maybe I'm not the only woman. But his words on the weekend made me feel special. And him reaching out to touch me made me melt into a puddle.

Am I the fool here? I was thinking he cares for me and hearing him answer the phone and call another woman *vixen* makes my blood boil.

I need to ask him who that is. There is no point in me falling for him, for me to end up being the laughingstock of the company.

George whistles softly and asks, "What was that about?"

I turn to the sound of his voice, having momentarily forgotten he was there. Something clicks in me, and I answer him with honesty. "I don't know, George. I'm really not sure."

He frowns, but doesn't say anything.

An idea pops into my mind, and I ask, "Maybe we should go out shopping this weekend?"

I tuck thoughts of James and me away and decide to do something for me.

"Yeah? I'm free. What are you shopping for?" he asks.

"I need new work clothes. I hate these ill-fitting ones that make me blend in with the small-town folks—that my parents insist I wear. I want to feel sophisticated and city-like." And, I add privately, I want people to look at me the way I looked at Ava when I first met her.

His lit-up face has me cracking a huge smile too.

He rubs his hands together. "I have a few places we could go."

"Don't get too excited. I don't have a lot of money. Can we go to the thrift stores here?"

He waves his hand in the air and says, "Got it. We can wander through the other shops if we don't find anything, but I'm sure we will find some good pieces."

I smile. "That sounds amazing."

I need some time alone. It's my break hour and I'm drinking a coffee across the road from my work building, to get some privacy to call home.

"Hello?" my brother Rhys answers.

I smile. "Just me. And before you ask, I'm fine. There isn't anything wrong. I'm simply calling to check in."

"Good," he grumbles down the line. He's always been a small talker and very protective of me. He has never had to say much, but the way he acts shows he cares.

"How's work?" I ask, deciding that if I ask him about work, I will get more than a one-word-answer conversation out of him. He loves his job as a local cop.

"Alright. Same old."

"That's good. I'm loving it here. I actually got moved out of contracts early and into the next rotation."

"I'm proud of you."

I break into a bigger smile, loving that he is supportive of me. At least someone in the family is.

"I know Mom wants me to come home for my birthday this weekend, but I'm staying here. So I won't be back to celebrate."

"Yeah, I heard all about it."

I giggle, but the smell of heavy sweet musk hits me and I close my eyes tightly and take a deep inhale. *It's him.* I tremble at the memories, and I pinch my lips together as I look up, expecting him to be at my table. But much to my disappointment, he's already seated in the back corner and his eyes are fixed on me with a hard glare.

I frown.

"Are you there?" Rhys asks.

"Sorry. Yeah, I know Mom isn't happy but I can't afford too."

The phone vibrates in my hand, so I pull it away from my ear and see James has messaged.

I glance over and he lowers his phone to the table and talks to his friends.

"She'll get over it. Crap, works calling. I'll let you go and I'll talk to you on the weekend."

"Okay. Bye." I hang up and open the message James sent.

James: It's your birthday this weekend?

He must have overheard the conversation with Rhys just now. I type back.

Abigail: Yep. I'll be twenty-five! And I'm here in the city.

I hit send, but a moment later, a message is already back.

James: What day?

Abigail: What do you mean?

James: Saturday or Sunday?

Abigail: Saturday.

James: Why didn't you tell me?

Abigail: It's only a birthday.

James: It's a big deal. I can't believe I didn't ask you when your birthday was.

Abigail: We have been busy.

I chuckle to myself as I hit send.

James: True. But you're different and I want to know everything about you.

Abigail: When's your birthday?

I peek over at his table and see his grin as he types. I look back down to the text that I just got.

James: You will have to find out on our date.

Abigail: Our date?

James: This Saturday. I'm picking you up and taking you to dinner and a night away. So pack for the night.

Abigail: James, dinner would be enough.

James: I want to celebrate you this weekend.

I can't help but feel the nerves swarming me. He is so different and so unexpected. I want to go away and spend time with him too. But I have to talk to him about the vixen because it's still playing on my mind.

Abigail: That sounds fun. Thank you.

I tuck my phone away and stand. He is watching me, and his friend turns his head with a smile before returning to James. I smile and grab my coffee cup to walk out. If my birthday weekend wasn't already going to be wonderful, it just got a whole other level of incredible.

CHAPTER 18

ABIGAIL

I'M WEARING THE HOTTEST yet elegant outfit I have ever owned. Thanks to the thrift shopping with George today, I'm feeling my best for my birthday dinner with James.

I turn off the hair straightener when my intercom chimes. I let James in and put my long gray coat on; the black dress underneath is too cold to wear alone.

He knocks on the door and I open it. The man makes me choke on a breath. He's wearing the sexiest expression. I take a look at his outfit, which is more relaxed: an open white shirt, no tie, and black suit. But it doesn't help the desire simmer. It intensifies the longer we stand here, and then his masculine scent takes over and I want to fall into his arms.

His eyes slide over my outfit before he meets my gaze.

"Hi," I say in a whisper.

"Abby. You are extraordinary." His deep, silky voice strokes my skin. "Happy birthday."

The sound of my heart beating is louder in my ears at his compliment. Will I ever get sick of them?

Never.

I run my hands down the front of it, admiring the soft fabric. "Thank you."

He hands me a gigantic bouquet of flowers. Our hands touch, which sends my heart into a flip. A smile trembles over my lips and I look down at the stunning arrangement of roses in all different colors and sizes, with green leaves to compliment. I lean in and close my eyes and take a deep inhale. The fresh, rich floral aroma hits me and I sigh.

I open my eyes, and he is watching me with an unreadable expression.

I lick my lips nervously. "These are beautiful. Thank you."

"You are beautiful," he says in a husky whisper.

He kisses me gently on my lips, and a twitch hits my core. He pulls away and I say, "Thank you. So are you."

I turn around and he follows. I go hunting for a vase to put the flowers in and once I have, we head out.

We hold hands and inside his car I ask, "Where are we going?"

His hand is still holding mine and I love this feeling. It's like he needs to touch me just as much as I need him.

"It's a surprise."

I don't push, knowing I'll be wasting my breath. The drive isn't as far as I thought. We slide out of the car, and we're standing in front of a small row of restaurants. I don't know which restaurant is the one we'll be eating in.

I close my coat tight against the breeze and he leads the way. A buzz of excitement is coursing through my veins as we walk together. We enter an Italian restaurant. I can smell the aroma of garlic and freshly cooked food so I suck in a breath, my mouth watering. I can almost taste it. This reminds me of how hungry I am.

The waiter ushers us into a private dining area, and I look at the stunning room with a table set for two, flowers in the middle, candles everywhere, and bottles of wine surrounding us.

I take my seat and he sits across from me.

"Have you been here before?" I ask.

"No, I only go out with clients or my friends. Otherwise, I eat at home."

His intense stare doesn't falter, and I shrink a little under his stare.

"This looks amazing," I say.

I drop my gaze to the menu and open it. My mouth is dry and I need a drink. I find a glass of red that sounds nice and when the waiter comes over, we order.

She fills our glasses with water, and I gulp mine down.

"Thirsty?" He asks.

"Yeah, a little." I blush. "I'm taking it easy tonight. I will not be drinking myself to a throwing up state tonight. I won't do that to myself again. That was not a fun time. And the next day"—I shiver with the memory—"was even worse."

The images of James rubbing my back flash in my mind and I push the hair off my face. I definitely don't want to be like that again. It's not a pleasant memory.

He nods, and the waitress brings the glasses of wine and takes our dinner order and leaves again. We toast and I smile at his longing gaze. I then take a large sip, not taking my gaze off him, drinking him in.

I want to ask him about what we are and who is *Vixen*. These back-and-forth mind games aren't working for me. I want him to make sure we are on the same page. But for right now, I lower my glass to the table and I ask, "So when is your birthday?"

"February fourteenth and I'll be turning thirty-five. Ten years wiser." He winks.

I choke out a laugh. "You're so full of yourself. Lucky you are smart and sexy."

I bite down on my bottom lip, cursing to myself that I accidentally slipped. No flirting until you get answers. The guy unravels my brain cells and turns me to mush.

He rubs his jaw and leans forward to grab my hand, the simple gesture hitting my heart like an electric storm.

His eyes soften but they don't leave mine. "What are your goals for the future?"

With his other hand, he grabs his wine to take a sip. I do the same and when I lower my glass, I clear my throat. "At first, I had thought I would return to Riddell's Creek and help my parents turn their business around to become profitable."

He tilts his head and asks, "And now?"

"Now I'm not so sure. I have loved the opportunity the training program has offered me, and I want more. In Riddell's Creek, there's no opportunity for career growth."

He gives my hand a gentle squeeze. "Since I've been working with you, I can see your passion and drive. It would be a shame for you to go back and not live *your* life."

I smile back at him. "Yeah, just thinking about going back and working for my parents causes me to feel dread, but I wouldn't say that's the only reason."

He frowns.

"I would miss you too. You have been a surprise since our first meeting at the airport, and getting to know the real you and the business you...well, I feel lucky. You're smart, kind, and giving."

He smirks. "So it's not just my good looks."

"No. What you are inside is sexier to me."

"It's because I read, isn't it?"

I giggle and nod. I'm loving this playful side of him.

"I want you to stay. I'd miss you too—"

The waiter comes to check on us, breaking up the conversation. The thundering of my heart hits my ears and I sit there, opening and closing my mouth, surprised by his words. It's unexpected but also a relief that he has feelings for me, too.

When the waiter leaves, he doesn't continue, so I take the opportunity to ask.

"Who's Vixen?"

His brows creases as if I'm asking if I have two heads. He shakes his head and says, "It's my best friend's girl-friend, and it's a joke name. I didn't think about it until now."

He reaches out and covers my free hand. I glance down and then back at him. His gaze is as soft as one of his caresses. He hypnotizes me, making me unable to concentrate on anything other than his hand."I'm sorry. I should have known it's not appropriate when you're seeing someone."

His words are creating an erratic rhythm in my veins and hearing that lets me know he likes me. I get it loud and clear now.

———————————

When we leave the restaurant, he holds my hand. I grip it tight and I love how just by that simple movement, I feel protected.

I tilt my head and catch his eyes on me.

"What?" he asks as we stroll back to his car.

"I'm just thinking about how you and I are now officially dating. And how I've taken you out of your playboy ways."

He pauses, his gaze fixing me to the spot. "Yes. I'm only seeing you. I don't want anyone else. Only you. You are mine."

He leans his forehead against mine and his words tickle me, causing my own breath to quicken and my lips to part. "There is no one else and will be no one else that could ever light a flame like you do. I don't know what you have done to me, but I don't think I could stop even if I tried."

I giggle, feeling lighter than ever. Knowing I bring this incredible man to his knees and make him jelly, makes me feel high.

He's standing so close and uttering sweet words. I lean up on my tiptoes and lay my hands on his firm torso, bringing my lips to his in a soft, loving kiss. His hands cup the back of my head, cradling it in his hands and holding me delicately to deepen the kiss.

When he pulls back, he breathes across my lips, "Mine." And then returns to the panty-soaking kiss, but this time, his tongue twirls with mine and we taste each other.

The next time we pull apart, I'm panting hard, trying to catch my breath. We hold each other in the night air, neither of us speaking, just enjoying standing with each other, cuddling.

His words vibrate under my ear. "I have something else for you."

I pull my head away from him, my nose wrinkling.

"What is it?" I ask, glancing around, expecting something to come out.

His deep chuckle erupts before his tone returns to serious and he says, "No, it's not here. I have it at home. I was hoping I could give you it there."

I feel my sex tingle with approval. My damn body is on his side.

"Okay," I answer in a gentle voice, although I'm excited to return to his house.

Butterflies are back in my stomach because I want to know what it is. He is full of surprises.

When we arrive at his house a little while later, he grabs my hand with a smile and ushers me to his bedroom. I feel my heart beat faster. It feels intimate and thrilling to be here with him, as his girlfriend. He moves to stand in front of me, holding both of my hands. My heart is now hammering and I'm thinking we are about to have sex again. But he leans forward, brushing the hair off my shoulders and kissing my neck in the most tender of kisses. The anticipation is causing my breathing to constrict.

He pulls away from my neck and kisses my lips in a soft caress before walking past me and into his walk-in closet I shudder from the kisses and stand there awaiting his return. A few minutes later, he holds out a present.

I blink rapidly, thinking it can't be real. He actually brought me flowers and now a gift. It's a lot. No man has made such an effort for my birthday before.

He hands me the present and I carefully take it with shaky hands, glancing at the gift and then at him. I say in a whisper, "I can't believe you did this."

"It's your birthday. Everyone needs a gift on their birthday."

I smile in awe at him.

He reaches out and tucks a lock of hair behind my ear. Moving his finger to under my chin, he tips my head back and kisses me once. My eyes flutter closed, but he pulls away and I snap my eyes open in an *Are you kidding me? Keep kissing me* vibe.

He smiles and says, "Open your present first. I need to make sure you like it."

I stare into his eyes unmoving, his finger still holding me up. "I will love it. You didn't have to."

He kisses me and then drops his finger and says, "But I wanted to."

I reopen my eyes and look down at the present and slowly tear the wrapping. He takes it from me so I can remove the lid. I open my mouth in shock as a pair of diamond earrings stare back at me. The kindness makes my eyes sting with threatening tears. Not even my parents have ever bought me anything this special.

"This is too much," I choke.

"It's not. Let me help you put them on."

But I shake my head and lean forward, closing my eyes, and I kiss him. I pull away an inch to say, "Thank you."

He moves his lips to my neck, nuzzling his nose into the crook of it, nipping and licking his way to my lips. When he gets to them, he sucks on my bottom lip. All the emotions running through me cause my head to spin. I let them all out in a frenzied kiss. I explore his body with my fingers, running up his biceps to his shoulders, grabbing his neck to bring his face back down to mine to capture his mouth.

His hands grab my ass and squeeze it. I slide my jacket off and slip my new black dress off over my head and toss it across the room, his hands going straight to the straps of my bra and removing them before tossing it completely. The bra drops and I struggle to breathe; I need him inside me now. I work on his pants, and they drop to the floor; he then pushes down my panties before he glides his hands over my skin, leaving me to shiver with desperation. He leans down and takes a nipple into his mouth, twirling his tongue around and popping it out of his mouth. His fingers trail down painfully slowly to my opening. He runs his hands through my wet folds, bringing my wetness to my clit and rubbing it in circles. I surrender to his touch, opening my legs farther, giving him more access.

"Good girl," he says and continues the lazy strokes. It causes me to whimper.

He dips two fingers inside my pussy and I moan with pleasure, my back arching into him. He moves quicker and I need more—I need him.

He continues pumping and rubbing my clit with his thumb.

"Your pussy is so greedy," he whispers into my ear, and I feel like I'm about to snap if he doesn't take me.

"Fuck me, James," I say as I tremble, struggling to stand on my weak knees.

"Whatever the birthday girl wants, she gets."

"Well, if that's how it is, I have a request." I bite my lip and watch him falter in surprise.

"A request? What type are we talking?"

I don't want to explain because I don't want to lose my nerve. And I really want to do this.

"Sit." I point to the bed.

He narrows his dark eyes at me and I lean in, kissing his lips in a brief caress. I wish I could mind read, because I want to know how he feels when I ask him to give up control to me.

Will he ask me to stop?

Or say no?

I pull back and open my eyes and say, "Please, sit. Trust me."

He turns and sits. Clasping his hands together in his lap, he watches me grab the lube from his drawer and sit between his legs. I peel his hands apart and lay them on his thighs. His chest rises and falls with every deep breath, his attention solely on me.

I capture his lips and kiss him. He kisses me back, and our tongues twirl. At the same time, I slide my hand over his thigh. His muscles quiver under me. I brush my fingertips along the crease of his groin and sweep down to where my fingers and knuckles touch his balls briefly and slide down his inner thigh before sliding back up to repeat the motion again. He breaks our kiss, breathing heavily, and looks down and groans.

"Is this okay? Or should I stop?" I whisper.

His eyes meet mine, but I brush his balls with my knuckles again and he whimpers, "No, keep going."

His skin is hot to the touch, matching my own body temperature. I glance down, and his cock is rock hard, the vein visible, and I want to run my tongue along it, but not yet. In time. I first want to feel him in my hands and bring him to the brink that way.

My gaze flickers back to watch his face. I stop the lazy circles and he stiffens as he sucks in a breath. I move my hand to stroke his balls and he lets out a hiss and opens his legs wider. Encouraging me, I fondle his balls gently while watching him for every reaction. He moans when I caress the skin between his balls.

"Fuck," he says, closing his eyes and tipping his head back.

I open the lube and squeeze it in my hand before discarding the bottle and wrapping my hand around him. He tenses and shifts to sit back up and watches me pull him down and back up, repeating the motion. I increase the pressure after a few strokes and he mumbles, "Yeah, that's it."

He drops his hands behind him and lifts his hips up, matching my strokes. This time, I twist my grip slightly and he groans again. "Fuckin' hell."

I smirk, watching his reactions to see how he's feeling, but the noises coming from him are encouraging. His cheeks are flushed, and it urges me to keep going, my own sex aching and becoming wetter as I explore him.

His body tenses and he grows tighter in my hands. I continue bringing him to the edge, but when he jerks, I remove my hand. He stares at me, blank, amazed, shaken.

I wait a few seconds before I shift off the bed and drop between his legs on my knees. He takes a sharp breath and I keep my gaze locked on his as I take him inside my mouth.

I'm enjoying the feel of him inside. My tongue is flat against his bulging vein and it's hot knowing he is hard for me. I pull him in as far back as I can before withdrawing and then bringing him back in. I take my time with every suck, enjoying the way his breaths are louder and his moans are more drawn out.

He moves to grip my hair as tightly as I hold him. I use the same twisting motion as before, and he groans loudly. "Baby, I'm going to come if you don't stop."

"Mmm," I say around him, knowing the vibration will drive him crazier.

"Fuck." He thrusts his hips up and his balls withdraw again, and I know he wants to come, but I drag my mouth off him and watch him as he realizes I did it again, bringing him to the edge of an orgasm but not letting him have it.

His eyes are dark and full of desire. His shoulders rise and fall with each breath. My pussy is wet, heavy, and throbbing for relief.

I move my hands between my legs and he watches, but when I glide my fingers through my slick folds, he pushes off the bed and my eyes widen. I sit up as he scoops me up and carries me to the bed, lying me down. His skin is flushed.

"Was that fun?"

I nod and bite my lip seductively, staring at his sweat-beaded forehead. A warmth spreads in my chest knowing I did that, and that he let me have control over him.

"You're fucking perfect. I'm so fucking horny, I could explode. That was so intense."

He gets a condom and rolls it on, then he grabs my leg and drapes it over his shoulder. The cold air hits my warm entrance, and it sends a shiver down my spine. I move the other one wider and he steps forward, stretching me and lining his cock up before he thrusts inside. I tip my head back and moan in pleasure. The feeling in this position is so different, so intense, it's making me dizzy. I'm glad to be lying down. He moves out slowly and thrusts in hard again, showing me just how well he knows his way around my body. He reaches around to my clit and rubs it in circles at the same time he's thrusting, and it isn't long before I'm calling out his name and begging for my own release.

I'm building so quickly that I'm clenching around him, loving the full sensation. He moves faster now and I can feel myself climb, chasing the release. When he changes his angle slightly and his body hits me again, pleasure ripples through me as I shudder from my orgasm. Deep, heavy pants leave my mouth and I feel him jerk, emptying deep inside and him saying, "Oh, fuck."

When his body stills, he pauses before slowly pulling out. His chest is glistening in perspiration, and I swallow hard at the vision. He discards the condom before he lies down to hold me tightly while we both recover, but I know him and he will be ready to go again.

"There is something I have read about and always wanted to try," I say between breaths. My heart is thundering as I speak.

"Mm?" He encourages me as I lift on one elbow to look deeply into his eyes. He strokes my cheek with his finger. "Anything."

"I want to know what it would be like with nothing between us. I wouldn't do it with anyone else. I just want all of you tonight."

His face softens and he asks, "You mean no condom?"

I nod. "Yes. I'm on the pill and I've never tried it."

"I have always used condoms, too, but are you sure? You don't have to do anything for me. I'm more than satisfied."

I kiss him, loving how he is so damn caring. "I want this. I want you."

He kisses me and he lowers me so I'm underneath him. I feel him at my soaking entrance. He smiles down at me and I squirm, trying to move him. He chuckles. "You really want it. You're such a naughty girl, but I love those fucking books you read."

I blush and I can't wait much more. I'm achy with anticipation but luckily for me, he thrusts in at once and I moan and clamp hard at the intrusion. He is all the way in, and I feel so full of him. Our gaze locks and his face softens in pleasure as he hovers above me. He pauses, waiting for me to adjust. The feeling of him bare is more exquisite than I imagined. When I relax, he withdraws and then thrusts back inside, repeating this motion over and over.

"I will not last long," he puffs.

Wanting to join him at the same time, I link my ankles behind his back, and it makes his body hit me at yet another new angle. I feel my lower back tingle and my whole body shudder. I unravel underneath him and his cock swells and jerks inside of me—we come together. Our bodies are both perspiring, and I'm quivering from the overwhelming emotions. The backs of my eyes sting as the entire night hit's me. Tonight has been beyond perfect, but this moment right now feels like home. The sensation without the condom was more pleasurable... I felt warmer and came harder, and with no barriers, it was amazing. He is my everything.

His eyes open and he stares deeply into me with adoration. I feel so much for him, my heart feels like it could combust. He lays a soft kiss on me and we cuddle, trying to recover. There is something about us that when we are together, we are like magnets, drawn to each other and fit perfectly as one.

CHAPTER 19

JAMES

I WAKE TO THE smell of her light summer fragrance and the taste of her on my tongue. Abigail, in my bed, is the best wake up I could ask for. Her body fits perfectly beside me and she is currently sleeping with her arm draped across my chest.

I try not to wake her as I check the time and see that we have slept in. I want to explore the city, so I put down my phone and stroke her hair, hoping to wake her gently. A few minutes later, she stirs, and her lashes tickle my skin. She lifts her head up to look at me.

I pause my hand in her hair and say, "Good morning. Did you sleep well?"

She sits up, mumbling, "Mm-mm."

She stretches her arms over her head. Her delicious body is on show for me. I want to take her again, but I know we don't have time, so I ignore my morning erection and say, "Let's get ready and explore the city."

Her face brightens, and she leans forward and pecks me in an all too brief kiss. "Yes."

"That has you perking up."

My phone rings. I look at it. "Fuck." The word slips out of my mouth. I grip my phone, turning my knuckles white.

"Are you okay?" she asks, clutching the clothes for today.

I rub the back of my neck and then lay my phone down on my bedside table. "It's my father, asking for more money."

Her mouth drops wide open before she shakes her head and says, "He asks you for money. What for?"

I feel my gut tighten as I force out a breath. "Drugs and alcohol. He says he is off the drugs, but I don't know if I can believe them. I give them money weekly for food, but it's not. I just can't seem to say no or to stop."

"Oh, my God."

"Mmm."

"I'm so sorry. That sucks. I only send my parents' money while I'm not able to work for them."

I tense and whisper, "You do?"

She nods.

"But you're the child."

"So are you," she says, reminding me I shouldn't do it either.

We are both stuck in the same predicament, wondering what we should do, but neither of us has any ideas.

I want to get off this topic and enjoy the day I have planned for her.

"That's true. Well, enough sad talk. We have to go soon, so go get your sexy ass ready."

I cup her face and cradle it, like she's fragile, and if I hold her too tight, I might break her. Even though she is nothing but the opposite, I can't help but want to protect and love her.

She turns and kisses my hand.

Her eyes glow with a savage inner fire. And I know if we don't get out of here soon, we won't leave this room.

"Let's get ready," I say huskily.

She slides off the bed, pausing at the end to look at me before dipping her chin and entering the bathroom with a pink flush staining her cheeks. I flop back, close my eyes, and rub a hand over my face before resting it on my chest. I need to wait a minute to cool down and collect myself, because it's not just my cock that's pulsating on its own... no my heart beats it's own rhythm for her.

We walk through the local streets hand in hand, walking into shops and being complete tourists. This is all new for me, the hand holding, being in a relationship, the flutters in my stomach, and the goddamn ache in my chest. We are standing in line to grab an ice cream when I see her face turned away, distracted.

"See that woman there? She went to my school back home." She points to a woman with red hair and a blue dress crossing the road.

"The one with the red hair?" I ask, narrowing my eyes, trying to get a closer look at her face as she passes by.

"Yeah, that's her. It's strange to see someone I know in the city. I wonder what she is doing here."

I look at her, still staring after the woman. "Do you want to go talk to her? I can grab the ice cream," I say, not wanting to hold her back.

She peers up at me and shakes her head, saying, "No. We weren't close friends. And it was many years ago. She won't remember who I am."

"Are you sure?"

I can see her thinking about it. Her gaze returns to the woman, clearly distracted by her. Waiting for her to answer feels like forever and I hold a breath, waiting. She lets out a deep sigh and her gaze meets mine. "I'm sure. The city is my future. I've got a good job and now you."

We share a brief kiss and I pull away grinning at her answer. *I'm in her future.*

We are at the front of the line, so we order our ice creams and begin walking the streets again. As the vanilla sweetness hits my tongue, I'm still thinking about her answer.

"What about a family and marriage? Is that something you want?"

I stare at her and watch her lick her rainbow ice cream. It's dripping all over her hand. And I have to hold myself back from telling her how to lick it properly or lick her hand free of the droplets.

She laughs and it distracts me.

"I haven't thought about it and definitely aren't planning to anytime soon. Are you asking me to be your baby momma, James?"

"No," I say back as a sea of emotions fill me.

Why am I asking then?

Because I'm in deep, that's why.

———

I enter the coffee shop where the boys are waiting for me. But as I wait for the order, I'm scrolling through my phone, and a picture that I took of Abigail yesterday stares back at me. A slow grin spreads across my face as I take in her eyes, which are glowing with enjoyment. *She is magnificent.*

My phone rings in my hands. My mom's name is flashing. The sweet is replaced with sour instantly. I grip the phone and exit the shop to take her call. I don't need anyone to hear it. Most of them see me on the phone a lot, but they do not know that it's to my parents. The constant asking for money and help is draining.

"What do you want?"

The gurgling sound on the end of the line has me running a hand through my hair and my stomach tensing.

I shake my head, trying to get rid of the vivid memories, and say, "Mom?"

The way my house smelled growing up sends shivers down my spine. I remember walking into my house, which was filthy from dishes piled in the sink, the empty food packets, the empty bottles of liquor, and the unwashed clothes.

And on occasion, I found Mom or Dad on the couch or in bed after school, gurgling the same noise because they were choking on their vomit.

If I hadn't had wealthy grandparents who left money for my schooling and care, I would have been in a terrible situation. I count myself lucky to have had them, but sometimes I wish they could still be here to help me with Mom and Dad. The constant phone calls and money demands are tiring. I have tried many types of rehabs, but nothing seems to stick. They stay sober for a week and then the next minute, they are back buying and consuming.

I'm waiting for them to ask to go to rehab. I can't force them to change. They need to want to go, not do it to please me and shut me up.

I'm about to grab a cab when I hear Mom's voice say, "Roll over." She breathes heavily down the line. "Come on."

I hold the phone to my ear, hoping she can manage to get him on his side.

"Oh, that's it," she says in a huff.

When the line is silent, I say, "Mom." I notice people looking at me weirdly as they pass.

The fumble on the phone makes me catch my breath. "Hello?"

"Mom, is Dad okay?"

"Yeah, he is on his side, and he is breathing. He just needs to sleep it off."

I rub my eyes and let out my breath. "Okay, but I'll call you in half an hour to check. Call me if he isn't doing well and I'll come."

"Yes, dear. And thanks for being on the phone incase I needed your help."

I hang up and run my hand through my hair. When I feel I can breathe again, I get back inside and pick up my order, which is now lukewarm.

Fucking great.

I stroll over to the boys and take a seat. "Hey, boys."

I'm relieved to be sitting and talking about something else to take my mind off what just happened. I accidentally spill some coffee on my pants. I dust it off with my hand and set the coffee aside for a minute until I am more in control of myself.

"What took you so long?" Benjamin lifts his head up and sips his drink, eyeing me.

"Work," I lie.

"Sure. I saw you on the phone out there." Joshua elbows me playfully and says, "I bet it's your girl."

I shake my head. "You're dreaming. Some people have to work. How else do you get to be the top developer? I don't need distractions."

Those sexy green eyes and pouty, bowed lips are the best and worst distraction for me. But I'm not ready to tell them right now. I want a bit of time with her alone before they all want to meet her.

"Speaking of work," I say, grabbing my drink. I take a long sip before lowering it back down and looking at Joshua. "I have a new restaurant and apartment building that will need your wiring. I still need the plans tweaked, and then I'll email them over."

"Yeah, sounds good," Joshua says.

"I got news, boys." Benjamin rubs his hands together and wears a big shit-eating grin.

"Yeah?" I say.

He bounces in his seat and says, "I got a call from the coach. Guess who the new starting quarterback might be?"

"Are you kidding me?" Joshua says.

"So pumped for you," I say.

"Congrats, man," Joshua says.

"Thanks. Levi might be out for the year after the last game." He still looks like he can't quite believe it. But his talent is exceptional, and this would be the only time he could play this position before he retires. Truthfully, he hasn't got long left in his career.

Joshua shakes his head and says, "That's insane."

I reach out and squeeze Benjamin's shoulder and say, "So proud of you."

"Thanks." He beams back at all of us.

"I think we need to celebrate," I say.

"Good idea," Joshua says.

"When will you know?" I ask.

"Not sure," Benjamin says.

"Keep us updated," Joshua says.

We nod in agreement before I got up to order another round of coffees. I decide to call Mom and see if Dad's okay, but after I hang up I'm suddenly overwhelmed by torment. Knowing only Abigail can ease the cold, deep, unaccustomed pain in my chest. I call her.

I call home.

CHAPTER 20

JAMES

IT'S MONDAY NIGHT AND Thomas requested us to be at his house instead of going out to the local bar. Thomas is the only one out of the four of us with kids. Watching him lose his wife and do it all on his own was tough. The strength he showed us and the life lesson we all took away was to love hard those who love you back because you could lose them all in a blink of an eye.

"Uncle Jay," says Lily, Thomas's oldest daughter.

She comes running and his youngest daughter, Rose, follows closely behind her as I enter their house. These girls are so precious and have a piece of my heart.

"How're my two favorite girls?" I ask.

"Present?" Rose asks, knowing I always bring them a gift.

I smile. "Of course."

I hand over the present to each of them. The girls take them from me and take off down the hall while I wander into the kitchen.

I turn the corner and Thomas stands with his hands on his hips. He says with a hard glare, "I told you to stop spoiling them."

I smile, and step over to give him a man hug. "I hear you, but I can't help myself. They are like nieces to me."

He pats my back, and when we pull apart, he stares back at me, then dips his head. I take it as a silent thank you for loving his daughters. "I know. It's just I worry they will always expect gifts."

"Tom, they are good kids. Me spoiling them is different to you parenting. You're doing amazing," I say.

Hell, I don't even know if I could do as good of a job with what life has thrown at him.

"I agree with James," Jennifer says as she comes out of the hallway where the girls' rooms are, carrying clothes in her arms.

I smile and kiss her cheek and say hi.

She immediately looks over at Thomas with adoring eyes. These two would make me sick with how perfect and in love they are, but after Thomas lost his wife, he deserves to be happy, and Jennifer definitely makes him happy. He tried to deny his feelings, but the way she was with his kids sealed his fate. She and the girls have this bond that only a mother normally has. It's so rare and special that I'm glad he came to his senses.

"I'll take the kids to have a bath and put them to bed. Let you guys have some time together," Jennifer says.

Seeing the girls reignites a longing in me. I want that... the wife, kids, and the white picket fence, but I haven't found anyone who would make me stop and see a future with them. However, since I met Abigail, there is now a flicker of hope that maybe she could be the one? That I can trust a woman and have the dream future that I thought I wouldn't have.

"What time are Josh and Ben coming?" I ask Thomas.

He grabs some drinks out of the fridge and says, "They should be here soon."

Jennifer wanders off with the girls following, and someone knocks loudly on the door.

"Just us," Benjamin calls out as he enters the house with Joshua.

Their heavy footsteps come down the hall and stop when they arrive in the kitchen. They are smiling broadly.

"Boys," I say and they say hello back.

Thomas hands us a beer and we all move to Thomas' game room to gather around the TV.

"Are you pumped for your game next week, Ben?" Joshua asks.

"Yeah, we should beat them. They have a few players still to confirm. Tonight's game will be close and I'm betting first, and I say a three-point win by the Sharks."

"I bet ten points," Thomas says.

"Dammit, Ben. You stole my bet. I'll go four," Joshua says.

"I'll go five. And how are the cheerleaders? Are you dating yet?" I ask Benjamin.

He doesn't sleep with them, or anyone for that matter, but I like to poke fun at him.

He rolls his eyes. "No thanks, dickhead. I don't sleep around like you; I like to keep my dick clean."

I grimace and say, "Gross, man. I feel my cock and balls shriveling up at the thought of a dirty cock."

We laugh in unison, and I take a drink of my beer. My phone vibrates in my pocket, so I pull it out and see it's from Abigail. I smile unconsciously at her name and open the message and read it while the boys chatter amongst themselves.

> **Abigail:** It's been one day at work and I didn't bump into you, *boss*. I know you're with the boys, but I just wanted to say hi and I miss you.

I can't help but wear a stupid grin on my face as I read the words *miss you*. It's how I feel about her, even though I had her for most of the weekend. There isn't a moment throughout the day that I don't think about her and wonder what she is doing.

I type out a response.

> **James:** I can show you who is boss Miss you too, baby. I used to love watching the game, but right now I want you more...

> **Abigail:** I want you too, but it's okay. I have a really good book boyfriend that is waiting for me. I just wanted to say hi, have a good night, and I'll talk to you later.

> **James:** No, don't go. You can't replace me with a fictional character. I'd rather be talking to you than watching sports.

> **Abigail:** Aww, you're such a big softie. But it's okay. No book can replace you.

The words almost cause me to chuckle out loud. These aren't words I would use to describe myself.

James: I have something else that's big and hard. Please don't tell the boys. I have a reputation to uphold. They will never let me live it down if they find out I'm a softie who is falling for a trainee and I read crime and thriller books.

Abigail: You dirty boy! I won't. Trust me. Your secret's safe with me. You can tell them when you're ready.

James: Why are you so sweet?

"James, you're missing half the game," Thomas says.

I peer over at him, his curious expression flicking between my phone and me. I grip the phone tighter, not wanting to share who I am talking to.

"He has caught the love bug," Joshua says with a laugh.

I narrow my eyes at Joshua and say, "Jesus, I'm not in love! I like her. Quit it."

I can't love her... Can I?

Do I?

Fuck.

"Bit defensive, are we?" Joshua asks.

Through gritted teeth, I say, "No. You boys are just fucking annoying."

They all laugh in unison, and I feel a tick in my jaw. Thankfully, I'm saved by my phone. A text message comes through, and I know it's her. I pull the phone out and read her name on the front. I smile as I read it, the tension easing. It's something only she can do.

Abigail: I'm just me. Who likes you a lot.

I read that line over and over.

She likes me too.

I wonder if I'm falling in love... could she be too?

James: I like you a lot.

Abigail: And you say I'm sweet. Go enjoy your friends. I'm going to have a bath.

Now I have a sudden urge to leave Thomas' house and go to hers. I want to join her in the bath. The thought alone has the pulse in my cock jerking awake. But then—that will cement what the boys think.

James: Why did you say that? Now all I can picture is your sexy body in a bath full of bubbles and how much I want to join you. Send me a pic.

Abigail: Sorry, no nudes. You get me in real life enough.

James: I can never get enough of you.

Abigail: You're insatiable.

James: Good night, baby. Sleep well x.

Abigail: Goodnight x

I tuck the phone away and lean back in my chair, returning my focus back to the game.

Work is busy and money is better than ever. There is a little heaviness in my chest, and it's because I haven't seen Abigail. I was flying to the conference today and I fly back tomorrow. But it feels too long to wait. I want to see her face now. I need to meet a client, but I have an hour yet, so I'm back in my room, planning to see if we can have a quick video call.

I sit down on the end of the neatly made king bed and call her. She answers and her face fills the screen and I see she is in her living area. I can't help but beam when she smiles a hello.

"What are you doing? I thought you were working. I didn't expect a video call."

"I have some time before a work dinner and I missed you."

She groans and says, "I know. I haven't seen you at work this week."

"I've heard you're kicking ass in project management."

"Eleanor giving you updates?"

"About you and George...yes."

"Well, thank you. I'm enjoying it. It keeps me out of the office more than contracts, though." A hint of disappointment laces her voice so I change the subject.

"What are you doing tonight?"

"Before you called, I was watching TV."

"I miss you."

She smiles into the camera and I feel it in my heart. I love her smile. I will never get sick of it. "I miss you too. The weekend can't come quick enough."

"You're telling me. I've never missed anyone or counted down to the weekend before... I think something is wrong with me."

Her smile widens and she says, "Must be something wrong with me too then, because I need you."

"Are you wiggling your brows at me?"

"Mm-hmm."

"I miss that too. I'll make it up to you this weekend at your house."

"I'm excited. I'm going to cook."

"Cook? You're going to cook for me?"

"Yeah, why?"

"You aren't going to poison me, are you?"

"No, silly. I actually love to cook." She says.

"The more I find out about you, the more I lo—like."

Fuck. It nearly slipped out.

She runs her hand through her hair but doesn't call me out or act like she heard it. She sits in her brown sweats and with her hair draped messily over her shoulders. The gnawing ache in my gut wants to be holding her as we watch TV. But I get back to being focused on where I am.

"Well, baby, I gotta go get ready."

"Alright. See you on the weekend."

She blows me a kiss through the camera and fuck, do I wish I could have her lips on mine for real.

CHAPTER 21

ABIGAIL

I'M BUSY TYPING AWAY on my computer, lost in a report when George walks in.

"Well, hello, miss Abigail."

I spin at the sound of his voice. An easy smile plays on my lips. "Hi. How are you?" I ask.

"I'm good. I just went out on the weekend. Drank way too much and danced till I couldn't stand it anymore. The same, really."

I giggle and say, "I don't know how you do that every weekend."

The memory of my drunk night is enough to remind me never to drink that much again.

He shrugs. "It's easy when there isn't anyone in your life, but let's not talk about that. I see you're wearing one of your new purchases."

"I am. I had to pair it with a few pieces from my older clothes. I cannot wait for the day when I have a regular decent paycheck, so I have a whole new wardrobe," I say as I rub my hands over my new pants.

"How come?" he asks and drags his chair over.

"I'm gaining confidence now, the way we are performing above expectations, and now with clothes that match how I feel. I don't want to be dragged down or reminded of my past."

"We really are kicking ass. Maybe we can get a job here when we are finished."

I laugh. "Don't get ahead of yourself. We still have a few rotations left."

"Didn't you just say a moment ago you are gaining confidence? That isn't a confident person's thought."

"I'm gaining confidence, not full of confidence yet," I say, giggling.

"Oh, so that's just me? Damn. Well, it's break time. Let's grab a coffee together."

I love the sound of that, so I grab my coat off the back of the chair. As George and I approach the cafe, James comes out of the shop with another brown-haired suit and my breath hitches. No matter how many times I see him, it's like it's the first time all over again.

My stomach flips with excitement, and I openly smile his way. When his gaze meets mine, he offers a small smile back, but otherwise his work mask is on. I understand why; we both are trying to see where this goes without anyone from the company finding out. I haven't told George because what if he turns on me and thinks I'm sleeping with James to climb the ladder? The thought makes me sick. I'd never do such a thing, but from the outside looking in, it could look like that.

I sigh and try to shrug off the weird feeling as if I'm reading too much into it. I don't want to be needy or one of those girls who needs to be social media official. I just need to know that he and I are on the same page. At the moment, we have only just made it official to ourselves. To me, that's the most important thing. My relationship is risky, I know that. I could lose this very job, but I don't want to lose him either.

He doesn't stop to talk to us; he just walks past with the guy without a second glance. I try to focus on what George is talking about, but my phone rings, distracting me. It's Mom. I pause and frown. It's unusual for her to call during the day. Even if they ask for money, it's at night after work.

"Mom?" I answer.

Her breathing is quick and I can hear her heavy pants.

My frown deepens. "Mom, are you there? Are you okay?"

I hold my breath, and the silence isn't helping my pulse, either.

"Sorry." She sniffs and the hairs on the back of my neck rise. "Your dad is in the hospital." She wails, and I feel my heart squeeze in pain.

I cover my mouth and let out a breath. "Oh my God, Mom. Is he okay?"

"I don't know." She mumbles down the line before saying, "I need you here."

With that, I squeeze the bridge of my nose and blow out a breath. "Okay. I'll get there as soon as I can."

She splutters, "Please hurry." And hangs up on me.

I hang up and George hands over my coffee. He asks, "Are you okay? You're awfully pale. Do you need to sit down?"

I shake my head. "It's okay, thanks. My mom just called and said my dad is in the hospital. I need to get back to the office now and book a flight home as soon as possible. Can we go back to our desks so I can pack up and talk to Eleanor and James?"

He wraps his arm around my shoulders and rubs my upper arm and says, "Definitely. Let's go."

I lean into his offer of comfort, needing the support. We walk back and as soon as I get to my desk, I drop myself in the chair and search for flights, booking the earliest one I can.

"George, I have to go." My voice breaks and my eyes fill with tears at the thought of my dad being hurt and I'm here in the city, being happy and selfish. I just hope I make it in time. At that thought, tears trail down both cheeks. "I need to go talk to Eleanor and James now so I can get home."

He opens his arms and I step into them and sob. He rubs my back and tells me everything is going to be okay. He doesn't stop until I sniffle and pull back. I wipe my face and take some good cleansing breaths.

"Let me know how you are going. I want updates while you are there."

I nod. "I won't be long."

"I'm sure Eleanor and James will give you all the time you need. Now go; I'll talk to you soon."

Nodding, I pick up my belongings and trek to the elevators.

I first talk to Eleanor and she says if it's only a couple of days, there won't be issues, but if it's longer than a week off, it's an issue. I can't guarantee it will be only a week.

What state is my father in?

I don't know. So I can't give her a straight answer, but I promise to keep her updated. The next person causes more tears to stream and my heart to ache.

I need him... His warm cuddles... His soothing word s... His everything.

Arriving upstairs, I approach Sophie and say, "Hi, Sophie. This is unannounced. Is he free for a quick chat?"

She picks up the phone. "Hi, Abby. Let me check." He must answer because she says, "Hi, James. I have Abigail here to see you." Then she hangs up and nods at me, and says, "Go for it."

"Thanks, Sophie," I say as I offer a weak smile.

I turn and open his door. He's already looking at the door, probably wondering what I'm doing here. I walk up to the chair in front of him, dragging the chair out, feeling myself become heavy.

A deep frown settles between his brow and he asks, "Are you okay?"

"My mom called. She said my dad is in the hospital. She wants me to come home," I whisper.

His brows shoot up, his face slackens, and he says, "I'm so sorry. Is he okay?"

I rub my hands up and down my pants in a repeating motion. "I don't know, to be honest. Mom was upset on the phone. I could barely make out what she was saying."

"What are you going to do?"

"I booked a flight for this afternoon. She needs me," I say.

His face flickers with an unreadable expression. He leans back in his chair and says, "Of course. Did you need me to do something?"

I lift my lips in a crooked smile. "No thanks. I will be back in a few days."

"Okay. I'll see you then. I hope your dad is okay."

He stands and walks around the table and scoops me weightlessly in his arms and I snuggle into his chest, feeling safe in his arms, wishing he could come with me, but I know he can't.

Mumbling into his chest, I say, "Me too."

I close my eyes and enjoy the smell of him. I want to savor these moments before I go.

He strokes my hair and I gently pull away.

I stare into his dark eyes. "I'll keep you updated."

"Please."

I stand on my tippy toes, clutching his chest, and kiss him. I quiver at the sweet tenderness of his kiss. He then kisses my forehead and I close my eyes, standing still in silence. Before pulling away and leaving his office, I pause at the doorway and look back. His hands are deep inside his pockets, his wide stance as usual, his face somber, and I dip my head and leave.

Getting home from work is a blur. I throw my stuff in a bag and then walk over to Gracie's, knocking on her door.

She answers and glances at the bag I'm holding, then back to me, and asks, "Where are you going?"

"Home. My dad is in the hospital and Mom wants me to come. I won't be gone long."

"Is he alright?"

"I don't know. Mom didn't give me any details. But I really have to go and catch my flight. I just wanted to tell you, so you know where I am."

She steps off the door and offers her open arms. I step into them and we hug momentarily.

"Take care. Message me when you get there, so I know you arrived safely."

I pull out of her arms and wave.

I return to the airport with a heavy heart. I'm of two minds. I want to leave to see if my dad is okay, but then I want to stay because this has been the best time of my life. The new people and new job have been the best life decision I have made. The heavy hearted feeling won't help deal with going home, so I push any more thoughts I have away. But when I see the café where I first met James, it's like someone has stabbed me through the heart with a knife. I will miss him this week. I look at the table and spot others eating and drinking, and I dip my head and walk off. I need to get far away before I don't get on that plane.

I check in and the lady informs me I have been upgraded. I ask her to repeat herself, thinking she has made a mistake, but sure enough, she repeats that I'm in first class.

I pull out my phone and send a quick text off to James with a smile on my face.

Abigail: Thank you for the upgrade! I owe you :) x

James: Anytime. Have a safe flight. x

I hurry off the plane and see my brother standing like the broody man he is, waiting for me. He stands still in his navy uniform with a scowl firmly plastered on his face.

I giggle at myself, knowing he will never change, and rush up to him and hug him, saying into his chest, "Hi."

He hugs me back before pulling away and asking, "How was the flight?"

"First class, so it was amazing."

His eyes bulge and he asks, "How much money are you making for first-class tickets?"

I feel a flush creep up my neck and onto my cheeks. I look down at the floor before peeking up under my lashes at his hard face. "Well, I didn't pay for the upgrade."

"Abigail. Who are you taking money from?"

"No one." I scowl back, hating his assumptions. "I have been seeing someone, so he upgraded me when he found out about my flight."

His jaw tightens like he is trying to hold back, and I'm glad because I don't want to hear it.

"Take me to Dad. Mom says he is in the hospital." He looks at me, then away and back again. "Mom asked me to come back because Dad is in the hospital."

His lips thin as if he is holding something back. I can tell because he used to do this all the time. He used to say it was to protect me. Instead, it annoys the crap out of me.

"What aren't you telling me?"

"Nothing. I'm taking you to Dad." He spins and walks off. That's his way of saying it's the end of the discussion.

I hurry and tug on his arm. "No. You're hiding something."

"I'm not. I just—you will see. Let's go."

I squeeze my eyes shut and blow out an exasperated breath. God damn you, Rhys Crawford. I storm off, following his grumpy ass.

We get to his car and I pause. "You have a dog?"

I could almost laugh. Rhys hates animals, so to see an animal in my brother's car is making me giggle.

"No. It's not my dog. And I don't want to talk about it."

"Touchy today."

"Abigail."

I smirk at his warning tone and open the back door so I can sit with the big yellow Labrador. I turn and the dog licks me repeatedly. I giggle loudly.

"Toby. Toby, stop that right now."

Hearing Rhys and having the dog lick me has me in a fit of giggles. When I recover, I say. "Okay, Toby. Sit down." He follows my command and then I buckle up and Rhys takes off.

I stroke the soft fur until he drops and I ask, "Who's dog is this?"

"I don't know."

"What do you mean?"

He doesn't answer, instead going silent.

"Maybe a dog would be good for you," I say, knowing my brother is guarded and grumpy and that puppies are the best way to cheer up even the saddest of people.

"No. I don't want a dog."

He really isn't giving me much, so I give up and just stroke the dog until we arrive at the hospital.

We step inside, and nausea instantly rolls in my stomach, so I rub my arms from the sensitive feeling that comes with places like this. I follow Rhys and watch as the nurses look at him and wave. He gives them a small nod but looks away and I see their faces fall.

My poor grumpy brother. What will I do with him? If he keeps this up, he will be alone forever. Looks won't stay forever.

Being a small country hospital, it's not that big, so I don't have to walk long to see my dad. He is sitting up, talking to Mom, and he has a cast on his arm. But otherwise, he seems fine. I glance at Mom, who is fluffing his bed, but is smiling up at him.

A tightness forms around my eyes. I swear the distress was more than what I'm seeing. Rhys clears his throat and Mom and Dad's faces light up when they see me.

"Oh, Abigail. So glad you're here. Your dad will be out for at least six weeks, so I'll need your help."

She hugs me, and then I hug my dad awkwardly around his cast arm. When I pull back, I flex my fingers, trying to stop my body from tensing up. Surely, she didn't call me here for work?

"But you sounded upset. I thought Dad was..."

"Dead?" says Rhys from behind me.

I wave my hands up and down at Dad and say, "Well, not exactly that, but not—this."

"Oh, no. I just fell over at one of the farm properties. Landed on my arm."

I suck a breath through my clenched teeth. I left work in a panic, thinking my dad was sick when really, he was fine with just a few small broken bones. The accident still worries me, but, it wasn't urgent enough to flee the city, and risk loosing my job for.

"I'm tired. I need to lie down. It's been a long day, and the flight took it out of me," I say. It's not entirely lying because I am exhausted; mentally, I need sleep. I have felt too many emotions for one day.

"Okay. Rhys will take you home. Make yourself comfortable."

I stare back and open my mouth, but only say a small, "Okay."

I turn my back and walk out and feel Rhys beside me. He doesn't speak, which I'm grateful for. I really don't want to speak to anyone right now.

His behavior about makes sense now. He obviously had no clue what Mom did. She wants me to help with the business while Dad is off. Why didn't she just ask? Why the dramatic phone call?

Well, I know that's her, but I would have come back to help. All she had to do was ask and maybe I could have organized something with Eleanor. I climb into Rhys' car, and Toby immediately gives me affection and loving licks. I stroke his fur, but remember I need to send some texts to let them know I arrived.

I decide on a group message to George and Gracie.

> **Abigail:** Arrived safe and sound. Dad's good. I'm so tired from the flight, I'm going to bed. Goodnight x.

But I send James his own text.

> **Abigail:** Hi, I arrived safe and sound. Dad's good. I'm so tired from the flight, I think I'll go straight to bed. Miss you x.

I sit back and when we get to Mom and Dad's, I walk the familiar steps into my house and straight down to my old bedroom. Anger still spirals in the pit of my stomach as I drop my bag on the floor with a thud, and I fall straight on top of my bed, thrumming my fingers on the mattress and thinking how I'll move forward with this situation. I'm deliberating when my phone rings and his name flashes on the screen.

I prop my chin in my hand, feeling brighter just because he's called. "James."

"It's too early for you to go to bed, so I just had to call to hear your voice and to make sure you're really okay."

I'm totally surprised by him picking up on my subtle clues. He pays more attention than I realize. I take a quick breath and say, "You're right; it's too early and I'm not okay. I just didn't want you to worry."

"I want you to be honest with me. Please don't hold back."

"But you're busy."

"Never for you."

His words are hitting me full force and the tension dissipates into a longing for him. I want to go back and be in the city bubble that fulfilled me.

I'm still silent.

"Tell me what happened."

"Mom dramatized Dad's fall, and he only has a broken arm. She wanted help with the business, so she overreacted to get me to come home."

A disapproving sound leaves his throat, and he asks, "How do you feel about helping her out?"

I sit up and bite down hard on my lower lip and think about it.

How do I feel?

"If she had asked me and I could have spoken to Eleanor, I would have been happy to do it, but right now, I'm still angry at her actions."

"You have every right to feel that way. Just do what's right for you. You said you have a friend there, so hang out with her. Take some time. A couple of days or the week won't be a problem."

"It will be nice to see my brother too."

"But only do what you want to do. Don't help your parents unless you want to. You went to the city to become independent; don't let them change that."

I lie back down on the bed and say, "You're so right. I need to live my life and my new job and you are what I want."

"I like the sound of that."

"I like you."

"I like you too."

CHAPTER 22

ABIGAIL

I STARE OUT MY old bedroom window, hearing movement in the kitchen, but knowing someone is awake doesn't make me want to rush out. Instead, I roll onto my back and cover my eyes with my hands, wishing I could wake up in my apartment in the city.

Unable to avoid it any longer, I sit up and look around my childhood bedroom. I walk over to the same timber dresser with a mirror resting on top of it. Pulling the top drawer open, I see my clothes are still how I left them, messy and shoved in the drawer. I close it again and grab my bag and lift it onto the bed, pausing before I open it.

Everything is still the same, yet I am not the same person I was when I was last here.

I'm different.

I was drained, hollow, and lifeless the last time I was in this bedroom. And I feel this way again.

In the city, I felt alive; I felt free, and I felt—love.

How does one person make you feel safe and also give you the strength to find yourself?

That one person is James, and I stand here with the burning imprint he left in me.

I push myself to move to find some clothes. I need a shower to feel the heat on me and to wake me up. I didn't sleep well last night, not being able to calm the sea that's brewing in me.

When I move the bag, I find a package underneath addressed to me. I hesitate, blinking with bafflement. I don't remember seeing that. Mom or Dad must have left it on the bed and I hadn't noticed. I grab it and tear off the card and read the words.

Miss you x

His kindness causes my eyes to gloss over. I remove the wrapping to see what the present is. It's a book. Two, actually. One of my favorite authors, and the other is the New York book I was reading in the bookstore. I flip the books over, not believing it's real. Stroking the covers, I sit on the edge of the bed staring at them in disbelief. I can't believe he did this for me. My heart squeezes inside my chest, and I grab my phone to text him.

Abigail: Are you awake?

My phone rings in my hand, so I answer it with a smile.

"Hi."

"Are you okay?"

"Yes, I'm more than okay. Thank you for the books. It was the best surprise."

I feel lighter now that I can hear his voice; the heaviness I felt in my chest disappears. He has this way of making me giddy and yet calm at the same time.

"So, I did good?"

I giggle, breathing a little easier. "More than good."

"I'm glad I can make you smile again. How's your dad?"

I close my eyes. "I haven't been out of my bedroom yet. He has Mom fluffing around him, so I'm sure that will drive him mad soon enough."

"What are your plans today? I miss you," he whispers into the phone.

The sound is causing my breath to catch.

I breathe. "I miss you too. I'll talk to them and go from there. I don't have any set plans."

"Good idea. Now I better go. I have a meeting to get to, but I'll talk to you tonight. Unless you need me. You call me."

I drop my chin, wishing I could talk to him for longer. But I understand he can't do that—he has a company to run—so I sit back up and say, "Yes, I will. Thanks again for my books."

"It's to remind you of your own goals. Keep yourself at the forefront of your mind when you talk to them."

I hang up, wishing I was with him at work right now and not here. I still haven't asked my mother why she acted like my father was dying; I'll never understand my parents. I'm green with envy that my brother doesn't have to live here. Why do I have to suffocate by being here? The alternative is to go to stay at his house, but with his lack of talking, that doesn't appeal much either.

I carry my clothes and go straight to the bathroom. I stand under the hot shower until someone must use the water, and it goes ice cold. I jump back, squeeze my eyes shut, and roughly wipe at them.

Seriously?

I should have told them I'm showering to stop them from using the taps. I take a deep breath and try to regain control. Ever since I have been back here, I haven't been myself. I feel like I'm a rubber band getting stretched until I snap. I'm thinning and not hanging on by much. I know my dad didn't mean to hurt himself.

Speaking of, I need to find out how it happened and let them know I need to get back to work in a few days. I finish my shower, get dressed, and find them both in the kitchen. Mom is sitting with Dad in the kitchen. At the sound of my shoes, they both look up.

Mom looks at the clock and returns my gaze. "We thought you would never wake."

I stay silent, biting my tongue as I walk farther into the kitchen and begin making coffee. "Did you want tea or coffee?" I ask.

Dad lifts his cup in the air and says, "No thanks. I have one your mom made."

I nod and ask the question that has been playing heavily on me. "What happened to your arm?"

I finish preparing my coffee and sit down at the table, staring at my dad over my cup as I take a sip of my coffee. It's the only comfort I have found since being here.

He looks the same as he always has, longish light brown hair and his favorite red flannel-check shirt. His cast arm is on the table while his other hand lifts his cup to take a sip. When he lowers it, he says, "I was on the ride-on mower and my foot got stuck. Came down like a sack of potatoes. Luckily, your mother was home. She helped me up, but the swelling came up straight away and I knew then something was really wrong."

I drink my coffee, trying to understand the panic of Mom's call. I feel my muscles coil with tension and I say through gritted teeth, "Okay, but Mom called me, and I thought you were dying."

He tips his head back; a deep laugh leaves his chest, and he says, "Yes, your mother has a way of thinking I'm going to die if I hurt myself. But I don't have plans to go anywhere."

I ease back into my chair, rubbing my jeans. This is the same pair I wore the first time at the football game with James. Wearing them gives me added confidence, as if he's here with me, encouraging and supporting me. When I told him I didn't know what I was going to do, it was the truth. I don't know if I'll leave today or stay for a few days. But one thing I know for certain is I'm not staying here.

God, I miss him.

I stroke my leg, loving the calming effect it has on me.

"Are you ready?" Mom says, interrupting my daydream.

I turn to face her with a pinched expression, trying to understand where we are going, but I'm still unclear, so I ask, "What for?"

She chucks a bottle of water and food in her bag. "Work. Let's get in the car. I don't want to be any later. There will be enough to catch up on as it is." She says hitching up her bag up on her shoulder and then crosses her arms over her chest.

"Hang on one second." The anger swells in my gut again.

Surprise is written on her face. I know she hasn't heard me stand up for myself, but this is the new me, the one who wants a choice with her life.

I don't want to be told what to do. I want to be supported.

Like James does.

"Let's discuss this. And then I'll decide about what I want to do."

"The city has changed you," she mutters under her breath.

"For the better."

Her brows rise.

"Yes, I heard that. Now, the city has changed me, yes, but for the right reasons. I love my job and new life there. I'm miserable here. I will not be back—ever."

My mom gasps loudly, while my dad is silent, with a sullen expression. A pain is forming in the back of my throat, but I swallow repeatedly, refusing to accept the guilt.

"I would say I'm sorry, but I'm not. I'm twenty-five; I can do what I want. And what I want isn't here. Now, Mom, I'm disgusted with your actions and false pretenses to get me here. Moving forward, I will stay a couple of days, maybe, but then I'm flying back. No arguments or fake dramatics. I want you to accept it. You don't have to support it, but accepting it is enough."

She grumbles but doesn't say anything.

"We can accept it," my dad says as he glances at my mom and nods before looking back at me.

"Good. Mom, when you talk about work, this is what will happen. I will come and help you sort out contracts and property management and any financials I can, but that's it. If what I've learned, and will teach you, doesn't turn the business to become profitable, I think you need to look at selling it."

I flick my gaze between them. Both are wearing a tight expression and their mouths are firmly closed.

Finally, they are listening to me.

I blow out a deep breath. I'm exhausted just from this damn conversation, but it was way overdue. "Give me a minute to get ready."

I go to my room to grab shoes and a sweater before following her out to the car.

The drive to the office is only a few minutes. Everything in town is close to each other. I stare out the window, my head on the headrest, just listening to the radio and bouncing up and down in Mom and Dad's old truck.

She pulls up outside the office and I slam the door shut behind me. We have spoken little, but it's not unusual. I have the same blonde hair and green eyes, but I'd like to think that's all that we have that's similar. My brother is my parents' favorite. I should be happy they meddle in his business and not in mine, but sometimes I wish they cared for me the same way they care for him.

The mess of the office has me pausing mid-step, glancing around at the paperwork, unorganized and left in piles. Why? How do they know which are old contracts and which are new?

What a mess.

I force myself to move forward and go to my father's desk. I let my bag drop to the floor and run a hand down my hair. *Where do I begin?*

"Mom, what system are you using?" I ask.

I can see myself spending the next few days organizing this place. And this is coming from me, who is not very organized. But this... this is chaos.

Mom steps over next to me. "Well, there isn't one. You know your father and I don't have a system."

I pick up papers and read their contents. "Okay," I say. "But you will have one."

She nods and wanders back over to her desk, listening to voicemails and calling people back.

I step over to the filing cabinet and see that it's barely used, so I sort through the pile on top of the desk until I lose track of time and my stomach growls loudly. I peer up at the clock and notice it's past lunchtime. I need food for energy to finish dealing with the desk.

I grab my bag. Mom is working at her desk, so I say, "I'll grab lunch at the store. Is there something you feel like?"

She doesn't move her eyes from her work. She just says, "No. Anything will be great."

I slink away and leave the office. Stepping into the street, I walk in the store's direction. I can't help but enjoy the pretty town and what it offers. It has the warm, homely feeling the city doesn't offer, but even with the familiarity, it doesn't warm me. There is still something missing.

Or should I say—someone is missing?

Before entering the store, I call Charlotte to arrange to catch up with her. I'm now smiling at the other person other than my brother that I'm excited to see now that I'm back.

I grab lunch for me and Mom and walk back to the office. We eat and then I finish more of the filing.

"We need to get home. I need to cook your father dinner and check on him. We will be back tomorrow. There is no rush now that you are back." Her voice has a sense of calmness that sets alarm bells ringing.

"Did you not hear me this morning? I said only a couple of days. Dad is fine; let's finish organizing so I can start setting up a new system. There will be a lot to learn. But I have a contract and a job to get back to."

I hate that she doesn't take my job seriously.

She shakes her head. "We need a lot of help. We are drowning." She waves her arms around the office. "Your dad and I are struggling. You know your brother can't help."

I feel my chest tighten as my lungs constrict, making it hard for me to breathe. They let my brother do what he wants to, but they treat me differently.

"I'm sorry, but that's not my issue. This is your business and I'll do everything I can to show you how to turn it around, but after that, it's up to you and Dad to figure the rest out. I'm out."

"And you think you haven't changed."

"I have, but for the better," I say and return to organizing the office.

CHAPTER 23

ABIGAIL

TWO DAYS LATER, I'M still sorting their mess of a business. I'm answering calls, booking inspections, and sorting through the contracts.

'Mom, I have a contract here that I want to discuss."

"Okay. Hang on a sec. I'll finish this email."

After a couple of minutes, she sits down beside me and I say, "I want to show you some new changes we should add to the financials and deposit."

"Okay."

I run through the property contract and explain what needs to be changed and why. I sit staring at her with a high chin and a satisfied smile. Everything I've learned from White Estate is coming into play now and I couldn't be happier.

After discussing the contract and working on a few more with her, I go for a small walk on my break, choosing to sit in the town square. I want to check in with George and send a message to James.

I send James a message first.

Abigail: Guess who showed her mom how to write better contracts and has organized the office?

James: I'm so proud of you. Showing them what you have learned is empowering and you should be proud of yourself. Now, you organizing them? This I wish I could see...

Abigail: Hey! I'm not that bad. It's messy neat.

James: There is no such thing. But I gotta run. I have a meeting.
I can't wait to see you. I need you. X

Abigail: I need you too. Counting down the days.

When I read the words *I need you*, they make my stomach flutter. I need him too—more than I imagined was possible, but I now know it's true. Being here makes me feel so low. The high of being with him feels like a distant memory every day I spend here. I'm just filling my days with so much work that I'm too busy and exhausted to think. I speak to him and go to bed, and that's my plan until I'm able to get back to the city.

I call George next before I return to work.

"How's your dad? What happened?" he asks.

I forgot he doesn't know what happened because the last time I was with him, I was a blubbering mess in his arms, thinking my dad was dying. I'm almost too embarrassed to tell him the truth.

I groan. "Well, I got here, and he broke a bone in his arm falling off the ride-on mower."

"But—"

I can understand his confusion, so I cut him off. "Yeah. Mom acted as if he were dying. But he is fine."

"I'm glad he is okay. But are you going to come back? Work is boring without you."

I smile and say, "Soon. I'm sure you're doing both our work, so it would keep you busy enough not to miss me."

"Pfft. No chance. We are learning maintenance until you can come back. They want to wait to discuss tenants until you're here too."

"Oh fun. I can't wait to get back to work."

"What are you doing there?" he asks.

I giggle again, but it ends with a sigh. I have to try to not be negative when I speak.

"Helping my parents' business; it's real estate, but it's kind of messy, so I had to organize it. And today I'm teaching Mom what we have learned at White, so she and Dad can make the business profitable."

He cracks up laughing and says, "You are organizing an office. Are you shitting me?"

"Hey! I'm not that bad, mister." I pretend to sound offended, even though I know I'm not the most organized person. But he and James have both commented on it today, so it must mean I really am bad. I can't help but have a lopsided grin at the thought.

"If you say so," he says before continuing. "If you have organized it, can't you come home now?"

"That's the plan. I can't wait. The fresh air here beats the city, but I feel—lonely."

Saying I'm lonely out loud was one of the hardest things to do, but with George, I feel comfortable being honest.

"Shit. I'm sorry you feel that way. You better get back to us soon, then."

I stretch, my back getting sore from sitting on the wooden bench. "I will. I better get going; I'm seizing up here. I need to keep walking," I say.

"Ha, okay, you old lady. Call me soon and I expect you back here soon or else you may find me in Shitty Creek, dragging you back."

I laugh. "Okay, okay. I hear you loud and clear. Bye."

I hang up and just lean back, looking around a moment longer, feeling better for talking to him.

A few hours later, I'm packing some of my things into the suitcase because I want to get back to James in two days. It's time to leave. I have helped them with the business and Mom should be fine to handle it on her own until Dad can get back. I just can't be away from James a moment longer. He gives me a rush and a longing that I can't deny myself anymore. I need him, like I need air to breathe.

I'm humming a tune while folding clothes into the case. Mom walks past and pauses by my bedroom door. I look over at her. A frown sets on her face and her gaze flicks between the case and me. As she straightens her body to take up the entire doorframe, she asks, "What are you doing?"

I stop packing and face her. "I'm packing to go back to the city. I'm leaving in two days. I start back at work on Monday."

She crosses her arms over her chest and steps farther into the room. "No. We need you here, Abigail. You can't leave yet."

Nobody here cares about my desires. Where is this thing we call love? Is this what parents are supposed to do?

I can't think straight, and I cross my arms over my chest, mirroring her stance. "Does anyone really care about how I feel? And what about what I dreamed of? No, I don't think you do."

She drops her arms and reaches out to grip my shoulders. I stare back into her gaze as she blows me away with her next statement. "Don't ruin our dreams. Your grandparents handed the business down to your father. Don't disappoint them or him. If you don't help us, we could lose the business. Do you want that?"

I squeeze my eyes shut, feeling my breath burning my throat.

"Please," she whispers.

And her selfishness causes my pulse to speed up and I open my eyes as my temper flares.

Her cold look is not helping the fury building in me.

"If you haven't learned from my time here and me organizing your office, then the business's failure is on you and Dad, not me! Don't blame me."

She shakes her head vehemently. The silence between us is back to unbearable, but I stand tall, angry, and proud.

Her face pales and then she walks out of my bedroom, leaving me standing there on shaky knees. After collecting my thoughts, I decide I need to call James and let him know what's happening here. I grab my phone and scroll through until I see his name. Before I hit call, I make sure my bedroom door is closed and I take a seat on the side of the bed to look out at the garden as I talk. I take a calming breath and stare at the call button. I close my eyes, trying to calm the heart palpitations and the threatening tears.

CHAPTER 24

JAMES

"HEY, BABY."

"Hi." She whispers.

I sit back momentarily in my living area with a cold knot forming in my gut. The tone of her voice is causing an alarm in me.

"Are you okay?"

"Not really." Her voice is barely above a whisper. I feel my heart and soul splinter. I can't bear sitting here, hearing her break down without wanting to book a flight to get to her. But I can't save her; she needs to do this for herself. Part of why she wanted to come to the city was for independence, so I need to let her do it on her own. I can only offer my support and encourage her with everything I have.

I stand and pace circles around the room, my hand rubbing my forehead and I say, "Tell me what happened. I'm here for you."

She sobs and the sound of her in pain has my throat closing, so I clear it to regain control. She needs me. I need to be calm and in control to help guide her.

"You're always there for me. I wish I could say the same thing about my parents, mainly my mom. She just doesn't support my independence, or the city move. I had hoped that by helping her with the business and explaining I want to go back to the city it would be enough for her to support me—"

"But she doesn't," I say, finishing her sentence.

"Not one bit. I know we don't have a perfect relationship, but I've never felt so hurt."

Hearing her say she is hurt makes me want to lose my fucking shit. I close my eyes and suck in a deep breath to calm the anger and torment swirling in me.

"I'm sorry she can't support you. But just know I do. I believe in you, and I'm here waiting for you."

"You have no idea how much that means to me, and knowing I have you strengthens me," she says through tears.

I squeeze my eyes and drop my chin. I'm still pacing the room, unable to stop, fearful I'll crack and go to her.

"You are strong without me. I'm just helping you see what I know is inside you. You can choose to live the life you want. We all have choices in life, and this is you making one. You won't regret living the life you dream of."

"You're part of the dream," she whispers.

My fucking dream too. One I didn't know I wanted, and I shouldn't have wanted but now I've had her, I'm refusing to let her go.

She is part of my dream.

Part of my future.

Part of me.

"You're the first man to care."

"Always."

The raw emotion between us is palpable and I can't wait to hold her in my arms.

"I might go. I'm mentally drained." She breathes. "I want to shower and read before bed."

"Good idea. And tomorrow you wake up and go fight for yourself, baby, and remember I'm waiting for you."

"I will. I promise."

I hang up with a thrumming heart and still too much energy, so I get changed into running gear and go for a long run to tire myself out.

I sit at my desk with my head in my hands, cursing every swear word possible. I rub my hands along my forehead roughly, trying to understand what the fuck just happened.

How did I lose a job to him? (My ex-business partner.) I have to figure out why. I need to make sure it can't happen again.

I pick up the phone and ask Sophie for the file.

She rushes in not long later and hands it to me.

I'm grateful for the distraction because I need to focus on something that makes my heart race and my palms sweaty for a different reason.

The temptation to go to her is so strong that I had to run extra miles this morning because I couldn't sleep.

I have been checking my phone and seeing if she has called or texted me. I'm trying to give her space, but the sounds of her sobs still echo in me.

The gut-wrenching sound shook me. And I so badly want to comfort her. And that is something I haven't wanted until her. Without her, I lose myself in work and remember I'll see her again soon.

I shake my head to refocus and flick through the file. Afterward, I get on the phone to organize a meeting for an hour's time.

The meeting goes according to plan, and I have a better understanding why we lost the job. And I managed to win another contract with them, and this one is for even more money, helping me climb to that top position.

Despite reaching my goals, I now have another one, and that is to make Abigail happy. Sitting here in the back of this car, I get memories of her being in here. I grind my teeth together and stare at my phone until I arrive. The gaping hole that's left in my heart is still wide open, waiting for her to come home.

Yes, I have more money, but I'm still seared with anguish. The pain in my chest is still beating with its own pulse and rhythm. I'm still a very empty man, craving to be whole.

Later that night, John is driving me to meet the boys to watch a game at a local spot. As I stare out the window looking at the city, I hold my breath when the coffee shop I took her to passes by. I tear my gaze away to focus on my phone that's gripped tightly in my hand. She makes me love this city. I can't help but smile at all the memories of us here already, and I can't wait to make more.

I arrive at the bar, and as I'm walking in, I roll my shoulders back, and take my seat in the empty chair. "Boys."

Joshua frowns, looking curiously at me, and asks, "What's crawled up your ass?"

I settle into my seat and say, "Nothing."

He knows me too well, and the worry for Abigail must be etched on my face.

He chokes on a laugh and winks at Benjamin.

I grind down hard on my teeth to prevent biting back and egging them on further, but feeling them watching me irks me, so I stand abruptly. "I'll get drinks."

I don't wait for an answer. Instead, I head to the bar and lean on it for support as I wait for the bartender to take my order. She tries to flirt with me, but I don't take a second glance at her, happy to just return to my friends.

When I return, I take a seat and drink half my beer in one go. The refreshing taste hits me the right way.

"Woah, now you're scaring me. Are you sure you're okay?" Benjamin asks.

He tries to snatch my glass from me, but I clutch it tighter and frown at him. I'm an adult and I don't need his help, and I already have a father, but I'm sure drinking would make him proud. The thought alone causes bile to rise at the back of my throat.

"I told you I am," I say.

I hug the glass, but I don't take another sip. I give myself some time to calm down. I thought being here with the boys would help soothe the turmoil, but it's not. It's making me snap and give away how I'm feeling. I don't share my life or feelings. I help people; they don't help me.

Something passes in Joshua's eye, some form of understanding, then he says, "Anyway, before you got here, Ben was telling me about a house he bought near his team's training field."

A small smile forms for Benjamin. I'm so proud of him. "That's awesome. I can't wait to see it," I say.

"Definitely soon," Benjamin says with a smile.

My phone vibrates and I pull it out and I think it's her for a second, but it's a work email. I don't bother responding, just tuck my phone away and drain the glass.

I rise, and I ask them, "Do you want another?"

The boys look at their glasses and then back to me, and then Joshua says, "We have only just touched ours and you already drank all yours?"

"Yeah," I say.

"No, I'm good," Benjamin says.

"Me too, but one more and then we are out of here," Joshua says.

"Why?" I ask, hating that he is telling me what to do. It's normally my job to boss his ass around.

"Because you don't drink over two and I won't let you. I'd rather go to the gym and let you beat me up than drink," he says firmly.

That makes me smile. "Don't tempt me."

He shrugs. "I'll let you, if you leave after your next drink."

"Deal, but don't say I haven't warned you. I'm in the mood to punch shit up," I say. I prefer this option to relieve the stress.

Joshua gives me an enormous grin, and he drops his chin with approval.

"I'm coming for a workout. I need to sweat off this beer," Benjamin says.

"I'll grab another drink and I'll be right back."

I walk off and text John to pick us up to take us to the local gym.

———

The next morning, I'm at the airport on my way to catch a flight. I take a seat in the same café where I first met Abigail. The seats we were in are now occupied, but it makes me want to talk to her.

James: (Picture of café)

James: Makes me think of when we first met.

Abigail: I wish I was with you.

Abigail: The real question is what book did you bring with you?

James: Who says I brought one?

Abigail: Come on. Tell me. I know you did.

I open my bag and snap a picture of the book that's sitting in there.

Abigail: No way. You keep the same book there? The one you were reading when we met?

James: It's my lucky charm. A piece of you is always with me.

Abigail: One more sleep.

James: Thank fuck. Are you okay?

Abigail: Yes. I promise. I'm good.

James: Good. I need to catch my flight. I'll see you tomorrow. Message me when you get home and I'll come.

CHAPTER 25

ABIGAIL

I WAKE UP TO the trees blowing and the birds talking outside my window. It's one of the many positives of the town. The humble people and the special town are gorgeous, but that's not enough for me.

It's Friday morning and after barely getting a solid four hours of sleep I'm utterly exhausted. Most of the night, I replayed moments of bliss with James and then the painful memories of my parents. I don't know how to process it and with no work because I'm catching my flight later, I roll over to check the time. It's early, so I decide to go for a walk.

I put on some shorts and a tank top with my running shoes and pass my parents sitting in the kitchen. "Going for a walk, I'll be back."

I leave without waiting for a response and jog down the steps, welcoming the warm breeze that hits me. After pausing at the bottom of the steps, I decided to walk the big loop around town.

I have been walking for an hour and I'm perspiring when I hear my brother's voice say, "Abby?"

I turn around and stop walking, squinting from the sun until I see his face clearly. He jogs up to me and slows to pause in front of me.

His hands are on his hips, and he's gasping for air. His forehead is coated with sweat, showing he's been out for a while.

"I was going to come by and see you later. I'm going back to the city today."

"You didn't want to come back?'

I hold on to my arms, hugging myself and I say, "No. I have a fantastic job in the city, with great potential to learn more. And I met someone."

He rubs the sweat off his forehead. "You mentioned that. How long have you been together?" he asks as he eyes me critically.

"It's new, but he, um, actually owns White Estate."

"Hence the first-class tickets."

I nod.

"Is he good to you?"

A warmth hits me just thinking about James.

"He's wonderful."

"That sparkle in your eyes had vanished since being here. So if he can bring that back and makes you happy, then I support it. Just take it slow and be careful," he says, and he pokes my nose playfully and I offer a small smile at his kind words.

"I will. I haven't told Mom and Dad, and I don't know when I'll do it. But for right now, I don't want them to know."

His gaze meets mine and his lips thin before he says, "They shouldn't have called you. It was selfish; you should go back and chase your dreams."

I blink slowly, unable to believe what I'm hearing. My brother, the man of few words, my parents' golden child, is standing up for me, encouraging me.

I rub my lips with one of my hands, willing the words to come to me. "Thanks. Well, you better get back to your run," I say in a shaky voice.

Relief floods my brother's face; he clearly needs the space too.

I'm on my way to see Charlotte for coffee. Between the both of us working, today was the only opportunity. The bell above the door chimes as I enter. It's still early and only a few tables are taken.

Charlotte comes rushing over. "Oh, hi. I've missed you so much. Give me a hug. It's been too long."

I giggle at her exaggeration. She pulls me into her chest, and I hug her back. She has a heart of gold. I pull back, but she still latches onto the back of my upper arms to look deeply into my eyes, and she says, "Are you sure you can't stay?"

I dip my chin down with a wince. "No. I need to get back to work. But I don't have any plans until my flight. After here, did you want to go to the stores?"

"Yes. Totally I would love that."

I glance around for a table away from the other locals. I want to speak to her with no one eavesdropping. Pointing to one of the free corners, I say, "Let's grab a seat."

We sit and order coffees and I get a piece of today's cake.

Her eyes shimmer. "I always loved your sweet tooth. It's so good to have you back. Now tell me how amazing the job is."

"It has been so hard but yet so rewarding. The other trainee, George, and I are excelling, which hopefully means we can get a job there afterwards."

"Look at you go. I'm happy you're settling in and enjoying it. I bet they offer you a job afterwards. They would be crazy if they didn't. And now I want the real gossip. What about the guys? Are you dating anyone?"

I bite down on my lip and look away. "Well, I'm seeing someone."

She gasps and covers her mouth.

I giggle.

"Who, where, how? Tell me more."

"He, um, is actually the owner of the company."

"You're kidding me."

"Nope. But I didn't meet him at work. I actually met him at the airport after my interview with his HR."

"No," she says as she shakes her head.

"Obviously, we had a shock when we found out we would be working together."

"Is he the one?'

James' face flashes in front of my eyes and it causes my chest to tighten. He is a man who makes me feel like I can get married and have children, the type of man who lets you feel free but carries you in his arms when you need lifting. I can picture being with him every day and being the happiest woman alive.

I nod. "Yeah. I can't see myself without him."

She beams at me.

The waitress comes over carrying the cake and the coffees.

I peer down at the large slice she served me. It makes me smile. The city serves a lot smaller, and I need comfort food right now. Not having James' arms around me to warm and comfort me, I have to eat my feelings until I see him.

"How're your parents taking it?"

I grimace. "Not good. They want me back."

"But that's not right. You don't want that," she says.

"No. Never. I love the city and my job at White. I helped set my parents' business up, so it's now up to them."

I pick up the spoon and eat some cake. The lemon hits my tongue and I briefly close my eyes, savoring the taste.

"Exactly. It's their business; they can figure it out. You shouldn't be miserable for them, even if I wish you would be here for me."

I smile. "I'll miss you too. If you ever want to leave or even visit, my doors are always open."

"I'm definitely coming to visit. The way you speak about the city has me hooked."

I giggle and we enjoy the rest of our coffees and my cake before walking to the shops.

The feeling of the delicate red lace between my fingertips has my stomach fluttering. Imagine how it would feel on me. I turn the price tag over and sigh. It's way too much. I need to watch my money since I paid for my flight home.

"That's gorgeous," Charlotte says over my shoulder.

"Mm, I know, but it's over my budget." I turn the tag over, showing her the price of the matching set.

"Oh, sugar."

I giggle and say, "Yeah. My thoughts exactly."

I drop the lace, and we move to the next shop. I'm browsing the clothes, but there isn't anything that matches my new pieces and I only want to buy clothes that make me feel good. Here, it's my old clothes—and I'm not looking back anymore. I'm only moving forward.

A selection of books catches my eye. I move forward, reading the titles until one stands out. I smile. The J.D. Robb book is here. I can't help but snap a picture and send it to him.

> **Abigail:** Look what I found in Riddell's today. You're following me everywhere.

> **James:** It's bringing you good luck. I can't wait to see you. Not long now.

> **Abigail:** I'm counting down.

James: The seconds—me too.

I feel my heart swell at those words and I can't help but stare at them for a moment longer. After a minute, I tuck my phone away and continue browsing.

Half an hour later, I say to Charlotte, "I better get back home. I still need to finish packing and get to the airport."

She moans. "I wish you weren't, but I'll be in the city soon."

"Please. That would be amazing."

We hug and I practically run home. I haven't told James about my flight details because my plan is to surprise him. The ache in my chest for him is too much to bear anymore.

I need him.

CHAPTER 26

ABIGAIL

I CALL MY BROTHER to take me to the airport. I know my parents will refuse or make some excuse or accident happen and I don't want to deal with their behavior anymore. If they can't support their daughter's dreams and hold her back on purpose, then they won't be involved in my life anymore.

After hanging up with him, I send a message to both George and Gracie, sharing my news.

Abigail: Get ready. I'm coming home.

George: Can't wait to have you back.

Gracie: Best news I've had all day. Can't wait to have you back. I'll be at work all weekend but come over Sunday and I'll have Ava join us for a wine night.

For the first time since stepping back into Riddell's Creek, I feel I have lifted the heavy weight off my chest. I'm breathing easier with every inhale and exhale, knowing I am about to be closer to him.

Now to say goodbye to my family.

I pace the room, thinking about how I want to say it. Once I'm ready, I roll my shoulders back and leave my room, walking to the lounge where the television is playing.

They both sit on the couch and turn their bodies at the sound of my footsteps along the tiles.

I stop with a pasted-on smile. Taking a seat, I clear my throat and say, "I need to talk to you two for a minute."

"Is everything okay, Abigail?" my father asks.

"Yes. I just need to tell you Rhys is coming to pick me up now and taking me to the airport."

My mom gasps loudly and my dad eases back on the couch, not saying a word.

"You're actually doing this," she says.

I turn away, speechless; I glance at the television before I return my gaze to hers, but now mine is hard. With tension forming, my muscles twitch, so I clutch my hands together and say, "Yes, I am. This is about me following my dreams. I'm twenty-five and I still do whatever you want, but you have not once let me chase my dreams or let me be happy."

And James makes me happy.

"That's a lie," Dad says.

"How? You tell me how you have let me be happy. I was hardly in the city before Mom called me up, acting like you were on your deathbed to get me back here."

"Abigail," my father warns.

"Don't Abigail me. I have been the perfect daughter, but this daughter is no longer a doormat. She is fighting for her happiness. I haven't even told you I met someone, someone I had to leave to come here."

"See, I knew this would happen. Those city people are changing you. They are toxic. I noticed the new clothes they make you wear," Mom says.

I hear my ears ringing with the blood pumping through them, and I shake my head. "They haven't. I chose the clothes; I wanted to feel confident. It wasn't about anyone else. It was about me. I needed to do this. I've grown up, but if you can't accept that, that's not my problem. Find a new doormat," I say.

I don't bother waiting for a response because they have already chosen their side, and I have chosen mine. I turn away and once I'm back in my room I close the door, leaning against it with my chin in the air and my eyes closed, huffing and puffing.

I have never had a disagreement like that, but it was refreshing. Standing up for myself felt exhilarating.

I hear voices, so I know Rhys is here. I had been reading on my bed, waiting. Grabbing my case, I leave my room. Rhys is standing in his running gear in the kitchen. His usual scowl is on his face and his arms are crossed over his chest. I bet listening to my parents complain about me. I have to pinch my lips together to prevent a laugh from slipping out.

I exit the room and push my chest out to make sure I stand tall and let them know I'm staying firm.

"Hi," I say to Rhys.

He dips his head, but my parents just look at me and say nothing.

Well, this is just great. We all just stand there silently. *Awkward.*

"There must be something in the water. You're not feeling well," Mom says.

Mom is trying to play the victim and begin her guilt-tripping, but I'm not letting it go any further. She will not dampen my spirits. I feel like myself again, the person I found in the city, full of life and direction, not this woman sitting here in the darkness of her room.

"Mom, I'm fine. I'm sorry, but this is what I want and nothing you or Dad say will change it."

She nods and crosses her arms. I don't offer to hug them. Our relationship is strained at the moment. Now that I have taken the blinds off, I can see clearly that it wasn't a healthy relationship.

"Bye, Abigail. Have a safe flight," Dad says.

"Will do."

I grab my case and look at my brother and I say, "Let's go."

I smile widely when I say those words. I have to calm myself down before I skip out of here. I get in the car, and I have my elbow on the window ledge and my fingers are twirling the diamond earrings *he* bought me.

I can't wait to get back to him.

"I take it Mom and Dad didn't take it well," Rhys asks.

I drop my hand and turn my body to face him. His face is stony but his eyes have a little wash of pride in them, but just as quickly as he looks at me, his gaze is back on the road again.

"You can say that. But I need to make myself happy and follow my dreams and heart. So here I am."

"I'm proud of you," he says through a tight jaw.

"Rhys Crawford, you didn't just pay me a compliment, did you?"

His lips slam shut in a thin line, and it makes me chuckle loudly. I know that's all I will get out of him, so

I lean forward and turn the radio up and sing loudly to the lyrics.

He takes me inside the airport, and I hug him.

"Be safe. Text me when you arrive."

"I will. Thanks for your support," I say before I walk off, taking a quick glance back to see him standing with his arms crossed, staring at me. I wave with a smile and then turn back around.

He is the only family supporting me on my journey, and it means the world to me. My eyes fill with tears, but as I step on the plane, the adrenaline is back. I'm going back home to the place I truly feel offers me love and support.

The closer I get to landing, the closer I feel to him. I don't know how he will feel about my surprise.

Taking the taxi to the apartment, I glance up at the towers and I feel back to myself already. I grab a take-away coffee before stepping into my building. The first sip has my eyes closing to savor the taste. God, I've missed the coffee here. Not as much as I have missed him, though. My stomach is in turmoil with excitement and nervousness, knowing I'm seeing him soon.

I walk inside my apartment and straight to my balcony and look out, proud of me for getting here and standing up for myself. I pull out my phone, snap a picture, and send it off to Rhys.

Abigail: Arrived safe. x

I unpack and shower before changing into fresh clothes and walk out my door bumping into Gracie and Ava.

"I missed my neighbor. So glad you're back. You are back for good, right?" Gracie steps toward me, giving me a hug. Her friend Ava is beside her. Now, she has brown hair.

I giggle and say, "Yes, I am. Hi, Ava. I love this color on you. Your eyes stand out more." I hug her and then pull away.

"Aw, thanks, love. How are you?" she asks.

I smile and flick my gaze to both of them and say, "I'm good. So happy to be back."

"When do you start back at work?" Gracie asks.

I run a hand through my hair. "On Monday."

Ava has a strange expression on her face, then she asks, "Sorry. Who did you say you work for?"

I frown and don't recall telling her, and it looks like neither did Gracie, so I say, "Ah—James White. From White Estate."

Ava gasps, immediately covering her mouth. She drops her hands away to say, "Are you shitting me?"

I feel my heartbeat picking up and I look at Gracie and back at her, trying to piece it together, but I still don't, so I ask, "What are you talking about?"

"You're the girl."

I frown and wait for her to explain.

"His friend Joshua is my boyfriend."

I nod remembering Joshua. He was at the football game.

She laughs and says, "James and Joshua are best buds. Joshua has been saying he is in one foul mood but won't say why."

"Such a small world," Ava says.

"Yeah, it is. I'm actually on my way to see him now," I say, purposefully leaving out the fact it's a surprise.

She laughs. "I bet he missed you. You're way too kind and pretty for him, if I'm honest."

I blush at her compliment and say, "Thanks, but he has the biggest heart. I can't even explain, but trust me, he is the kind one."

"How long have you been together? I didn't know he was your boyfriend. You skipped out on that detail." Gracie says.

I peek up at Gracie and say, "Not long. You haven't missed much."

"Joshua said he hadn't seen James so wound up over someone before and that you were something special. I wholeheartedly agree with him there," Ava says.

"I don't know about special, but I'm different," I say proudly.

"You are, and that's why you caught his eye for sure. I'm excited when two people fall in love. I know what that feels like," Ava says.

I choke on air at her choice of words. I'm coughing my lungs up, trying to recover.

Love?

Do I love him?

As my heart beats with an uncomfortable rhythm at the thought of him, I know right now I love James, but the real question is—does he love me?

CHAPTER 27

AT THE WHITE BUILDING, the hustle and bustle make me exhale a long sigh of contentment. I can't get enough of the noise of the cars and the people all around me. I'm blissfully happy to be back.

Checking over my outfit, to make sure it's all in place. I smile at my jeans, knowing these are the ones I was wearing the day James introduced me to his friend Benjamin. The memory brings a new flutter in my stomach, but I push it aside to admire my pretty gray top and black blazer, completing the look with my city-bought black heels. I love the extra height it adds to my frame. I run my hand through my hair.

Taking a moment on the sidewalk to gather myself. I'm too eager, so I need to calm down. I push aside the nerves that are rolling in my stomach and head inside, aiming for the elevator. I hope he is in there; it feels like forever since I have seen him and knowing I'm so close causes such an overwhelming tug to my heart.

I reach the elevator and Eleanor steps out. Her face lights up when she sees me and she asks, "Abigail, how are you?"

"I'm good, thanks. How are you?"

"Good too. Just on my way out for a coffee break. James said you start back Monday?"

The question hits me at full force. I didn't prepare to see Eleanor and have my reason to be back here late this afternoon, visiting the boss.

I feel myself shrink, but I push through and think of something to say. "Yeah, I was planning to go visit you and go to my desk. And I'm hoping to talk with James briefly before Monday. I want to hit the ground running next week."

I can't believe I'm rambling like this. *Get it together, woman!*

A flash of surprise hits her face, but it's quickly replaced with a smile. "Well, good luck. It's nice to see you again. I'm glad to have you back."

"Thanks, Eleanor. See you Monday."

But when she nods and walks off, I stand there panicking. Maybe this is a bad idea. Bumping into her has rattled me and now I'm second-guessing surprising him.

I shake my head and stand straighter.

No. I didn't come this far not to do it.

The elevator doors open on his floor and my mouth is drying up as I try to swallow the lump that's formed as I walk toward Sophie. Her eyes widen at the sight of me, probably wondering what I'm doing here without a meeting scheduled.

"Hi, Sophie. Is James in?" I ask, knowing I haven't had a proper conversation with her in the short time I have been working here. And it makes a lump form in my throat and I make a mental note to make more of an effort.

I hope he isn't in a meeting.

"He is—he doesn't know you're here, right?" Her voice is barely above a whisper as she leans in and looks between his door and me, giving me the answer I need—he's in there.

I'm trembling at how close I am to him.

I step closer to her desk and rest my hands on it, feeling like I need to do something with myself, and the cool desk on my sweaty hands feels so nice. "Ah, no, but I'm hoping to chat with him."

She nods and looks around, and then a little smile breaks on her mouth. "I'll call him and check."

I nod, but no words come out. I'm choking on a breath. He is about to find out I'm here.

She picks up the phone and says, "Hi, Mr. White. I have Miss Abigail Crawford to see you."

"Yeah, it's her."

What did he ask her?

I want to know what he is saying, but I don't have long to think about it because she hangs up and looks at me. "He said you can go in."

"Thanks," I say and push off the desk, running my hands over my outfit to make sure it's all in place. Taking a few deep breaths, I step over to the door that separates me and him.

I unfold my arms and shake out my hands and knock hard on his door.

"Come in." His deep, smooth voice has me tingling all over.

I briefly close my eyes. God, I have missed that bossy, handsome man. I grab the handle as if it's my life and twist it, pushing it slowly open. I step inside his office, closing the door behind me. I turn and he rises from where he was sitting on the edge of the desk.

He is wearing a white shirt with the buttons at the neck undone, his gray tie loose around his neck and no jacket, telling me he is knee-deep in work. Even with shadows under his eyes, he is a delicious sight.

As the recognition hits him full force, his face breaks into the biggest grin. He throws his arms wide open. Heat radiates through me.

When I look at the man who has my heart, and the ache inside my chest is too much right now. I smile the biggest stupid smile and step into his waiting arms. I loop my arms around his neck and hold him close. I try to control my breathing, but I'm enjoying his musky scent again. His arms are wrapped tightly around my waist, pulling me flush up against him so that my feet don't touch the floor.

His nose tickles my neck, and he whispers, "I have missed you."

I swallow the lump that's formed and say, "I have missed you too."

We stay connected. Neither one of us looks like we want to step out of the embrace.

I just want to stay in this cocoon of bliss forever. But we are in his office, so I pullback. His hands skim my lower back and pause on my hips.

I smile awkwardly. "Hi."

A flush hits me at how he is staring at me right now.

He eyes me. God, this man is the king of unreadable expressions.

"I guess you're wondering why I am here early." I laugh loudly, but more to myself because his lips don't move at all. His expression is still unreadable and I wish I knew what he is thinking.

"When we spoke on the phone, I knew I wanted to surprise you." I pause, trying to slow down my breath and erratic heartbeat before continuing, "I was hoping you would be excited to see me."

His face softens and a small lift to his lips finally eases me. His hands leaves my hip to touch my face in the most tender of touches. He rubs his thumb over my glossy lips and instinctively my mouth drops open from his hypnotizing movement.

I'm panting when he brings his face close to mine and squeezes my hip. I whimper. God, I have missed his touch.

"You have no fucking idea how much I have missed you and how fucking excited I was to hear Sophie say your name. I had to get her to confirm it; I didn't believe my dreams were coming true. But here you are. Back where you want to be. Following your own dreams and your own life. I'm honored you want me as part of it."

I'm speechless. His touch on my face stops and he pulls me closer, and he kisses me like never before. It's raw and real; I missed his talented lips. His tongue hits my lips and they open, ready for when his hot tongue massages against mine. I savor his taste and kiss him back with everything I can. I thrust my hands into his hair and pull him closer. I need him. I never want to be apart from him again.

We touch just to remind ourselves that I'm back and I'm really here. He strokes my back. It's soothing yet scorching. Our lips part, and our breaths are hard and fast.

I peck my now swollen lips to his and glance up into his eyes. "I can't tell you how hard it was being there."

I'm holding onto him, needing support to hold up my trembling legs. His gaze flicks over my face and then back up to hold mine.

"I felt suffocated, and I knew I couldn't live my life forever in that town and take over the business like they wanted me to. But do you know what I felt the most, being there?" I whisper, staring into his dark gaze. "Utterly heartbroken and missing you terribly. I knew I was falling for you, but it wasn't until I left and I thought, this is not truly living, this is just existing. You've made me feel a genuine happiness that I've never had before, and even wish for things I never thought were possible for me, but it's because of you that I dream now, and I'm not talking about work. I want a future with you."

I feel my eyes sting, but I shake my head softly.

You will not cry.

This isn't about sympathy. I'm just laying it all out for him.

I'm breathing heavily, feeling exposed and vulnerable, unsure if I shared too much.

"You're falling for me?" he asks and slowly shakes his head. "I—" His desk phone rings and he lays his forehead against mine and says in a groan, "Damn it. I better get this, even though I want to ignore it right now."

I check his watch, and glance back at him.

"Go and work. I'm back now. We have plenty of time to catch up." I say through a painful tightness in my throat.

He drops his hand from my face, and he reluctantly pulls away and I have to swallow a whine. I don't want him not focused on work. We both encourage and support each other at work. And after how supportive he was while I was away, I don't want to distract him anymore.

He picks up the phone. I watch him say, "Sophie."

His eyes don't leave me and the air is now clear of his intoxicating scent, reminding me of the way he held me moments ago.

He hangs up the phone and walks back to me and grabs my hands. "I have one more meeting left for the day. Can I come over after? I'll bring dinner."

I grin at his offer. "Of course. I would love that. I hope you're planning on sleeping over too."

He raises a brow at me and then a wicked grin takes over his face.

I watch his Adam's apple bobble as he swallows hard. "Oh, I wouldn't have it any other way."

"Thanks for your time. Bye, James." I wink and turn, swaying my hips. I hear his soft growl and I don't turn around; I just open the door and say goodbye to Sophie.

I step into the elevator on shaky legs. When I get inside, I slump against the wall, desperately needing support to hold myself up. He makes me feel everything. It totally consumes me.

I hit the button for my floor to visit George, who is at his desk. His mouth drops open, and he rushes to me, squeezing and lifting my feet off the floor. I squeal and for the first time since I arrive in this building, I feel like I can breathe.

"Abby, I missed you so much. How was your flight?" he asks as he lowers me back down and steps back.

I shake my head. "My flight was good, but I'm grateful to be back." I laugh, but it's strained. I'm hiding my pain of knowing my relationship with my parents is in a really toxic place.

"I'm grateful you're back. We get into tenants next week. However, I need to run you through maintenance first and catch you up on what you missed."

I smile at the sound of the prospect of work, so I say, "I'm free now if you have time?"

"Of course. Come sit."

I follow him over to his desk and pull up another chair beside him. He runs me through the maintenance database and properties and after he finishes, he turns to me. "Did you want to grab a coffee? I'm due to go home and I want to tell you about my weekend plans. I have a date." George turns to close his work.

I smile. A genuine relief floods me and my shoulders sag, and I say, "Ah—that would be amazing."

He nods and grabs his wallet. James said dinner and I don't have to cook, so I'll have time for a cup of coffee and a catch-up.

We head to the elevator in silence and when it arrives on our floor, the doors slide open. I freeze momentarily mid-step when a pair of black eyes stare back at me. They widen when they notice me, but James' posture remains unchanged. The relief I felt merely moments ago quickly turns to panic. A wave of apprehension sweeps through me and I flush miserably. I know no one knows about us, but there is always a deep fear. We need to discuss what we will do about work. It's a situation we need to sort out.

George enters and ignores my hesitation. I have to follow, biting down hard on my lip and feeling his glare burn through me. I move so George is in the middle of us.

"Hi, James," George says.

"George," he says.

I don't turn toward James. I keep my focus on the elevator buttons and watch them count down until we arrive on the ground floor. He takes off first, and I watch him in his tailored gray suit. I know exactly what that body is capable of, and it causes me to shiver with desire. I just had him wrapped around me not that long ago and soon I'll have him all night. The thought makes me breathless.

"He is one glorious bastard."

I giggle, throwing a hand over my mouth, not wanting others to hear. "Shhh, in case he hears you."

"He is too far away—relax."

I feel a light swelling in my heart. I am back in the city and with people who care and support me.

We walk across the road and into the coffee shop to enjoy a much-needed catch up.

CHAPTER 28

JAMES

WHEN SHE WALKED INTO my office, I thought I was hallucinating. She is even better than my nightly dreams or any memories I had of her. She had me dizzy and fighting the pain hitting my chest as I watched her enter.

God, she is so beautiful, making me weak. I hate my lack of control over my emotions. When she opened up about her parents, I desperately wanted to offer to fix it, like I always do with everyone's problems. She proved not only to me but to herself that she can fight and stand up for herself.

When she said those things about me, it sent my thoughts spinning inside my head, causing spots to flash in front of my eyes. The emotions flooding through me prevent me from focusing on any work. It's been like that all week, where I sit and wonder what she is doing. Even when we had spoken, I couldn't help but want to be right there with her.

The issue we have is how will we move forward with work. Will people treat her differently because of our relationship? Probably.

I don't know how to handle it and where her head is with it, but we definitely need to discuss it.

It would be easier if she was training somewhere else, but could she train with me and then get a job somewhere else?

But why does my stomach harden at the thought of her working somewhere other than here?

Somewhere else, I can't protect and teach her. And deep inside me, I have this compelling need to look after her.

Fuck!

Why can't I just sort my shit out?

I can't keep working this way. I'm barely getting any work completed and the whole time I'm distracted by visions of her in my arms and that sweet taste of her on my lips.

I hold my head in my hands, trying to figure out who wins.

My head or my heart?

Logic or risk?

Brainpower or feelings?

I slam my hands on the desk, frustrated with the lack of answers.

After giving up, I grab my jacket from the back of the office chair. I straighten the collar and then call Joshua.

"Well, hello. Did you wake up on the bad side or the good side of the bed?" he says.

Unfortunately, I'm not feeling cheery at all, and his teasing grinds my gears.

"Fuck off. I don't need your shit today."

He chuckles and I can hear Thomas say in the background, "I take it he is still in a bad mood."

I squeeze my eyes shut and take a deep breath through my nose, trying to calm the chaos that's forming inside me. That's how much they are pissing me off. I have helped guide them and looked after them any time one of them called, making up for all the times they helped me crash on their couches or on their room floors growing up. I felt safer at their homes than in my own bed. I was cleaner and my stomach wasn't growling for food.

I was safe and full—two things my parents couldn't give me.

When I made serious money, I knew I wanted to help them succeed in their own lives. I would always offer any help I could, and when I helped Joshua fund his father's mess of a company, I felt like I was finally giving back. I still don't feel like it's enough, but for now, I have done as much as I can for him.

"We are in Thomas's office. Come join us," he says.

"I'll see you soon," I say and hang up.

I welcome the fresh air on the street, and I suck in a few good breaths before walking next door. I get stopped by a few people and I plaster a fake smile and answer, but tell them I have a meeting with Joshua.

When I arrive on Thomas' floor, Ava's there as I walk in, so I pause at her desk. She lifts her head up and away from her monitor.

"Ava," I say, no longer calling her *Vixen* because I know it hurt Abigail when I did.

She smiles, and it reaches her eyes, and then she says, "Hi, James. The boys are waiting in there for you. I have been told to have a break."

I frown. "Why?"

She laughs loudly. I'm standing there, not understanding why she has to leave when I can simply close the door.

"Something about your moody ass and a certain blonde girl with green eyes." She coughs out the word *Abby*.

I tense, my hands curling into fists inside my pockets.

Her face settles into a smug grin, and it pisses me off further.

"I think you need a long break," I say.

She winks. "I thought so. Bye, James."

I don't move, as she pulls out her bag out of the drawer and walks off, waving at me.

I shake my head and try to gather the strength that I will need to deal with my two friends. Now they know there is a woman in my life. The fact that they know there is one before I told them means I'm in for it.

I take a deep breath and walk into Thomas's office, saying, "Boys."

I take the empty seat next to Joshua. He sits there reclined in the chair with his ankle draped on his opposite thigh, his hands linked behind his head. The relaxed CEO and the complete opposite of me.

"You free to come to my place for the game? I want to watch as many of Ben's last games of the season as I can," Thomas asks as he sits forward, his elbows on the desk.

"Yeah, I'm free," I say, not wanting to miss any of the games either.

Joshua is at the edge of his chair now and he says, "So Ava told me your blonde friend is a neighbor of her friend Gracie. And that she is seeing you."

I bite my tongue at the stupid smug grin that's sitting on his face, the *told you so* written all over his face.

"It's none of your business," I say.

Fuck, I'm coiled up so tightly.

"Well, Benny boy told us in the locker room, you were looking at her differently. He said you were different with her, and there was no way you two were just friends. You know friends don't look at friends that way," Joshua says with a wink.

Surely, I didn't make it that obvious, or did I?

I remember feeling jealous and protective, but did I gaze at her like I love her?

"Fuck Ben and his big damn mouth. Why can't I have a bit of privacy?" I say.

"Calm down, you big doofus; we are only trying to help. This moody-ass behavior is why we are bringing it up. If you didn't care, it wouldn't hurt and you wouldn't be such a dick to us," says Joshua.

When I peer over at Thomas, he nods in agreement.

I drift my gaze to the window and tug at my shirt collar, which suddenly feels too constricting. I take a pained breath. "I don't know what's going on. My head is such a mess. This pain in my fucking chest feels like I'm having a damn heart attack."

I rub my eyes with my fingers and turn my gaze to Thomas, who is staring back at me with a gleam in his eye. He says, "You, my friend, are joining the love club, whether or not you like it. Those are the feelings of a smitten man."

I glance over at Joshua who's smirking and I say, "Thomas, you make me want to vomit."

Joshua chokes out a deep laugh. "I gotta agree with James. That word isn't something I like to be called. I prefer pussy whipped; nothing wrong with a good pussy."

I shake my head and stand in disgust. "That's my cue to leave. I really wonder how Ava puts up with you." I swat the back of his head.

He chokes out a laugh.

"Wait, now that you have your answer. How will you deal with the work situation?" Thomas asks.

"That part I don't know. She is in the middle of her training, but after the year is up..." I shake my head and continue, "I don't know how to work with her. I don't want people treating her differently because she is with me." I sigh.

"I would be interested in interviewing her and seeing if she'd be a good fit here," Joshua says.

"You would?" I say.

"Of course. I'm always looking for skilled employees."

I rub my chin and deliberate that option. It's not a bad idea. I still don't know if I want her working with another company, but it's not my choice—it's hers.

"I don't know if it's something she would want, but I will ask her tonight."

"No rush. What are you two doing tonight?" Joshua asks with a raised brow.

I don't answer his question. I just leave his office and wave, saying, "I'll talk to you boys later."

As I take the elevator down, I think about what they said.

I wouldn't class what I want as crude as pussy whipped, I just want a love that lasts. Is there something wrong with me?

Deciding there is only one person who can answer that, I go to her.

I stand at her apartment intercom, rubbing the back of my neck with my free hand and a bag in the other. I press the buzzer and stand back. It feels like I have been waiting a while and I wish time would hurry up.

"Hello?" her delicate voice finally answers.

I glance over at my car and then back to the intercom, and I say, "Abigail, it's me. Can I come up?"

She doesn't hesitate. "Hi. Yep, I'll buzz you in."

My hands are sweating, and the bag is slipping, so I adjust my grip as the buzzer sound goes off and I know she has let me in. With every step closer to her, I feel my heart banging inside me. I can't believe she is back, but my thought vanishes when her door opens and that electrical current runs between us.

"Hi," I say as I stand in front of her, staring down into her magnificent green eyes. I run a hand through her hair and tuck the stray lock hanging over her face behind her ear. Her silky blonde locks always hide that beautiful face.

She smiles and leans into my hand before stepping back and breaking our eye contact, saying, "Hi. Um, come in."

I dip my head and kiss her, my heart thrumming madly at the smell of her perfume. She kisses me with hunger, so I kiss her back greedily. I can never get enough of her soft lips and hot mouth, but I'm breathless. I pull away and try to capture my breath, and I can't help but smile at her flushed cheeks.

I enter her apartment, pausing to put the bag down on the table that she set up for us. I raise a brow and say, "You set the table for us."

She stands next to me and her cheeks are now crimson. *Adorable.*

"Ah. Yeah. I figured if I didn't cook, I could at least set a table."

"I love it," I say and kiss her cheek.

Her smile is brighter than ever and it hits me in the center of my chest. This woman has me in the palm of her hand. I'm completely putty when it comes to her.

I don't like how we are seated opposite each other, so I drag her closer to me. She frowns.

"I want to be close to you. I have spent enough time with distance between us."

I sit down and she sits beside me.

"Oh, sorry. I totally forgot to ask. Do you want a drink?"

She goes to stand, but I reach out and gently grab her hand. I feel the jolt of electricity between us, but I ignore it and guide her back down. "No, I'm fine. Please sit."

She seems as nervous as I am, so I gain control of the conversation. The relief washing over her face tells me it's helping her calm down.

I stare down at my hand, which still holds hers, not wanting to let go of her, and I say, "I'm proud of you."

She snorts. "Proud? Why?" I flick my gaze up at the sound, and her other hand covers her mouth. Her eyes widen. "I can't believe I just snorted."

God, she is so fucking cute.

I reach out and run my fingers over her face. Her eyelashes flutter with the sensation. "The way you stood up to your parents. It couldn't have been easy. If anyone understands how hard it is—"

Her eyes open wide, she cuts me off, saying, "You do."

I drop my hand and run it through my hair. "Yeah. I've always focused on work to be better than them. Not making time for anyone because I don't—"

I struggle to say the words *feel worthy of love.*

So, I don't. I just watch my thumb trace circles on the back of her hand.

She whispers, "Imperfect is perfect for me."

I lift my gaze back to meet hers and see the green is much clearer. My heart thuds harder from her words and her beauty.

"You are too kind and smart for me. I don't deserve you. But I also can't let you go. I'm a selfish man. I have fallen in love with you. Having you walk back in my office today confirmed what I knew I was feeling—you're mine." My voice cracks.

I clear my throat. Unable to stop the honesty that's rolling off me, being here with her, just us, I can be my raw self.

Our eyes lock and she says, "I love you too. I knew it as soon as I left the city and I was in Riddell's Creek. There was a hollow feeling in my chest, and it didn't stop until I was in your arms today."

I bring our joined hands to the middle of my chest so she can feel the thrumming rhythm of my heartbeat. I sit unmoving, my ears ringing. Surely, I heard wrong, so I ask, "You love me too?"

I want to hear it again.

She nods, a nervous smile on her lips and a worried expression etched on her face. "Yes, so much. Why is that so hard to believe?"

I'm struggling to breathe; my lungs are burning with every breath I take. My brain is trying to absorb the words she is saying. It's a lot to take in; it's more than I wanted.

It's perfect—just like her.

I bring our joined hands to my mouth and leave a soft kiss before lowering it and saying, "It's not. You just take me by surprise. And truthfully, I didn't expect to fall as hard as I did." I take a breath before continuing. "It wasn't until you left that I knew I was head over heels for you. I'm angry at myself for not telling you sooner, but now that I have you, I'm not letting you go. I can't live my life for another second without you. You belong with me in my arms and bed every night."

Her smile is so wide, it reaches her eyes. I reach out and press my lips to hers like she is the most delicate thing in the world and if I'm not careful, she will shatter in my hands. She kisses me back and I grab the sides of her face and tilt her head back to thrust my tongue inside and taste her. I moan loudly, having missed her sweet, delicious taste.

When she pulls back, gasping for air, I remember our food on the table.

I peek down and she blinks, saying, "Let's eat our dinner. We need the energy for tonight."

A small frown knits between her brows as she watches me rise and grab the bag and bring it toward her, saying, "I hope it didn't melt."

She takes it and opens it and her mouth drops open and when she tilts her head to look up at me, her eyes light up, saying with shock, "Rainbow ice cream and peanut butter M&M's. I'll have to have it later; thank you. You're so thoughtful."

We sit and eat our pasta for dinner.

I take the opportunity to ask, "Have you heard from your parents since you left?"

She shakes her head. "No. But I'm fine about it."

I nod and chew my food, trying to think about how best to approach work without changing how the mood is right now. She gets up and grabs water. I take a large sip and then ask, "Now that we are in an official relationship, have you given any thought to how you will feel when everyone finds out?"

She lowers her cutlery and sits back in her chair and says, "I won't be telling people. If they find out, I won't deny it, but we don't work directly together, and so long as you don't give me preferences over George or anyone else, I don't see why anyone will find out."

"Even George?"

She shakes her head. "No. I don't want anything to change between us. Don't get me wrong: If he asks, I won't deny it, but I think at work, we work."

I beam.

"What?" she asks, tilting her head.

"I like that nothing changes at work; it's exactly what I wanted to say. I love how we think the same."

"Great minds think alike."

"After the training program, did you have any idea on where you wanted to work?"

She frowns. "I was hoping with White, but should I be worried?"

"No. I'm asking because Joshua would be interested in interviewing you and seeing if you'd be a good fit for his company."

She stares at me wordlessly for a minute before saying, "Really?"

I chuckle. "Yes. Really."

"Wow, that's so kind. Did he mention what position he is offering?"

I shake my head. "No. Is there something in particular you would like?"

She shakes her head. "No. I'm just wondering what he has."

"It will be good to have opportunities at the end of the program, in case word's out about us and it's too much on you."

She nods.

"You don't have to take the job at either of our companies. Either way, I would support you. I just want a company to help teach and guide you; you're intelligent and I want them to give you the best opportunity to reach your full potential."

She rapidly blinks and I see her eyes gloss over.

"Are you okay?"

"Yes." She grabs the water and drinks some before saying, "You say the nicest things."

"Only for you."

"Only for me," she whispers and reaches for the ice cream, lifting the lid and I notice it's melted, so she closes it and stands, walking over to the freezer to pop it in.

I follow her into the kitchen. I need to be close to her. She spins to face me, and I have the compelling need to erase the distance between us, so I wrap my arms around her, burying my nose in her hair. Her arms wrap around me in a tight squeeze, seeking comfort, too.

But despite holding her in my arms, it doesn't feel like enough.

I need more.

I need to claim her as mine, the one I love so deeply it aches.

CHAPTER 29

I STAND THERE IN my kitchen with my hands wrapped around his toned middle, breathing him in. I never want to be apart from him ever again. He's staring at me like he can't wait to have me, and the feelings are totally mutual. I'm overwhelmed, so I close my eyes and enjoy the unexpected release of all the tension I had coiled up inside me.

"So, does this mean you're staying in my bed tonight?" I ask, smirking against him.

"Definitely. I want you with me tonight. I like this apartment."

"But it's small?"

"It's got your touches, and it's calming to me." He looks around and adds, "It's surprisingly not messy."

"I may have tidied up before you came," I say through a laugh.

He chuckles, "Well, thanks, but it's your space. You don't have to change for me."

"I know, but I want you to feel comfortable here."

"Wherever you are is where I'm comfortable, baby."

I bite my lip at his sweet words and mumble, "I'd rather your house. Nothing beats your office with all the books."

"Use it whenever you'd like. You can even help me add books to the collection."

What?

I lift my head off him and look up into his gaze, which is heavy with tenderness and longing. I smile. The words he speaks makes my heart jolt and I stand on my tiptoes, my body feeling heavy and warm, the ache between my thighs intensifying. He must sense the change in my body because the kiss turns from passionate to crushing. He grabs my face and kisses me with such a hunger that a whimper slips out of my mouth.

At the sound, a growl leaves his chest and he says, "Fuck, I missed you."

He picks me up and I wrap my arms around his neck and lock my ankles around his back, where my breasts sit close to his face. He carries me smoothly across the apartment into my room where he lowers me into the middle of the bed, and settles between my legs. I stare up at him, unable to believe this brilliant man is mine.

I slip my hands into his tousled brown hair and lower his head to me. "Make love to me."

I lean in to softly kiss him.

He pulls back, staring down at me with hooded eyes. He's breathing heavily, as if he's trying to restrain his usual hard fuck back. I love his dirty mouth and rough hands, but tonight I need this—I need him to make love to me.

He strokes my face with his fingers, his thumb tracing my bottom lip, and then trails down the middle of my breasts to the bottom of my top, dragging it up slowly. I lift my arms up and he takes it off; he looks down at me with adoring eyes. I smile up at him and he leans forward, kissing my neck. I tilt to offer him more of my exposed skin, which he kisses and trails more down over my collarbone and in between my breasts to the top of my jeans.

With anticipation, my chest rises and falls. I watch as he pulls back and carefully unbuttons and unzips my jeans, pulling them over my hips and taking them all the way off. I lie there in my bra and panties while he is still completely dressed. Goose bumps appear on my body from his intense gaze.

I run my eyes over his suit, his hard length straining in his pants. I swallow, my sex throbbing with a need for his touch. He takes his suit jacket off and tosses it onto the floor. I'm aching with excitement at my very own strip show. Grabbing his tie with both hands, he urgently tugs it off, and I run my tongue over my lips, my breath catching with anticipation. I'm trying to be patient and hold myself back from ripping the shirt off him. But thankfully, he reaches up to his neck and begins unbuttoning it until his shirt is hanging open, his muscles half-covered by his shirt. He shrugs it off and my breath hitches at the sight. I twitch, wanting to touch that soft, toned skin.

He stands at the end of the bed, removing his belt, and whips it off in one quick stroke. I feel I'm about to combust from need, so I close my eyes briefly, and when I reopen them, he has a knowing smile on his lips. When he pushes his pants down and I see the enormous bulge, I almost choke. The strip show is causing my mouth to water, and it is testing my patience. Luckily, I don't have to wait long.

He pushes his briefs down and I quiver, his thick, heavy cock between his thick thighs leaking with pre-cum on the tip. He fists himself, sliding his hand up and down. When he reaches the tip, he drags his thumb over it to smear the liquid. It's so damn sensual, I can't wait to have him. Having my own personal show has made me wetter.

He climbs on the bed, so I lower myself back down. Hovering over me, our heavy breaths the only noise between us. He lowers his mouth to mine in a demanding kiss. At the same time, I feel his hand on my back, unclasping my bra. Once it's undone, he pulls his hand out along with the bra and tosses it across the room. His chest is rising and falling, and his eyes are so dark with desire, I wonder if he desperately wants to attack me in a controlled frenzy, but he is respecting my wishes and going slow tonight.

He sits back and drags my wet panties down my thighs and settles back between my parted legs.

Leaning over me, he trails kisses over my collarbone and up to my ear, and he whispers, "Are you wet for me?"

"Yeahhh." I slam my eyes closed from the sound of his voice and my need to have him inside me.

He reaches down between us and his feather-light touch on my pussy has me arching into his hand to seek pleasure. I whimper as he slides two thick fingers through my slick folds, moving his fingers over to my clit, where he rubs in hard, slow circles. My breath catches at the slow, torturous pace.

"James," I gasp, desperate for release.

"Does it feel good?"

"Yes, but I need you."

"Okay. I got you, baby," he says and lines himself up. Our eyes are on each other and when I nod, he thrusts slowly until he is all the way in, filling me completely. We both groan from the pleasure, my eyes roll back, from the intensity. He stills inside me, allowing my walls to adjust. I open my eyes slowly and his forehead rests on mine, waiting for me to give him the go-ahead to move again.

"Are you okay?"

When I nod again, he moves slowly, and I explore his perspiring body, needing to hold on to him. The sex opens the gate of emotions and with every thrust, I feel him fill me with love and adoration. Feeling myself climbing with every minute, I moan louder, my grasp on his skin a little tighter, my nails biting into him, but he doesn't complain.

"You're so beautiful."

His words are too much and cause more tension to build. He angles his body to hit my G-spot, and it drives me wild.

My back arches when his thrusts become a little harder and I clench down. "I'm close."

"Come; I got you."

And that's all it takes for me to come so violently that my toes curl. He grows inside me and pumps his hips a little rougher until I feel him still and chase his own orgasm.

He leans down and lightly kisses my forehead. "I love you."

I feel so exposed from the release of the orgasm that a tear trickles down my face. The emotions running through me are much more powerful than I ever thought possible.

We both don't want this to end. We want to stay here a little longer, lost in our love and emotions.

After a minute, he pulls out slowly, causing me to shudder at the loss of him. I crawl under the covers and wait for him to return from the bathroom. When he settles in my bed, I lean up and kiss his lips with a caress and settle back down, enjoying the feel of his arms wrapped safely around me.

Finally, I feel like I'm home, with everything I could have ever wanted. My heart is full of love for this man who is all mine. He lies here in my bed with me, treasuring me like I'm the most precious thing in the world.

CHAPTER 30

JAMES

IT'S THANKSGIVING AND WE are all at Joshua and Ava's for dinner. I cradle the only drink I'll have tonight and keep my gaze on my woman. She is laughing and talking to Ava, Gracie, and Jennifer. She picked out this emerald pantsuit thing, which makes those striking green eyes stand out. I love this color on her and I've spent any moment I have complimenting her. I'll probably hate it tonight when I can't get it off her and I want easy access, but she chose it and she loves it and I love her.

My phone vibrates in my pocket. I pull it out and grimace. The deadbeat parents. *Fuck off!*

> **Dad:** Can we have money for Thanksgiving dinner?

I tense at the message. No fucking *Happy Thanksgiving* to your son. Of course not. I want this conversation over and the tension to dissipate because Abigail will ask me what's wrong. She always has a sixth sense and can tell when something is wrong with me. I'm refusing to let my parents interfere with my first Thanksgiving with her. She is beaming at Ava, happily chatting, and I'm on the other side of the house with Thomas and Joshua, who are talking. I'm surrounded by my second family—my friends.

James: How much?

Dad: Two hundred.

James: One hundred and it will be in your account.

Dad: Thanks.

I stuff my phone away after transferring the funds and take a sip of alcohol.

"Who was that?" Thomas asks.

"Dad."

His eyes widen and he asks, "What's going on with them? I haven't had a chance to catch up with you."

"No changes; they are still fucking addicts," I say with a shrug.

"What's a fucking addict?" I hear Thomas' little girl Lily ask.

I freeze. What the fuck do I say? I glare at Thomas and silently send an SOS for help. He nods.

"Nothing, sweetheart. Just ignore your uncle Jay; he's naughty. Where is your sister?"

Her face bunches and she looks lost. *Thank fuck.* I need to remember to be careful when little people are around. I don't need them learning bad language from me. Thomas would kill me.

"I don't know. She is boring," Lily says.

"Just go play with her. Dinner won't be much longer. Will it, Josh?" He looks at Joshua with begging eyes. We need him to find food fast. We need a distraction.

Joshua coughs and splutters on his drink. Recovering, he says, "I'll see if we have something for you to eat, Lily. Follow me."

They walk off and I swallow the hard rock that's sitting in the back of my throat. Turning around to face Thomas, I say, "I'm sorry about that."

"It's okay; she snuck up on us. But try to rein it in next time. That was a little too close," Thomas says.

"It was way too close. I don't know how you do the whole two kids, partner, and work. You do it all, man. How?" I ask.

"I love everything you just said, so with that, it's easy to juggle. It won't feel like work if you love what you do. Don't get me wrong: The kids are hard some days, but I have Jennifer, who is a big help," Thomas says.

I'm glad he found her; she has been an angel to him and the girls. Thomas said from their very first meeting that the girls really loved Jennifer. Rose, who struggles with separation, really took a liking to Jennifer and it wasn't long before she became his girlfriend.

"I'm ecstatic for you, man. Jennifer has been the perfect fit for you and the girls," I say.

"She really has. I actually said I'd have another child with her," Thomas says with a hint of hesitation.

I feel my mouth drop open in utter shock. I know he was adamant he wasn't having any more, out of fear of losing another mother of his children and raising more children on his own. So, this is a big fucking deal.

"Why the sudden change?" I ask.

"Part of being in a relationship is compromising, so this is me meeting her halfway."

I frown in confusion, needing him to explain it to me.

"She understands how hard it is for me to be willing to have another child, but it's also unfair not to allow her one that she desperately wants. We agreed on the middle and that was one," he says.

"Let's hope it isn't twins then." Joshua slaps Thomas' back with a laugh.

"God, that sounds like hell. I barely can talk around kids, let alone two babies at once," I say, suddenly feeling a headache forming. This topic isn't something I have discussed in detail with Abigail.

Would she want kids soon? If so, how many? How would we be as parents? It's not like I had great role models but then, hers are only slightly better. I have thought a lot about an engagement ring and taking that next step but talking about children is unsettling to me. I don't know how to feel. My stomach is twisted in knots at the thought.

"Dinner is ready," Joshua says, saving me from my thoughts.

I slip away and head to Abigail. My arm snakes around her waist, resting on her hip. I tug her to me so her body is flush up against mine. Leaning down, I whisper in her ear, "Are you okay? Do you need anything?"

She tilts her head back and smiles up at me. I peck her glossy lips and she pulls back slightly to say, "No. I have everything I need. Thanks for checking on me."

I lick my lips, tasting her strawberry gloss, and I say, "Always."

Everyone moves to the table. Once we are all seated and before anyone dives into serving and eating food, Joshua stands, hitting his glass with a knife.

"Thank you all for joining Ava and me tonight. I hope the next year brings us all love and happiness. I know a few of us are settling down and working hard. I hope established businesses continue to flourish and new adventures become successful. And for the final part of my toast... Let's all cheer for our Benny boy, who will win his game tonight. Cheers, everyone."

As I look around this long rectangle table, decorated with a white cloth and mini pumpkins and lights running down the middle, I can't help but be grateful for my life right now. All the losses have led me here and I wouldn't have it any other way.

I sip my drink and turn to Abigail. I lean into her ear and whisper, "I'm so grateful for you. Thank you for showing me how to love and be loved. I promise to be there for you every day and next year is our year of growth. Growing together in life as one."

Her eyes are glossed over and when she blinks, a tear sits on her bottom lashes. An ache hits my chest at the sight. I lower my glass to the table and dust away her tear with the pad of my thumb before kissing her tenderly. It's not a greedy kiss, it's a *You're my world* kiss.

I pull back and her mouth stays parted, and when she opens her eyes, she stares back at me brightly. "I love you."

I smile at her words. They are only three words, but leave a mark so deep, it aches.

"I love you too."

She smiles back. At this moment, it's just us and I'm thankful to be with each other, surrounded by love and food.

"Gross."

I chuckle and turn to face Lily, who is pretending to vomit.

"Lily, please," Thomas says.

"One day, Miss Lily Dunn, you won't be saying gross," I say.

"She won't be dating," Thomas says.

I laugh again. As if he has any chance of stopping Lily from doing whatever she wants. Thomas has his hands full with that one.

I'm surprised he hasn't learned that you can't stop love when it enters your life. Whether or not you want it, the universe forces two people together. Just like him and Jennifer.

"Have you thought about what you will do after your program, Abby?" Joshua asks.

I sit back and tilt in her direction, curious about what her answer to him will be. I don't know what she has chosen to do post-program.

She sips her wine before lowering it to the table and says, "To be honest, I haven't. I want to stay at White, but then how long will it be until our relationship is out to the entire company?" She reaches out to capture my hand and holds it. We both cannot keep our hands off each other, always seeking the other person out. She is the first person I have ever just wanted to just hold. It used to just be all about sex, but with her, it's different. I just want to feel her warmth on me.

"I think maybe I should leave before it's out," she adds.

"I don't think you should leave unless you want to. I think when people find out, they might not care because of how hard you work and they know you're not getting special treatment," I say, not wanting her to feel forced out if she genuinely wants to stay at White. I support Abigail in whatever she chooses. And of course, I'd love her to stay at White, but I've always encouraged her independence and will never stop it. This is strictly her choice.

"What do you think?" Joshua asks me.

"I want Abigail to do what makes her happy. It's her career, and she needs to work that out on her own," I say and turn to her. She is looking at me and smiling.

After dinner is eaten and cleared, we all move to the living area to catch Benjamin's game. Not one of us wants to miss a second of his game.

"Now, is everyone right for drinks before it starts?" Ava asks.

"Yes, babe. Just sit your ass down," Joshua says.

"It's polite to ask. We are hosting, remember?" she says.

Abigail tugs at my top. I lean down and she whispers, "Are they always like that?"

I smile and peek over at Ava sitting in Joshua's lap before returning to face Abby and I say, "Yeah, that's them. Fiery, aren't they?"

"Intense."

I nod, understanding what it looks like to her. I'm about to speak when the game starts and the cheering for Benjamin begins.

"Come on, Benny!" I say, joining in.

The room is ecstatic to watch our friend on Thanksgiving.

Later that night, Abigail and I are at home in bed at my place. She is curled up beside me as I feel myself drift off to sleep.

"I have this crazy idea." Her voice cuts through the quiet house.

I open my eyes and twist to look at her. Now, I'm wide awake. I lift my brow and say, "Yeah?"

She shakes her head. "No. It's stupid. Forget I said anything; just go back to sleep."

I know she wouldn't be thinking and saying anything if it was nothing, so I say, "Not going to happen. Tell me."

"No. It's fine. Seriously."

I tickle her rib cage and she squeals in laughter. I found her ticklish spots a few weeks ago and I love to play with her whenever I get the chance. The squeal is another favorite thing I've found of hers. I have a very long list of qualities I love about her now. The more I know, the more I love. But I'll still always have a soft spot for her smile. It's still my favorite thing about her.

"I wanted to see if I could work in the bookstore here."

Her work in a bookstore?

I shake my head of the dirty visions of her in a sexy librarian costume and focus on what she just said. I'm still baffled at how unexpected it is. I understand her passion and love of reading, but I didn't expect this.

"Are you sure you want to just work in one?" I say and sit up.

She moves positions to sit facing me and she asks, "What do you mean?"

"You have the potential to run your own. You're very bright and I could see your mix of city coffee, love of books, and small-town vibe doing really well in the city."

She thinks about what I just said before grinning. "Do you really think so?"

"Of course. But it's only a suggestion."

"I know you only want to encourage and support me. But I like this idea. I really do."

"I happen to know a guy who could help you find the perfect place."

"Do you?" she says with a smirk before leaning in to kiss me.

"Yeah, I think you might know him," I say, against her lips.

She pulls back and says, "Oh, yeah. I know him really well."

I chuckle at this playful side. I'm loving every second of it.

"Who?" I ask.

"Mr. James White."

I growl at the way she says my name.

"Yeah, that's it. He is a very smart guy. I'm certain he will find you the perfect location for this bookstore."

"Well, I can't wait to see what he finds."

I grin like the happy idiot I am and kiss her passionately, promising to deliver a place for her new goal.

CHAPTER 31

ABIGAIL

I'M WAITING WITH GEORGE for the barista to make our coffees. We've only got four months left of the training program. I check my phone to see how much time we have left on our break.

"How are you finding the marketing rotation?"

"Honestly, it's definitely the hardest one out of the whole program."

"Oh, thank God. I thought it was just me."

I giggle and say, "Nope. Not just you. But we only just got to the department, so I'm sure it will get easier every day."

He snorts and says, "We hope."

"I know. We didn't come this far to fail."

"I didn't say I'll fail," he says.

I raise my brow at him. "I didn't mean it to come across like that."

Our order is up so we grab them and leave.

"Have you applied for a job at White?" I ask.

"When the program ends?"

I nod and sip my coffee as we walk across the road.

"Not yet. I was waiting to see how I went with this final rotation but as of right now, I don't want a job in marketing."

I laugh, but I totally know what he means. It's hard, but it's also giving me ideas for the library.

"What about you? Have you applied?" he asks as we enter the White building.

"I have one idea but it's too early to talk about," I say and take a sip, but I miss my mouth and a drop falls on my jacket. I dust it off, disappointed I spilled it because I'm wearing one of my recent new black suits. Now that I don't have to pay my parents any money, I'm free. To buy what I want—finally.

I didn't realize how much I needed it and how liberating it would feel to have that toxic behavior gone. They are my parents, but it didn't stop them from hurting me. Even telling them repeatedly what I wanted didn't stop them. It was time to follow my heart and stand on my own two feet.

With my newfound independence, I've grown into a stronger woman who surrounds herself with people who support that. They aren't threatened or trying to change me and are definitely listening to what I want.

For the first time... I feel heard.

I don't know what my parents are doing. I don't ask my brother when I check in with him; I don't want to put him in an uncomfortable position. They haven't messaged or called, and neither have I. Despite that, I don't hold a grudge. I'm simply living my life the way I want to.

My life is filled with work, James, friends, and now this new goal of my own business. Ever since he suggested owning my own bookstore, I haven't been able to stop looking online at pictures for ideas, spending hours on Pinterest.

I show James every new idea and bless him, he is there with every bit of enthusiasm he can offer. Even after a twelve-hour day or a business trip, he acts just as excited. He gives me the time with a damn smile on his face. If I didn't love him already, I'd be a puddle right now. He has been the best surprise of my life and I can't wait to show him my gift for him later tonight.

We wait for the elevator. When they open and James walks out, I'm caught off guard, not knowing what to do. We haven't crossed paths much, because he has been in contracts and he's helped us enough, but he's hovering in the background. Always available if we have any questions, but we are both trying to keep a low profile at work. So seeing him is causing a surge in exhilaration.

His infectious grin is on display as he passes with a quick hello. Each time I see him, the attraction to him is stronger, and I want to fall into his protective arms. I can't help but run my gaze over his signature black suit and white shirt, matching me, and that stupid thought has a tiny warming effect on me.

Once he is out of sight, I'm trailing behind George and others into the elevator. My phone chimes and I pull it out of my bag and see his name on the screen. I still get a rush when his name pops up on my phone; I can never get enough of him.

I open to read his message.

James: You're looking very sophisticated and sexy today. I love the black suit on you.

Abigail: I had to match my boyfriend, who knows how to wear a suit.

James: I don't look as good as you in a suit. With your brains and looks, you are a force to be reckoned with. And I'm the lucky bastard who gets to be with you. When are you going to move in with me? I want you every night and not apartment hopping. I'm a greedy man and I need you.

Abigail: At the end of the program, my lease is up. Not long now.

James: Not quick enough.

Abigail: I need to get back to work. My break is over. But I'll see you tonight. I love you. x

James: I love you more. x

Those words will never get old. I could hear them a billion times over and still not be sick of him saying it.

Later that night, I hand James an envelope.

He takes it from me with a frown, and he asks, "What's this?

I smirk. "Open it and find out."

He narrows his eyes and hesitates.

"Come on."

He tears open the envelope and takes out the tickets. The pinched expression on his face softens the moment he reads what they are. I'm smiling like an idiot, barely containing my excitement.

"You didn't."

"I did." I say.

He's holding tickets to New York.

"After my training program ends, I want a trip together."

"You brought me something," he whispers.

The way he looks right now makes me want to buy him more sentimental gifts.

"I organized the time off with Eleanor and Sophie, so they know about us."

"I either need to sit the fuck down or have a drink." He rubs his forehead before continuing. "You did this all for me."

"Yes, as a thank you for helping find me a perfect location."

"It's my job."

"You spend more than the required time on it, and the hours of listening to my ideas hasn't gone unnoticed."

"That's what soulmates are for."

"See. That's why you deserve this."

"You're confusing."

I giggle at him. He doesn't understand how sweet and selfless he is. I grab his hand, dragging him to sit on the couch.

"You didn't even ask how Eleanor or Sophie took the news."

He runs his hand through his hair and says, "I was in too much shock. But tell me they were fine."

"Yeah, Eleanor was surprised but happy. She said it doesn't change my duties or performance, and I was adamant it doesn't get in the way. Today was the first time seeing you in a while."

"Yeah, it was. But you're in a different area now."

"Sophie said she knew it. She said you started whistling in your office."

"Because I whistle, she knew I was with you? That sounds ridiculous."

I giggle. "No. She said you seemed happier and assumed you had a woman in your life. She didn't guess it was me."

"Ah, okay. That makes more sense. Does George know?"

"I will tell him tomorrow. I want it to come from me and not someone else. I'm certain he won't care; we have a good work relationship, and he knows I work hard. And it has nothing to do—"

"With working the boss hard. Now, saying hard is getting me all excited."

I slap his chest and say, "No, let's order dinner. I don't want to cook tonight."

"I can cook," he says.

I shrug. "As long as it's not me, I don't care."

"I'll make pasta and tell you about the location I found for us to view this weekend."

"Really?"

"Yes."

I throw myself into his arms. He catches me... like he always does.

I'm at home, changing my clothes before James comes to pick me up. He hasn't shown me many locations because he wants to only show me the best ones.

The previous ones I have viewed have been over budget and the bank won't lend me that much. James has offered me money, but I want to do this myself with money from only the bank. He just needs to stick within budget, which I know isn't easy, but I believe he will find me one, and I really hope this is it. The butterflies are back in my stomach as I throw on a navy sweater.

My phone rings and I expect it to be him, but I see Charlotte's name. I smile as I answer. "Charlotte."

"Hey. Is this a good time to talk?"

"Yeah. Why? What's up?" I ask.

"I was planning a visit, so I wanted to run some dates past you."

"Are you serious?"

"Someone's excited."

"Of course I am. If I have it my way, you won't go back either," I say, giggling.

She laughs and I smile as my intercom chimes.

"Hang on a sec; I have to let James up."

"Ohhh, and how is that all going?"

I buzz him in and I only have a few minutes to get her up to speed.

"It's still picture perfect. We are actually visiting a potential rental space."

"What for?"

"A new business adventure."

"How does he have time?"

"This isn't for him. This is for me."

"Oh. What's the business?"

"A library and café in one."

"Oh, Abby, that sounds amazing."

The knock on the door alerts me. "He's here to pick me up. Can I call you when I get back and I'll let you know if it's the place or not? And we can work on those dates for your visit."

"Yeah, go. I'm home tonight. Good luck."

I hang up and open the door. James stands there in casual clothes of blue jeans and a charcoal top. The sexy smirk on his face has me stepping forward and grabbing his head and kissing him.

"Whoa, what was that for?"

"I missed you."

"I'll have to get you to miss me more if that's the reception I get."

"I need my fix now."

He chuckles against my mouth, and I feel it between my legs.

I want him.

"What time do we have to go?"

He checks his watch and says, "Now."

Dammit!

I drop my arms and turn to grab my bag.

On the drive, I sit nervously in the seat and ask him where it is and what it looks like, but he won't tell me anything. Not even one tiny hint.

Ten minutes later, he parks the car and we hold hands up the path until we reach a door. He opens it and we step into an abandoned space, off the main street. Goose bumps cover my skin, so I rub my arms.

"Are you cold?" he asks.

"No. It's oddly quiet."

"It's a big space and empty until it gets a tenant."

A big space?

"How expensive is this big empty space?"

"Within your budget," he says and brings our joined hands to his lips to kiss mine. "Relax."

It's very cold, but there are exposed brown bricks and archways that give the building character. The high ceilings would be perfect for rows of bookshelves.

"Walk around wherever you want. You can open doors, drawers, anything. It's ours to view. Take your time."

I nod, unable to form words. This is an older building, and I love the textures of this space. I can imagine the café near the front and the remaining space being the bookstore. There are rooms at the very back where I could add couches for customers to sit and read.

This is beyond anything I could have asked for.

"Do you like it?" He asks.

I jump and place my hand over my erratic heartbeat. "You scared me."

"Did you forget about me?"

"I was lost in how I could set this up."

"From the way your face is lit up, you can picture it?"

"Yes. But are you sure I can afford it? It seems too good to be true."

"It's definitely within your budget."

I narrow my eyes at him. "And you're not doing any shifty things, right?"

He tips his head back, laughing loudly.

"No. I will not give you money to fund it. This is your wish, remember?"

"I'm just checking."

"You're cute. I love the excitement on your face right now."

I blush and glance away at the space.

"Give me a tour. I want to hear about your plans."

I smile. Taking a step, I point and explain all my ideas. He follows along, nodding, and at the end, he asks, "What do you think? Did you want to put an offer down? The only reason people don't want it is because it's off the main street, but I think word of mouth and marketing—"

I groan at the word.

"What?" he asks with a raised brow.

"Marketing is hard. The rotation for the program is definitely the hardest."

"Oh, we finally found something you're not excelling in. I like that something is challenging you."

"And George."

He chuckles. "Either way, you will learn a lot and it will help you market this place."

"Let's do it," I say.

"Okay. Let's go sign you up for your new project. I think entrepreneur life will suit you."

"You think?"

"Your brains are one of the sexiest yet loveable things about you."

I gaze into his eyes, completely grateful to have found a soulmate who loves me for who I am and lets me be my true self.

EPILOGUE

ABIGAIL

I LAY A CHASTE kiss on his chest after another round of mind-blowing sex. He is still the most handsome man I have ever seen. I don't think I will ever get used to it.

He is mine—I am his.

He grumbles inaudible words and stirs underneath me. I'm smiling down at him, watching him lie there with his eyes closed, but when they pop open, my breath catches.

His eyes still have me weak at the knees. Have you ever looked into a pair of eyes and felt lost?

I do every time our gazes lock.

I'm unable to concentrate on anything other than those deep pools of love staring back at me.

"You're staring," he says with a purr. His post-sex voice vibrates through me. But he has to get up to meet Benjamin, and I am going shopping with Gracie.

I push off him and scramble out of the bed before he has other ideas. James White is insatiable, and I have never been with a man who has such an appetite. He makes me feel adored, and I truly don't know if I'll ever have enough of him.

"We better get ready; we have people to meet." I say.

He comes up behind me and wraps his arms around my waist and nuzzles his nose into my neck. He kisses the top of my head and turns to walk to his phone, and I move to the bathroom with a new spring in my step.

An hour later, I arrive at my old apartment complex and press the intercom to Gracie's.

"I'll be right down."

She comes down a couple minutes later and we walk to the shops. I have a dinner date with James tonight so I'm hoping to find a nice outfit and shoes.

We have been walking a while when we pass a store and I see a green glitter dress that twinkles in the shop window. I gasp and grab Gracie's arm and point to it. She looks at it and nods, grabbing my hand. We hurry inside, walking straight up to it.

"Hi. Can I help you?"

We turn to the saleswoman.

I smile. "Can I try that dress on?"

"Certainly."

I have to concentrate on walking slowly and not skipping. I have a good feeling about it. The price tag worries me because this is a boutique, but I haven't found a dress and time is running out. This one literally stopped me on the streets and if it does that, I can't wait to see how I feel about myself when I have it on.

The second I'm in the dressing room, I strip faster than I ever have and slide the dress over me. I look at myself in the mirror, twirling and posing. This is a dress! I smile to myself.

"Do you have it on yet?" Gracie asks.

"Yes," I say and open the dressing room door.

"Wow. That color is stunning on you."

I peer down at the dress and smile. The saleslady walks over and asks, "How are you doing?"

"I'll get this, but do you have heels that would go with this?"

"Good choice; it's beautiful on you. Yes, I know the perfect pair."

"Thank you," I say.

She rushes off to grab them and I whisper to Gracie, "I hope this isn't going to be crazy expensive. I'm expecting a bit more, just not ridiculous."

"Here you are." The saleslady hands over a pair of silver heels.

I take them and say thanks before slipping them on and standing to walk over to the mirror.

"They look great with the dress," I say as I spin to face them.

Both of them stand there beaming. I'm a little embarrassed, so I turn around and look at my reflection. I need to take it and get home.

"You look hot, Abby," Gracie says.

I peek over my shoulder at her and give her a nod and walk into the changing room and reluctantly remove it. Realizing I never checked the price and I have already said I'd take it, I find the tag and turn it over. I'm relieved at the number. It's not as high as I predicted, but it's more than I have ever spent on a dress. I deserve it and I love how sexy and confident I feel in it.

I check the shoes; they are a bit of a price stretch, but I'll make them work. I only own the black stilettos, so this would be a second pair.

With not much time to spare, I pay for both items and we walk home talking.

"How's the bar?" I ask.

"It's busy again, and I doubt it will slow down. I'm working overtime every week. I'm happy for my family but also, I'm desperate for some time off. I might look at going on a trip with the money I've saved by working so much."

"A vacation sounds nice."

"Speaking of vacations, you have your New York Trip with James coming up. I'm so jealous. I really want to go there."

"You should. You work so hard. You deserve a break." I check the time and add. "I better go. I need to walk home, shower, and do my hair and makeup."

"Yes, you do. Have fun tonight."

We part ways and when I get home, I hang the dress up. The way it reflects the bathroom light has me hurrying so I can put it back on.

But my phone rings and it's mom. I answer and we talk briefly before I need to go and get ready. Our relationship is still strained but we talk every couple of weeks. And I don't know what the future holds for us, but, at the moment, I'm happy with where it's going.

After the shower, I add a little makeup and some red lipstick. Thanks to Ava's tips, I apply it perfectly. And finally, I pop the dress on and put the shoes on. I run my hands over the sparkles; I can't believe the dress fits like a glove. I twirl in the mirror in total shock at my reflection. It's breathtaking, the whole outfit. As I stare at myself in the mirror, a wicked smile erupts, and I can't wait to see his reaction.

I walk out in my new outfit to find James waiting in a sexy black suit and tie, leaning against the kitchen counter on his phone, typing away, and my heart flutters at the sight. He is my real Prince Charming, the ones I always read about in my books and never thought I'd be able to have.

The click of my heels on the floors is so loud that his gaze snaps to mine and a large dazzling smile takes over his face. He stops typing on his phone and stuffs it into his pocket and comes to meet me, wolf whistling, which has me tipping back, giggling.

When we are toe to toe, I warm under his intense gaze and the way his gaze trails seductively over me as if he can see me naked. Is he about to devour me?

He clears his throat and says, "Look at you. How did I get so lucky?"

Clearing my own constricted throat, I say, "You like the dress?"

He shakes his head with a grin. "No, baby. I love."

"Thanks," I say.

He strokes along my face and then tucks my hair behind my ear. I gaze back at him, loving the feather-light touches and the adoring looks he gives me. He leans into me, inhaling my perfume, and he whispers, "Do you know how much I love you?"

I nod and bite my lip at the word *love*. It sends my pulse rising and I almost melt into a puddle. I don't get sick of hearing him say it; it's better than any physical present.

He glances at his watch and says, "We need to get out of here before we don't leave, and we have specific times to stick to."

I gaze at him with confusion but then shrug it off, knowing he is so organized that there is no point trying to work it out. So, I peck his lips and say, "I'll grab my coat and bag."

We arrive at a high-class restaurant and I'm clutching James' hand while walking through the restaurant. I feel like an imposter. I never went to places like this before I met James; it's a different lifestyle, one I'm still adjusting to.

Looking around, I soak in the romantic setting. I can't help but pause and stare. The soft warm lights and the gray tables and chairs are exquisite. All the tables have floral arrangements, and the couples are lost in their own conversations. I smile to myself, loving that I get to be the center of James' attention.

We are escorted out to a table in the back, away from others, but the set up is the same. James whispers to the server and I'm about to take a seat when he says to me, "Let's go upstairs first and have a drink. Then we can come downstairs. The sun will set soon."

I nod excitedly, saying, "Sure."

I shrug out of my coat and I'm about to drape it on the back of the chair, but another server appears to take it away for me. I smile and nod and he whisks it away.

James' gaze hits mine and he asks, "Are you ready?"

"Yes."

He steps to me and captures my hand, and I follow him to the elevator. Inside, he pulls me to the front of him and cuddles me from behind. His heart is thumping hard. I can feel it through me, and it causes my temperature to rise.

When the doors open, we separate and I almost groan, loving his warm affection, and I hate it when I have to leave it.

We walk hand in hand. Outside, the sun is setting, but the red rose petals sprinkled across the concrete floors and the lit candles along the edges have me beginning to sweat. I can hear the beat in my ears. He calmly walks me to the very edge, and I grab the rail in one hand to hold my trembling body up and I take in the view.

"This is incredible," I say with a waver in my voice.

"Not as incredible as you."

"Aw, aren't you cute?"

He grunts, which makes me smile. I know he hates it when I call him out on his sweetness, but bad luck. He is sweet and I want him to know how much I appreciate this and would never take it or him for granted.

The sun has almost set and he moves to hold me from behind. We stand silently, looking out across the city, listening to the sounds of sirens and cars. I'm so totally lost in the view that I don't hear him say anything until I feel the cool air hit me. He tugs on my hand and I frown, but as soon as I see his hand disappear into his pocket, my heart rate skyrockets and I'm internally freaking out.

He is going to fucking propose.

My heart is swelling. I can barely breathe.

His gaze is locked onto mine and a smirk hits his lips, as if he knows what I'm thinking. But I say it anyway.

"What are you doing?" I whisper.

He kneels and I gasp, a hand covering my mouth, and tears fill my eyes.

No way.

I'm shaking, probably ruining my lipstick, but I don't care. I can't get over this handsome man on his knees holding a box in front of him.

"Abigail Crawford, when I met you in the airport, I knew I'd met my match. I knew then it was only a matter of time until we arrived at this moment. I will always be there to support you and let you grow and love you indefinitely. Will you give me the honor and be my wife?"

My vision goes blurry from his words, and I blink rapidly. This man is crazy. Crazy for me, and I'm crazy for him. I can't speak through the tears. I just throw myself at him and he catches me.

We embrace and he says, "I guess that's a yes."

I choke out, "Yes."

I pull back when I have collected myself. I'm still shaking from the adrenaline, and his lips capture mine in a soft caress, sealing our hearts as one.

He pulls the ring out and offers it. I give him my shaky left hand and he slides it on. The sparkling princess cut platinum diamond stares back at me under the night sky.

I twirl my hand and stare at the gorgeous ring, unable to believe it's mine. I peer up at him and say, "I love you."

He smiles back and he says, "I love you too, baby."

BONUS CHAPTER

ABIGAIL

I TWIRL MY ENGAGEMENT ring around my finger. It's only been a few days since James proposed and I'm still on cloud nine. We have just landed in New York City. I'm holding his hand and in the other, I hold the New York book. Who would have thought I'd be here right now? Engaged to James and in New York City with him. Not me! But I plan to soak in every sight, sound, smell, and taste.

"Where to first?"

We grab a taxi and I say, "Let's check in and freshen up and go for a walk around."

"I like that plan. I need to spend some alone time with my fiancée."

"You had me this morning."

He leans down to whisper in my ear, "I can never have enough of you, baby."

"Bad luck. We have a city to explore."

"You really are ready to be a tourist and soak in New York, aren't you?"

"Mm-hmm." I stare out my window.

The city is more striking than any picture in this book. Nothing can prepare you for the vision. I sigh and lay my head on the window ready for the twenty-minute ride from the airport. We have a couple of sight-seeing trips planned, but otherwise, I just want to wake up and explore. Which, to James, is hard. He likes to plan but I think vacations are better left to just go with the flow.

He mumbles under his breath that it must be the small town in me, but it's not. Not everyone has to have a plan—some of the best times are unplanned.

When we arrive at the hotel, we check in, refresh, and I promise him attention later because I stopped mid-kiss before we left the room.

Walking hand in hand down the streets, I'm in awe of how high the buildings are. On the way, we find a pub who has a live band playing. Our cruise is booked for tonight, so we decide we could eat a little later to allow enough time to get more sightseeing in. James doesn't complain and I don't know if he is enjoying being a tourist and not working or whether he is doing it for me. Either way, I like this relaxed James. He works so hard and it's nice to see him switch off.

"There's an art gallery. Did you want to check it out?"

I smile at his offer. He is finding something that interests him, which is what I want to see on this break. Vacation James is a side I haven't seen before.

"I'd love to."

We spend the whole hour in there before we backtrack up to the pub with the live band. We take our seats and grab a menu.

"What New York food should I have?"

He looks up from his menu and says, "I don't know. I stick to my usual foods."

I gasp, covering my mouth with my hand before dropping it to scan the menu and I say, "We are about to change that."

"What do you suggest?"

I peek up over my menu and see his brow rising. "Let's grab some shared plates and try a few different things." I glance back down and see the desserts. "Oh, and for dessert, I want to try the cheesecake."

"That seems like a lot of food," he says.

"You don't eat it all."

He shakes his head.

"What?" I ask.

"Nothing. You just never stop surprising me."

"It's not about to stop now."

"Good."

We stare at each other lovingly. I cannot wait to be married to him. He is everything I didn't realize I needed.

Afterword

To keep up to date with my new books releases, including title's, blurb's, release date's and giveaways. Please subscribe to my newsletter which you can find on my website.

To keep up to date with me? Come join my Facebook reader group: **Sharon's Sweethearts**

This is a PRIVATE group and only people in the group can see posts and comments!

ALSO BY

Doctor Taylor
Accidental Neighbor
Bossy Mr. Ward

About Author

Sharon Woods is an author of Contemporary Romance. She loves writing steamy love stories with a happy ever after.

Born and living in Melbourne, Australia. With her beautiful husband and two children.

Acknowledgments

My husband you're my rock, I love you. And my two blessings, my children. Thank you for allowing me to write and watch you grow at the same time.

All my beta's, friends and family, without each of your support, I would be awfully lonely. I'm so happy to be supported by a tribe. Just know, I will be forever grateful. Love you all.

My readers, thank you for supporting me and purchasing my books. You are supporting my dreams and without you, my career wouldn't exist.

Thank you.

S x

Printed in Great Britain
by Amazon

44646638R00215